JADE PALACE VENDETTA

Death at the Crossroads

Death in Little Tokyo

The Toyotomi Blades

JADE
PALACE
VENDETTA

DALE FURUTANI

A SAMURAI MYSTERY

WILLIAM MORROW AND COMPANY, INC.

NEW YORK

Copyright © 1999 by Dale Furutani Flanagan

It is the policy of William Morrow and Company, Inc., and its imprints and affiliates,
recognizing the importance of preserving what has been written, to print the books
we publish on acid-free paper, and we exert our best efforts to that end.

Library of Congress Cataloging-in-Publication Data

Furutani, Dale.
Jade palace vendetta : a Samurai mystery / Dale Furutani.— 1st ed.
p. cm.
Sequel to: Death at the crossroads.
ISBN 0-688-15818-8 (alk. paper)
1. Japan—History—Tokugawa period, 1600–1868—Fiction.
I. Title.
PS3556.U778J33 1999
813' .54 dc21   99-18701
CIP

Printed in the United States of America

First Edition

1   2   3   4   5   6   7   8   9   10

BOOK DESIGN BY ANN GOLD

www.williammorrow.com

The "emperor" was
Akira Kurosawa.
An inspiration.

ACKNOWLEDGMENTS

It's rare that an author has the support of a string of great editors this early in his career. I have. The editor of this series, Zach Schisgal, has been a source of many improvements and much kindness. The editor who acquired this series for William Morrow, Elmer Luke, had faith in a mystery that broke the rules and had a protagonist with a very different perspective and character. At the publisher of my modern Ken Tanaka series, St. Martin's Press, I had a similar experience with Keith Kahla and Shawn Coyne. I wish to acknowledge the help of all these editors. Editors' names don't normally appear in a book, but the result of their hard work always does.

Thanks also to Sinya Shaeffer and the people in the map room of the U.S. Library of Congress, Nachiko Lee, Rick Hencken, and Neeti Madan.

MAJOR CHARACTERS

In this book, names follow the Japanese convention, in which the family name is listed first, then the given name. Therefore, in "Matsuyama Kaze" (Mat-sue-yah-mah Kah-say), Matsuyama is the family name and Kaze the given name.

Ando, the head of Hishigawa's household
Elder Grandma, leader of the Cadet Branch of the Noguchi family
Enomoto Katataka, head of guards for Hishigawa
Goro, a peasant
Hanzo, a peasant
Hishigawa Satoyasu, a rich merchant
Kannemori, a master swordsmith (also called a *sensei;* a master or teacher)
Matsuyama Kaze, a *ronin*
Noguchi Mototane, Elder Grandma's missing grandson
Noguchi Nagatoki, Elder Grandma's grandson
Okazaki Masamune, a master swordsmith from Kamakura's past
Okubo, a *daimyo* (lord) and Tokugawa retainer
Sadakatsu, a servant of the Noguchi family
The Sensei, Kaze's *kendo* (sword) teacher
Tokugawa Ieyasu, the new ruler of Japan
Toyotomi Hideyoshi, the Taiko and former ruler of Japan
Yuchan, Hishigawa's wife

EDO (ANCIENT TOKYO), KAMAKURA, AND THE TOKAIDO ROAD

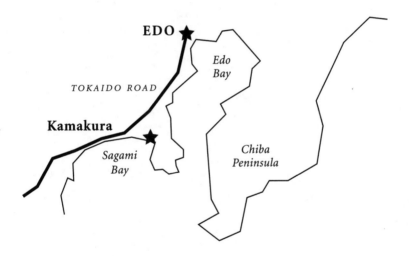

JADE PALACE VENDETTA

Puffed generals, vain
dolts and sly politicians;
Fools acting foolish.

Japan, the eighth year of Keicho, 1603

What do you want me to cut?"

The drunken *samurai* got unsteadily to his feet. He swayed from side to side, as if the platform beneath him were the rolling deck of a ship instead of the floor of a roadside teahouse. Pulling his *katana*, his long sword, from its scabbard, he held it before him like a necromancer's divining wand, waving vague circles in the air as he waited for spiritual inspiration.

His companion sat on the tattered *tatami* mats of the common room's floor. He was also a samurai, dressed in a creased gray kimono and holding a square wooden *sakè* cup in one hand. He looked about him, searching for a target for his friend's wavering sword blade. With a burst of drunken inspiration, his gaze fixed on the sakè cup.

"Cut this," he said, holding up the cup.

"The cup?"

"Yes, let's see you cut this. I'll toss it in the air and you slice it in half."

"In the air?"

"Of course! It's no challenge if I put it down." He gave a grin that revealed crooked brown teeth. "Wait a minute," he said, bringing the cup to his lips so he could drain it of the last dregs. The smell of the fragrant wooden cup enhanced the taste of the cheap, milky white rice wine. "Ahh, that was good."

It was early afternoon, but the two samurai had apparently been drinking for most of the day. In loud voices, they had challenged each other to a display of swordsmanship.

"All right," the sitting samurai said to his companion. "Now, get ready." He hefted the square cup with one hand. "*Ichi, ni, san,*" he counted; then he threw the cup up in the air. The cup tumbled in the air, with silver drops of sakè flying from it like the sparks from the pinwheels nailed to bridges during summer fireworks displays.

The standing samurai took a befuddled slice, and the wooden cup, untouched, tumbled to the worn tatami mats and bounced twice before coming to rest. The sitting samurai laughed uproariously.

"What's so funny?"

"You are."

"Well, let's see you try it," the swaying samurai said indignantly. He took exaggerated pains to insert the tip of his katana in his scabbard, his drunken state making this simple task, one of the most basic moves taught to beginning students of the sword, a sudden challenge. He finally got his blade into the scabbard and plopped back onto the mats.

His friend obligingly crawled over and picked up the cup. He stood as unsteadily on his feet as his companion had. Hefting the cup in one hand, he extracted his sword from its scabbard.

"Watch," he said, tossing the cup up into the air.

Taking a wild, one-handed slice at the cup, he gave it a glancing blow that hit the cup and set it flying across the room, like a shuttlecock batted by a decorated battledore in the game of *oibane.*

The cup landed near a person who was sitting, sipping tea. It was a *ronin,* a masterless samurai, dressed in the *kimono* and *hakama* pants of a traveler. Unlike the two other samurai, he didn't have a shaved pate. Instead, his hair was drawn back and tied in a topknot. He saw the cup flying toward him and, with nonchalant agility, he reached out with his free hand and grabbed the cup before it hit him. His other hand, holding the hot teacup to his lips, didn't sway or spill a drop.

"Hey, give me the cup back," the drunk roared.

"So you can play oibane with it again?" The ronin put his teacup down. Oibane was traditionally played by young girls on New Year's Day, so the drunk viewed this as an insult.

"I'm not playing oibane with it," the drunk said indignantly. "I'm trying to cut it. It's a show of swordsmanship!"

The samurai looked at the cup carefully, turning it over in his hand. Then he said dryly, "You haven't been too successful at it."

"What's your name?" the standing drunk demanded.

The ronin considered this question. The last time he had been formally asked this, he had been standing in the mountains. He had looked up and been struck by the beauty of the wind moving the pines on a mountainside. He had invented a name based on the beauty he had seen. He decided that the name he had given then was as good as any he could create today. "I'm Matsuyama Kaze," he said.

"Wind on Pine Mountain?" the drunk said. "What kind of name is that?"

"What kind of name is any name?"

"Well, whatever your name is, let's see you do better!"

"Why not?" Kaze said. In one fluid motion he stood and tossed the cup in the air without a second's hesitation; then he took his sword out of its scabbard and smoothly drew his sword through the center of the falling wooden cup. The speed of the blow and the sharpness of the sword allowed Kaze to cleave the wooden cup in two while it was still in the air. The two pieces of the severed sakè cup hit the tatami mat just as Kaze was returning his katana to its scabbard.

"By the Lord Buddha, what luck!" the first samurai exclaimed.

"Oh, yes," the second one said, "what a lucky blow!"

The ronin shook his head. "It was not a lucky blow. It's what I intended to do."

"It was a lucky blow," the first drunk insisted. "You couldn't do that again."

Kaze shrugged. "If you say so. But it was not luck."

"Come on. Come on. Let's see another demonstration," the second drunk said. He reached over and grabbed another cup.

"This silly game is not worth destroying the property of the innkeeper," Kaze said.

Having consideration for the property of an innkeeper was an alien idea to the drunks. "What are you talking about? This is just an innkeeper's cup. We're samurai!"

"Yes," the second drunk said. "We should be able to do what we want. And besides," he continued, "that cut of yours was simply luck."

Kaze smiled and shrugged. "If you say so."

"Are you still saying it wasn't luck?" the first drunk said argumentatively.

"It was whatever you decide."

"I'm drunk," the first samurai said, "but don't talk down to me."

"*Gomen nasai.* I'm sorry," Kaze apologized.

"Look, you couldn't cut something in the air like that again."

"I could if I wished to."

The first drunk laughed. "But you don't wish to."

"No, not really."

"That's because you can't do it," the second one said.

"But I can," Kaze said mildly.

"All right, let's see you do it again," the first one said. "We'll pick something for you to cut in midair and let's see you do it again."

"And if I do it will you stop bothering me?" Kaze asked.

"Of course, of course," the drunken samurai said reasonably.

"All right," Kaze said, "what is it you want me to cut in midair?"

The first one looked slyly at his companion, then pointed to a fly buzzing in the room. "Let's see you cut that," he said with a guffaw.

"Yes, cut the fly. Cut the fly," the second one laughed.

Kaze said nothing but stared at the two samurai for a few seconds. Then he walked away. Behind him he could hear the raucous laughter of the two drunks.

Kaze stepped out of the teahouse and looked up at the sky. It looked like a piece of rough, gray mulberry paper that had been streaked with an ink wash. The puffy dark slashes delineated clouds heavy with rain, much as a brush heavy with black ink would be used to paint such clouds.

Kaze could smell the thick scent of rain and feel the oppressive pressure of a gathering storm. He thought about returning to the teahouse to seek shelter. He knew he could will himself to ignore the two drunks; he would simply draw the internal curtain that allowed a Japanese to not see what he was seeing and not hear what he was hearing. Sometimes pretending not to see or hear was what allowed Japanese society to function.

Although he could ignore the drunks, he couldn't ignore himself. He was upset at himself for wanting to display his prowess with a sword, cutting a sake cup in midair. It was a weakness in himself, and he hated weakness. He could hear the voice of his sword teacher, his Sensei, saying, "When you play with fools, you act like a fool. When you act like a fool, you are one."

Kaze could ill afford to draw attention to himself by engaging in foolishness with a couple of drunken buffoons. There were fifty thousand ronin wandering Japan, most of them displaced by a great civil war when they ended up on the losing side. Some had turned to banditry, others had already given up the warrior's life for farming or trading, and many were still seeking employment with one of the victorious lords who had supported the winning Tokugawa clan. A few were still sought by the Tokugawas as enemies. Kaze was one of these few.

Kaze decided to continue his journey, and when it rained, he would simply get wet. Standing outside the teahouse, he stood looking up and down the wide dirt path that formed the Tokaido Road. This dusty strip of soil joined Japan's past with its future. At one end of the Tokaido Road was Kyoto, the ancient capital for almost eight hundred years and the home of the Emperor. At the other end of the Tokaido Road was Edo, the new capital and the stronghold of the Tokugawas, the new rulers of Japan. Kaze stood physically and metaphorically between the old and the new, longing for a happier past but unafraid of a harsh future.

Before the civil war, the Tokaido Road had been thick with traffic, with travelers sometimes walking shoulder to shoulder at congested spots. During the civil war traffic had dropped precipitously. Since the Tokugawa victory almost three years before and the subsequent uneasy peace, traffic was beginning to increase, although the danger from bandits made a journey still precarious. Often only a few brave merchants, ronin, ne'er-do-wells and bandits were found along the road. Sometimes it was difficult to tell one from the other.

Kaze had been wandering Japan for almost three years, searching for the kidnapped nine-year-old daughter of his former Lord and Lady. Recently he had come across a clue to the girl's possible location, a scrap of cloth with the Lord's *mon*, or family crest, of three plum blossoms. This cloth was given to him by an unlikely group, a trio led by a grandmother who was on an officially sanctioned vendetta. With a serious grievance, it was possible to get the government to sanction private revenge.

Apparently this grandmother had obtained such a sanction. She proclaimed her mission with a headband emblazoned with the *kanji* character for "revenge," and in his earlier encounter with her at another teahouse, Kaze had found her as fierce and willful as any samurai. The *obaasan*, the grandmother, was accompanied on her mission of vengeance by her fifteen-year-old grandson and an old servant who looked like a bag of bones.

The grandmother said she was looking for a merchant who traveled the Tokaido Road, so Kaze had also come to the great road, seeking the trio in an effort to learn more about where they had found the cloth with his Lord's family crest.

Now that he was at the Tokaido, he had no idea which direction to go; toward Kyoto or toward his enemy's stronghold of Edo? He had asked about the trio at the teahouse but had received no information from the proprietor. The teahouse owner had assured Kaze he would remember the group described, but it was only a matter of chance that any group traveling the Tokaido would stop at a particular roadside teahouse.

Kaze picked a stick off the ground. He removed the small *kogatana* knife that he kept in a groove in his scabbard and quickly cut a point on one end of the stick. Returning the ko-gatana, he threw the stick in the air, watching it tumble end over end before it hit the dirt road. The point was aimed toward Edo.

Squaring his shoulders, Kaze took his katana out of his sash and rested it on one shoulder, as one might carry a musket. He turned toward Edo and started walking down the Tokaido with the long gait of a man used to covering great distances on foot.

Once out of the village, the Tokaido Road turned into a wandering path that cut through forest, mountains, and fields. It usually took two weeks for a man to make the journey from Kyoto to Edo, although a fast dispatch could make the journey in three to four days, exchanging horses and sometimes riders at one of the fifty-three stations along the road.

Kaze had come out of the mountains near Edo. He had been in the mountains for months, methodically checking villages, looking for the girl. The tedious searching had not discouraged him. Now that he had finally come across the scrap of cloth that might be a connection to the girl, it was as if it was only the first day of his search, not almost the third year.

This section of the Tokaido was in rolling hills, with tall trees bordering the path. Sometimes the branches of the flanking trees merged, making the road a leafy tunnel. Kaze had walked sections of the Tokaido Road before, and he knew that in the heat of summer the wooded canopy that sometimes covered the road was a welcome shelter against the sun. Patches of blue were scattered throughout the branches, and spots of gold sunlight dotted the road, mirroring the bits of sky.

Today, with the threatening skies, the leafy tunnels were dark holes filled with unpleasant possibilities. Even in the open sections, the dark day made the road uninviting and gloomy. Kaze saw no others as he walked. He surmised that other travelers must be discouraged by the bad weather and holed up like badgers.

Kaze looked up at the roiling clouds and saw that the streaks of black were sweeping toward the earth. It was already raining behind him, and soon it would be raining on him. He decided that it would take a man driven by some great need, just as he was, to be traveling the Tokaido in this weather.

CHAPTER 2

I saved a red fox
from a snake. The fox bit me.
Good can bring evil.

Help! Somebody help! They're killing us!"

The plea was punctuated by the distinctive clang of sword blades crashing against each other. The anguished shout and the sound of battle floated over the hillside ahead of Kaze.

Curious, Kaze ran across a small stone bridge and up to the top of the hill, using the gliding run of a man in Japanese straw sandals. At the hill's apex, he stopped and looked down at the tableau spread before him.

Men were locked in desperate battle, like the *bunraku* puppets of a samurai drama. But in a bunraku the figures are coordinated. A black-robed master puppeteer moved each figure with one or two assistants, also clad in black, who trailed behind the puppeteer like the wings of a crow.

Kaze's practiced eye could see that here there was no coordination, no plan of battle other than brute force and the weight of numbers.

Eight men were attacking four. The four formed a tight knot around a pushcart. One of the four was standing on the pushcart, an older man dressed as a merchant. He was the one crying for help.

◆　◆　◆

Hishigawa could see that the situation was desperate. "Help!" he cried again. "Somebody help!" He had one foot on a large strongbox that was tied to the pushcart and in his hands he had a sword, which he was thrusting about inexpertly. He had been robbed earlier that same year and, although he came out of that experience with his life, he was desperate not to be robbed again. There was too much money involved this time. He was also fearful that he would not see his wife, Yuchan, again if he was killed.

The three men in front of him were supposed to stop a robbery. They were handpicked as experienced men who would act as his *yojimbo,* his bodyguards. With the sudden attack by so many bandits, they had jumped to his defense, but he could see they were being pushed back toward the cart by the strength of the bandits' numbers. The yojimbo were fighting hard. It was a fight rooted in mortal desperation.

One of the bodyguards fell, a large cut cleaving his shoulder and biting into his neck. With an agonized groan, he sank to his knees, a dying man.

The eight bandits pushed forward, squeezing the remaining bodyguards back against the cart. Instead of trying a pincer or flank attack, the bandits simply came crashing down on the two bodyguards like a giant tsunami smashing into the seashore. The guards crumpled under the attack.

Hishigawa looked to the top of the hill and he saw a lone samurai staring down at him, watching the fight. The man was of average height but seemed muscular. He carried a single sword instead of the two normally worn by a samurai. Instead of having the sword tucked in his sash, this samurai had it resting on one shoulder, a hand on the hilt. Hishigawa's heart sank, because he knew a single samurai could do nothing to stop the attack.

At that distance, Kaze could not read the man's eyes, but it was clear that the man on the pushcart had seen him. As he watched, the man made a plea that seemed to be aimed directly at him. Fear and desperation tinged the man's voice as he begged, "Please! Please help us!"

Sighing, Kaze took the scabbard of his katana sword off his shoulder and slipped the blade out of the plain black-lacquer covering.

One of the eight attackers was wounded and appeared to be dying, but that didn't stop the other seven from pressing forward and cutting down one of the remaining defenders.

"Please!" the man on top of the pushcart pleaded.

Kaze dropped the scabbard of his sword and started running down the hill. A lesser man might have shouted during his attack, but Kaze realized that surprise was as valuable as two additional sword blades in this situation. Instead of shouting as he ran toward the group, the only sound that came from him was the slap of his sandals as they struck the dirt road.

The attackers gave a yell of victory as the last of the defenders fell, slashed by multiple sword blades. They surged forward to surround the man on the cart. The merchant beat wildly at the bandits with his sword. The seven bandits should have been able to cut him down easily, but strangely they hung back, as if they were reluctant to rush the man and kill him. "Surrender," they called out to the merchant.

This hesitation allowed Kaze to arrive. First one and then a second of the attackers shouted in pain and crumpled to the ground. Surprised, the bandits turned just as a third man received a cut from the unexpected quarter. Kaze had cut down two men from behind and was finishing his stroke on the third.

The odds were still four to one, but in the illogic that marks battle, the four men scattered and ran. They dispersed to the side of the road, disappearing into the dense brush and trees that flanked the highway.

Kaze stood his ground, breathing heavily, unwilling to pursue the four bandits as they ran off. He saw no need to avenge the three dead defenders and had only entered the battle reluctantly, prompted by pity for the desperate cries of the merchant.

Suddenly there was a shout from a new direction. Kaze immediately spun about to see a lone samurai rushing toward the cart.

"It's the leader of the bandits," the man on the cart screamed to Kaze. "Protect me! He wants to kill me!"

Kaze stepped in front of the cart to protect the screaming merchant. In the split second between the time Kaze took his position and when the attacker was upon him, Kaze took the measure of the bandit chief.

He was better dressed than the other attackers. His forehead was shaved and his hair was pulled back with a sleek glossiness. On his young face was a look of pure rage. Both hands were on a sword held over his head and high in the air for a *shomen*, a vertical head-cut attack.

The new attacker brought his sword down, and Kaze brought his blade up to parry the blow. The sword blades, both finely polished and shimmering silver in the murky light, came together with a tremendous clang, and Kaze was pushed back a step by the combined momentum of the running man and the force of his overhead blow.

The bandit chief immediately turned his attention to the man on the cart. He seemed to lose interest in Kaze, intent on reaching the merchant, who was now cringing from the fury and hate of the man's attack.

"No!" Kaze shouted, making it clear to the bandit that he would first have to kill Kaze before he could reach the merchant. The bandit turned his attention back to Kaze.

"Let me kill that scum and you can go," the bandit said.

"No," Kaze answered, this time in a low voice. He held his sword in the aimed-at-the-eye position.

The bandit brought his blade back over his head for a second blow, and Kaze centered himself to respond, balancing evenly on his feet and bending his knees to bring his body low to the ground, making himself one with the earth so that he could withstand the furious attack.

The second blow was parried by Kaze's blade, but this time, instead of taking the full force of the blow, Kaze deftly twisted his blade to deflect the bandit's attack. This was to bring the bandit's blade low to the ground so that he would have a longer distance to draw his blade back for a third blow, giving Kaze enough time to set up an attack of his own.

Realizing what Kaze was doing, the bandit jumped back a pace, planting his own feet and lowering his center of gravity, at the ready to meet Kaze's attack. But Kaze didn't attack. He stood silently watching his opponent, noticing every characteristic of his stance and swordsmanship, looking for an advantage. The bandit stole a quick glance toward the man on the pushcart and once again rage contorted his face.

He looked back at Kaze. "I have no argument with you," the man spat out. "Get out of here and I'll let you live. I just want him." He pointed at the merchant with his chin.

"Oh, dear Buddha," the merchant groaned, "please save me!"

Kaze didn't know if the last request was directed toward Buddha or himself.

"He means to kill me. Please don't let him slaughter me! You can see I have no skills with the sword." This time the merchant was clearly addressing Kaze.

"That's right!" the bandit shouted. "I mean to cut your guts out and hang them on a tree with you still living and attached to them."

Another groan came from the merchant. "You can have the woman," the merchant said, "just let me live."

"It's beyond that," the man said. "Now I won't be satisfied while you still live."

"Please don't abandon me," the man pleaded with Kaze. "I'll give you anything, anything! Just don't let him kill me."

"Go on, get out," the samurai said to Kaze. A tinge of contempt colored the man's voice, as if Kaze was an object of disgust for defending the merchant.

"I'm sorry. I don't think I care to do that," Kaze responded coolly.

Instantly, the bandit attacked. He was a skilled swordsman, and

Kaze saw no apparent weakness in the man's attack. He put his own blade in motion to parry the blow.

Kaze caught the man's blade and deflected it. Then he pressed an attack of his own. He took a cut at the man's head, but the bandit managed to parry it. Without pausing, Kaze took a second and third cut at the young man. Although he was driven back, the bandit stopped the cuts before Kaze's blade could penetrate his defenses.

Kaze was impressed. The young man was an excellent fencer, sound in fundamentals and with the strength and agility of youth. The two men separated and Kaze launched another attack, shouting as he rushed toward the young man.

Kaze brought his blade down in an overhead cut with all his strength. The young man raised his own sword to parry the blow, just as Kaze had done at the fight's beginning.

When the two swords met, Kaze felt the force of the blow in his wrists, arms, shoulders, and throughout the rest of his body. But in the vibrations of this violent clash of steel, something felt unusual and false. Kaze heard a brittle metallic snapping sound and noted a peculiar feel, one he had never experienced before. He immediately knew that not only was something wrong, but that something was drastically wrong. The unthinkable happened.

To his utter amazement, Kaze's sword broke in two. The end of the sword flew off and went spinning through the air, hitting the dirt a few feet away from the combatants. The bandit gave a shout of triumph and took a cut at Kaze's shoulder and neck.

Kaze caught the blow in the fork of his *tsuba*, his sword guard, and the broken piece of his sword blade. After absorbing the brunt of the blow, Kaze took one hand off the handle of his sword and twisted forward. He grabbed the handle of the *wakizashi*, the short sword, carried by his opponent in his sash and drew it out of the scabbard. He thrust it back into the man's stomach, all in one smooth, reciprocating motion.

The man gave a grunt of surprise and then of pain. He drew his own sword back to take another cut at Kaze. Kaze then yanked the short sword, cutting the muscles of his opponent's abdomen. The man groaned and fell back on the ground in a sitting position. He looked up at Kaze with an expression that changed from pain to anger to sorrow. With a soft hiss of air, he crumpled the remaining distance to the earth and fell back dead.

Kaze stood with his opponent's sword in one hand and the broken stub of his own sword in the other. He was panting for breath from exertion, stunned by what had happened.

"Superb!" Kaze heard the merchant shouting. "Brilliant, absolutely brilliant!"

Kaze glanced over at the man. He was still standing on the cart, one foot on the chest bound to the cart. He was wearing a brown kimono with a white peony pattern. He looked to be in his mid-forties, with gray streaks at the temples. He had leathery brown skin, probably from spending many days on the road as he did his trading. He had a large fleshy nose, somewhat unusual for a Japanese. The cloth of his kimono was of fine quality.

The merchant jumped off the cart and walked over to the body of Kaze's most recent opponent. He spit on the corpse, and then he hiked up his kimono, moving aside his loincloth and making a stream of water on the face of the corpse in a gesture of utter contempt.

The merchant's act offended Kaze, but it was already in process, so Kaze saw no point in objecting. Instead, when the merchant was done Kaze walked over to where his opponent had dropped his sword and picked it up to look at it.

In almost every respect it was a standard Japanese katana. The sword did not seem remarkable in any way. There seemed to be no reason this sword could break Kaze's.

Kaze looked at the remainder of his own broken sword and shook his head in disbelief. The sword had been a faithful companion for years, seeing Kaze through numerous battles, both during the short and violent civil war and the years since as Kaze wandered Japan. That it should break was unthinkable. Yet the remnant of the sword in Kaze's hand showed that in fact this had happened.

"It was lucky you were so quick." The merchant had come up to Kaze after finishing his business with the corpse. "Grabbing a man's own wakizashi and using it to kill him! That's unbelievable. I've never seen anything like it!"

Kaze raised an eyebrow at the merchant but said nothing.

"Excuse me," the merchant said, bowing. "I am Hishigawa Satoyasu, the merchant."

Kaze noted that the merchant affected a double name, but said nothing. Instead, he pointed to the dead corpses littering the ground around the cart. "And who were all these?"

"Three of them were my yojimbo," the merchant said. "The rest were members of his gang." The merchant jerked his chin toward Kaze's last opponent.

"And who is he?" Kaze asked.

"He's Ishibashi, the chief of the bandits who attacked me. One of the most disgusting men you'd ever want to meet."

"And what was this fight all about?"

"A robbery, of course."

"You exchanged words. This is more than a robbery."

"Well, yes. There's that. It was also about a woman."

"What woman?"

"My wife, Yuchan," the merchant said simply.

"What?" Kaze asked.

"My wife. That man wanted my wife, and nothing was going to stop him from having her. He was obsessed with her. He decided the best way to have her was to kill me."

Kaze looked at the merchant again, taking in the roll of flesh around his belly and his bandy legs.

"I know what you're thinking," the merchant said. "How could someone that looks like me have a wife that's worth desiring? But my wife is much younger than I. A real beauty. I have businesses in Kamakura, Kyoto, and Edo. In Kamakura I've created a special environment just for her. I call it the Jade Palace. In it, I've crafted a separate world dedicated to the comfort and pleasure of my wife. Before I knew he was a bandit, I made the mistake of letting Ishibashi meet my wife, and he became obsessed with her beauty. He actually tried to buy her from me! But of course I refused to part with her. She's mine, and mine alone!" The merchant said the last words savagely. He shook with emotion.

It was a few seconds before the merchant could compose himself and continue. "He's been waiting his turn, he and his entire gang. He intended to kill me and then to take my wife as his own. But thanks to you, Ishibashi is the one that's dead now, and so is a good part of his gang. You were superb!"

Kaze said nothing.

Kaze took his opponent's sword and walked to the side of the road where a tree was growing. Seeing a likely limb, he took two cuts at it, trimming it to a piece roughly the length of the span of his hand.

"What are you doing?" the merchant asked, greatly puzzled.

Kaze made no answer. He walked up to the top of the hill and re-trieved his scabbard. Taking the ko-gatana from its place in the scabbard, Kaze started carving as he walked back toward the mer-chant.

The merchant waited for Kaze's return. His lidded eyes were heavy with curiosity. Kaze continued carving the piece with a practiced hand.

"What are you doing?" the merchant asked again.

"Easing some souls."

The merchant opened his mouth to say more but couldn't think of another question to ask in the face of such a cryptic remark. Instead, he watched as Kaze transformed the piece of tree limb into the figure of a woman, deftly creating the shoulders, neck, and head of the fig-ure by making rapid cuts to the soft wood with the sharp knife.

As the image emerged from the limb, the merchant exclaimed, "It's a Kannon!"

Kaze nodded and continued his carving. Under his skilled hands the image of the Goddess of Mercy emerged. Looking around, he realized he wouldn't be able to bury all the bodies about him. He took the image of the goddess and placed her in the crook of the tree that he had cut the limb from, positioning her so she could survey the scene of the battle and the dead bodies that littered it.

"Do you have water?" Kaze asked, suddenly thirsty.

"Yes," the merchant responded, scampering off to retrieve a water jug from the cart. Kaze looked up at the sky and reflected that he could soon get a drink of water just by opening his mouth and tilting his head back, but he gratefully accepted the water jug from the merchant and took a long swallow.

Returning the jug, Kaze examined the dead bandit's sword once again. Its sword guard was made of iron, with a cherry blossom pattern. Highlights of a cherry branch formed the outer edge of the guard, the edges of the branch picked out in gold. The individual cherry blossoms were tiny sweeps of silver, so it looked like the blossoms were catching the last rays of the setting sun as they fluttered to the ground. To Kaze and most samurai, life was symbolized by the falling cherry blossom, fragile and ephemeral.

The blade of the dead man's sword was about the size of the sword that had broken. Katana were long swords, but they were not forged to a set length. Often the length was adjusted to the size of the man. Kaze tentatively slipped the dead man's sword into his plain black-lacquer scabbard. It was not a perfect fit, but it would do until he was able to figure out how to get another sword made for him.

He tucked the scabbard into his sash and started walking off down the road.

"Where are you going?" the merchant said, alarmed.

"As you see, I am walking down the Tokaido Road. I'm resuming my journey."

"Wait! You can't go and leave me," the merchant said.

"Why can't I?" Kaze answered.

"I want you to be my bodyguard, my yojimbo."

CHAPTER 3

Travel makes strange friends.
Standing under a tree in
rain draws us too close.

You want me to be your bodyguard?" Kaze asked incredulously.

The merchant waved about him. "You can see my men are dead, and I still need protection."

"Why?" Kaze asked.

"Because that dog's offal still has men," the merchant said, pointing to the dead bandit chief. "They will gather others and they'll come after me again. Their obsession for my Yuchan knows no limits."

Kaze eyed the merchant warily for several moments. Then he said, "You said the bandit was after you because he wanted your woman. Now he's dead. It's true that an *obake*, a ghost, can still desire a woman, but it's not true that an obake can organize his men and continue to attack you. They can't all desire your wife the way Ishibashi did."

Hishigawa pushed on without the slightest hesitation. "It's just that I know his group and how they think. They'll never let me live. Of course, the group won't have the same passion for my woman that Ishibashi did, but they will have a passion for avenging his death."

"In that case, I'm the one who must worry, because I am the one who killed him," Kaze said.

"But his men won't know that," the merchant argued. "They'll think that I killed him. And they'll gather their forces and recruit new men and come after me."

Kaze looked at the merchant. The merchant stared back at him with frog's eyes. Instead of pursuing the argument, Kaze turned on his heels and started walking down the Tokaido Road again.

"Wait!" the merchant said.

Kaze continued walking.

"Please, wait! I'll tell you the truth," he shouted. His voice was tinged with fear and apprehension.

Kaze stopped and turned around, but he didn't come closer to the merchant. The merchant ran up to him, a look of desperation on his face.

"And what is the truth?" Kaze said.

The merchant sighed, saying more to himself than to Kaze, "I guess I have no choice but to tell you."

Kaze shrugged. "It's all the same to me. You can tell the truth or not. But if you don't tell me the truth I'll leave. If you do tell me the truth I still might not stay, but it would be nice to know the cause of all the killing I've just done."

The merchant sighed once more, as if telling the truth was difficult for him. "It is true that Ishibashi wanted my wife. It was an obsession with him, the kind of lust that spreads from the groin until it poisons the blood and then eventually crazes the mind. Yet there's something more involved in this particular story." He pointed to the pushcart and the chest that was strapped to it. "On that cart is gold. I have businesses in Kyoto, Edo, and Kamakura. I have to transfer funds from all those interests. Edo is growing so fast since the Tokugawa victory that it requires an influx of gold to keep up with the growth. I was transferring funds from Kyoto to Edo, and that's the reason I was attacked on the road. Ishibashi's personal animosity was directed toward me because of his lust for my woman, but the gang was motivated to attack because of their greed. Although the lust was killed with the bandit leader, the greed is still very much alive in the hearts of his followers. I'm sure they'll come again, and I'll be helpless here without you. You have to get me to the next guard barrier."

"Why?"

"Because I'll pay you."

Kaze tightened his lips in disgust with the talk of payment. Merchants loved such talk, but it was not in the nature of a true samurai to concern himself with such things.

When he was a castle samurai instead of a ronin, his wife handled the finances. She would outfit him in armor and assure he had proper horses and retainers to go to war. She and an accountant handled all the funds for the castle that Kaze ruled. Kaze knew the total income of his land in *koku*, the amount of rice it took to feed a man for one year, but he had absolutely no idea what his personal finances were like. It was beneath the dignity of a true samurai to worry about money.

Still, his life had changed in many ways over the past two years, and he had learned the importance of money. If he had no money, it would impede his search for the girl. Also, without money he would not be able to replace the sword in his scabbard with another one. As much as he tried to balance and calm his spirit, he was still greatly disturbed by the breaking of his sword and the fact that he was carrying a dead man's katana.

The katana was the soul of a samurai. It was shrouded in myth as well as mystery. One of the key symbols of Shinto was a sword. A samurai using a sword taken from a dead body seemed to violate the ideals of purification and spirituality. Kaze was uneasy about using such a sword.

As if he was reading Kaze's thoughts, the merchant said, "I'll give you enough so that you can buy another sword. A fine sword to replace the one that was broken. Kamakura has the finest swordsmiths in Japan. We'll go to my home there instead of continuing to Edo. You can have your pick of any sword in Kamakura, and I will pay for it!"

Kaze wondered about taking money for his services, but he realized that for most of his life as a warrior he had received some kind of payment for his services. The payment was often in rice or land or honors, but it was still payment.

"Until the next barrier?" Kaze confirmed.

"Yes, just until the next barrier. There I should be able to get some more men to help me finish the journey safely. When I get home to Kamakura I'll send the money on to Edo under heavier guard. You can accompany me to Kamakura, and I will pay you when I'm safely home."

"You pull on the handles of the cart and I'll push it," Kaze said.

Smiling, the merchant put away his sword blade and got between the handles of the cart, pulling it down the Tokaido Road with Kaze behind pushing. The cart was surprisingly heavy. Kaze thought that the chest must contain a substantial amount of gold.

As Kaze pushed the cart, he realized they were being followed. The bandits he had chased away had found courage in their greed, or perhaps they had realized that there were only two men opposing them. They flitted from tree to tree, remaining hidden in the brush along the side of the road.

"How far is it to the next barrier?" Kaze asked.

"We should be there by tomorrow," the merchant answered.

A day, a night, and part of a day again. Plenty of time for the bandits to regroup and plan another attack.

Kaze pushed the cart a bit faster. The cart lurched forward and struck the merchant in the back. He looked over his shoulder. "Be careful," he said. "Don't push so energetically."

"The bandits are following us," Kaze answered. "If we pick up the pace they either have to come out in the open and start following us on the road, where we can watch them, or they can stay in the woods and start slipping behind us. In either case the result will be good for us."

"You've seen them?" the merchant said, looking around.

"Stop looking," Kaze said. "They're trying to follow us in the woods in an effort to prevent us from knowing that they're following. If you make it clear that we can see them, then they'll start trying to be more clever. We don't need them to be more clever. We're the ones who should be clever."

Kaze continued to push the cart down the road while the merchant pulled it using the bamboo handrails. Kaze could tell the merchant was not used to extended periods of physical exertion and that they would not be able to keep up such a rapid pace for very long. He bent his head down as he pushed, not because he was already tired, but so he could peek under his arms and see the bandits who were following them. He caught brief glimpses of them through the brush and trees that bordered the road. It took several sightings, but he became convinced that there were only two of them following. He looked at the other side of the road to see if he could see the other two bandits, but either they were much better at following than the first two or they weren't there.

"How far away did you say the barrier was?" Kaze said.

"A day and a half," the merchant said, panting.

The barrier was a checkpoint along the Tokaido Road, a way of controlling and monitoring the movement of people. It was a place where there would be guards and large crowds and where the merchant would find safety. Kaze mulled over why only two bandits were following them and asked the merchant, "Do you know if the road ahead cuts back or curves?"

"It's fairly straight for quite a distance," the merchant said, panting even more heavily. Then he added, "I don't think I can keep this pace up."

"We're going to have to get off the Tokaido Road and move onto one of the secondary paths," Kaze said.

"What are you talking about?" the merchant asked. "Moving this cart will be even harder if we get off the main highway and onto some kind of side road."

"We have no choice."

"Why do you say that?" the merchant said, looking over his shoulder at Kaze, slowing down his pace with the cart.

"Because there are only two bandits following us."

The merchant looked puzzled. "What does that mean?"

"It means that if the road cut back or curved ahead, then the other two might be moving across country to cut us off and ambush us."

"But the road is straight."

"Yes. That means that the two have probably gone to gather more men. There's a day and a half of travel ahead of us. We can't move very fast with this cart. If we stay on the highway, there's ample time for them to get more men and attack us. The two following us are just to shadow us and make sure they know where we are."

"But what good does going off the Tokaido onto some side road do us?"

"It's simple. They have to leave at least one man where we branch off the highway to guide the rest of them."

"But one of them will still be following us."

"Then we can branch off again, and if he doesn't stop to direct them at our second turn, then I can take care of him. In any case, it will be hard for the bandits to find us if we are taking some of the side roads instead of the main Tokaido."

"But which side road should we take?"

"The first one that seems to be going in the general direction of the barrier. We'll eventually work our way back to the main highway."

"But on the main highway we might meet others."

"How many people are traveling the Tokaido today? If you do meet others, do you think they will help you?" Kaze asked. "Do you think another merchant will risk his life for you? Or perhaps you think a group of other ronin would be less dangerous than the bandits following you, especially when they find out you have gold in this chest?"

The merchant was silent, apparently considering his dilemma.

"What if you're wrong about where the other two went?" he eventually asked.

"And what if I'm right?" Kaze answered.

After a few seconds, the merchant said, "All right. If nothing else, if we get on a side path maybe we can slow down this murderous pace."

"No," Kaze said, "we shouldn't slow down. At least not yet. If the two men following us split up, as I anticipate, I want our remaining shadow to fall behind us more. I want a little time between us."

The two bandits following them had a short argument when Kaze and the merchant pulled off the Tokaido Road. The one who won the argument got to stand by the road waiting for his fellows to join him so he could direct them. The one who lost continued to follow the pushcart.

As the bandit followed, big, thick drops of rain started splattering the dusty surface of the road. Within a few minutes, the rain started coming down in a steady curtain. The bandit pulled his kimono about him tightly. But the rain made it a lot easier to follow the pushcart.

He could clearly see the fresh ruts of the pushcart's wheels going down the track. He slowed his pace and fingered a large scar on his cheek as he thought about the situation. He grinned to himself, because he could now follow them at his leisure. They couldn't get away leaving such an obvious trail.

The bandit had followed for a distance when the cart's ruts pulled off the road. Puzzled, he followed. He watched the ground before him, intent on following the ruts in the rain-soaked earth. It wasn't as easy as the road, but the ground was now sufficiently soft that he could continue his shadowing without difficulty.

The ruts continued off the road and into the woods for a short distance. He soon came to a place where a large tree was growing right in the middle of the cart tracks. A rut from one wheel clearly passed to the right and the other to the left of the tree trunk, and the bandit stood for a moment, stupefied, trying to understand how the cart could pass through a sturdy tree.

As he contemplated this problem, he heard a rustling in the tree above him. Blinking against the heavy rain, he looked up to see the soles of two straw sandals rushing down on him. Before he could get over his surprise, the feet hit him on the chest. The bandit's arms flew in the air, and he fell backward into the soft mud with a loud squish.

The breath was knocked out of him. Gasping, he looked up and saw the ronin who had killed his companions staring down at him. The ronin was holding a freshly cut staff, probably from a sapling growing by the side of the road. Fear gripped the bandit's bowels.

"*Konnichi wa.* Good afternoon," the ronin said pleasantly.

The bandit reached to pull his sword from its scabbard. The ronin used his staff to give the supine bandit a hard rap on his wrist, causing paralyzing pain. The bandit yelped and withdrew his hand from his sword's handle.

He then tried to sit up, but once again the staff came into play. The butt of the staff thumped the bandit on the chest, pushing him back into the mud.

"What?" the bandit finally was able to say.

"Not a very polite greeting," the ronin mused, "but I suppose it will have to do. Now, I see you are following us."

"No, Samurai-san, I'm—"

The butt of the staff struck the bandit sharply at the base of his neck, generating another yelp.

"Please don't insult me," the ronin said. "It's obvious you're following us, just as it's obvious that your companion is waiting on the Tokaido Road to alert your gang which path we took when we went off the main road."

Hearing the ronin's words, the bandit gave a snarl of defiance and knocked the staff away from his chest. The ronin simply twirled the staff 180 degrees and, using the other end, brought it down on the bandit's neck, pushing down on the man's throat and pinning him in the mud as raindrops pelted his face. Leaning on the staff slightly to keep the man pinned, the ronin reached down with one hand and pulled out the bandit's sword, flinging it into the bushes.

"Now," Kaze said amiably, "what we have is a very interesting situation. It's not often that we hold our own existence in our hands as clearly as you do at this moment. I have no particular desire to kill you, although I suspect that your dark life has been lived in a manner that richly deserves killing. But, on the other hand, I don't want you following us, either. So here's what I suggest. You tell your friends that when I dropped down on you, you were injured much more seriously than you actually are. Tell them you were unable to walk and therefore couldn't follow us. You can point them down the road in the direction we're actually going, so I'm not asking you to lie to them. But I am advising you not to follow us, because if you do, I'll kill you. Do you understand that?"

The bandit snarled a curse, and Kaze added some pressure to the staff, choking him in midword. The bandit grabbed at the staff to try to relieve the pressure. Tears formed in his eyes from the pain. Kaze eased off and leaned closer to the bandit, staring into the scarred face.

"Defiance is fine, but it's not called for in this circumstance. I have treated you reasonably, considering the situation. Now prove to me that you have some brains and simply answer my question. The choice is simple. Continue following us and you die. Stay here and you live. Now, do you understand?"

"*Hai*. Yes," the bandit croaked, the staff still pressing down on his neck.

"Good. Now remember, your life is in your own hands. If you don't want it to end today, this will be the last that I see of you."

Kaze dropped the staff and walked back to the path.

CHAPTER 4

Bitter memories
gnaw at my soul. How many
tears wash away pain?

Did you kill him?" the merchant asked.

"No."

"Why not?" Hishigawa looked annoyed.

"Because I didn't need him dead," Kaze answered. "If you need him dead, then you can kill him. I'm sure he's still back where I left him. I threw his sword into the bushes. Perhaps if you hurry, you can get to him before he recovers it."

Hishigawa was used to having his money buy him respect and the services of ronin. He was also used to a certain brusqueness from his aristocratic customers, but, because of his wealth, not from ronin, even though technically any samurai, including a ronin, was far above the merchant class. Only the handlers of the dead and animal carcasses occupied a lower social class than merchants.

Hishigawa would not have been a successful merchant if he didn't study men and their nature. It helped him to understand the weakness of a man when he was trading. He saw in the ronin a man of ordinary height, but extraordinary will and skill with a sword. The way he attacked the bandits showed that. Now he was helping to escape those bandits, and he was also helping Hishigawa bring the gold back to his Yuchan. He needed this ronin. At least for now. Hishigawa gave a quick bow and said, "*Sumimasen.* I'm sorry. I simply wanted to as-sure that the bandit wouldn't trouble us."

"If he does, then I'll kill him," Kaze said. "Some place up ahead we're going to have to actually get off the trail and move across coun-try."

"Why?"

"Because it's too easy to follow us when we stay on these trails. If we have to constantly cover up the cart tracks, we won't make progress at all. Once I've covered up where we get off the trail, we can proceed for some distance."

"To where?" the merchant said. "We have to get to the barrier."

"We will get to the barrier," Kaze said. "We'll only go across coun-try until we see another path going in the direction of the barrier. Then we'll use that. It will take the bandits quite a while to try to fig-ure out which path we're on."

"But it might take us days to get to the barrier that way," the mer-chant protested.

"Yes. But if the bandits catch us we won't get to the barrier at all."

The merchant saw the logic in Kaze's statement and said, "All right. I suggest we travel on this path a little way before we leave it. That way, even if the bandits surmise what we've done, it will still be harder for them to pick up our trail."

"Good," Kaze said. He pointed at the cart.

"You pull, I'll push, and we'll stop every fifty paces so I can go back and obliterate the cart tracks."

The merchant looked up at the heavens. "It's raining a lot harder now."

"Yes," Kaze said, "but raindrops won't stop men in search of gold."

At a likely-looking place, he and Hishigawa pushed the cart off the path and started threading their way through the woods. At some junctures they had to take wide detours to avoid thick patches of brush that would have totally stopped the heavy cart. It was hard, ex-hausting work, and at one point the merchant almost collapsed from fatigue.

"We can leave the cart here and take the chance that the bandits won't find it," Kaze said to the weary Hishigawa.

"Leave the gold? Never! This gold belongs to Yuchan as well as me. I'll never leave it." The merchant was intransigent about abandoning the cart, but the thought of leaving a fortune seemed to add fire to his muscles, and he tugged at the cart handles with renewed vigor. Kaze insisted they stop and rest a bit. Both men sat silently on the cart, drenched by the rain and too tired to speak.

Finally, Kaze got up and wordlessly took his position behind the cart. Also without words, a tired Hishigawa took up his position between the thick bamboo rails of the cart and started pulling as Kaze pushed.

It was the end of the day by the time the two men came across another path. It seemed to go in the direction of the mountains and not toward the barrier, but Kaze knew they had to take it. The two of them couldn't continue to manhandle the cart through the woods.

The rain was coming down like spears blanketing a battlefield by the time they stopped for the night. Kaze had found a ridge near the path they were on and placed the cart so it straddled it. This had the advantage of making the water run down on each side of the ridge, providing a somewhat drier space under the cart. He was careful not to place the cart in a north–south direction. Corpses were laid out with their heads in the direction of the rat, or north, and he didn't want to sleep in that position. Both men crawled under. They were exhausted, soaked, and cold.

"This is intolerable!" Hishigawa said, pulling his kimono around him tightly. Water dripped down through the cracks in the cart floor, hitting him on the nose. He jerked his head away, hitting it on the inside of a wheel. "Damn!" he said in pain. "I'm going to get out of here and find some temple or peasant's hut where I can get some shelter."

"*Dozo*. Please," Kaze said. "Find some building nearby and hole up like an animal in a warm den. Soon the hunters will come to sniff you out. Don't you think the bandits will search all nearby buildings first?

You'll be warm and dry until they capture you. And when they do, just don't tell them where I am, no matter how much they torture you."

Kaze turned his back to the merchant and closed his eyes. He listened to the grumbling merchant for a few seconds to satisfy himself that Hishigawa was not leaving the meager shelter of the cart.

"You said that bandit I killed was after you because of your wife," Kaze said, his eyes closed.

"That's right," Hishigawa responded.

"Why?"

Hishigawa smiled and closed his eyes, lost in reverie. "She is the most beautiful creature you can imagine. Exquisite skin, as white as a camellia and as silky smooth as the skin of a new persimmon. A mouth with lips as dark red as the most luscious plum. The nape of her neck is long, like a swan's." Hishigawa opened his eyes and looked out at the rain. "Even Yuchan's hands are the most perfectly formed things you've ever seen," he exclaimed. "Delicate, small, and extremely graceful in every movement she makes."

Kaze turned and looked at the merchant. He had a long, horsey face and baggy eyes. He hardly looked the part of a lovesick swain, but it was obvious that he was enchanted with his wife.

Hishigawa's hair was shaved like a samurai's, and at one time his family had undoubtedly been samurai, which was why he affected two names. Commoners, including merchants, were supposed to have only one name; only samurai and nobles were supposed to have two.

After the great battle of Sekigahara, fifty thousand ronin samurai were left without a use for their sword except mischief and banditry. More and more of these samurai, in despair and desperation, were taking their hand to different endeavors, such as farming and other occupations. Many were returning to the soil, maintaining farms. Two generations before, almost all samurai had been soldier-farmers. A professional class of warrior was a relatively recent development, spurred by the wars to unite Japan into a single country. From the looks of Hishigawa, however, the decision to follow the path of the merchant was not a recent one.

Kaze had mixed feelings about the choice of becoming a merchant. As one of the lowest trades in the social class, the grubbing for money seemed somehow beneath the dignity of a warrior. Yet, he knew one of the foundations and strengths of the Tokugawas' ascendancy was the legendary tightfistedness of Tokugawa Ieyasu.

Ieyasu knew that money could be translated into men and arms and power, and he waited, biding his time and gathering his resources until the previous ruler of Japan, Toyotomi Hideyoshi, died, leaving a young son and a widow to try to protect his legacy.

Then Ieyasu acted. He attacked the forces loyal to the Toyotomi at Sekigahara during the month that has no Gods. It was the largest battle ever fought by samurai.

At the start of the battle, Ieyasu was outnumbered because his son had been diverted besieging a castle, and one-third of Ieyasu's army was not on the field. But Ieyasu had two secret weapons: betrayal and greed. He used some of the money he had gathered over a lifetime to bribe forces on the side of the Toyotomi before the battle. They agreed to remain neutral or to turn on their allies in the heat of battle and fight on the Tokugawa side. Ieyasu started the battle seemingly outnumbered, but as the long day wore on, key Toyotomi forces would not attack when ordered to. At the critical moment of the battle, the disloyal troops under the command of Kobayakawa attacked their erstwhile allies. By the end of the battle, Ieyasu was the undisputed ruler of Japan.

To Kaze, Ieyasu's victory was based on promoting disloyalty. This lack of loyalty and honor struck at the very heart of *bushido*, the warrior's code, the core of Kaze's beliefs.

Now Hideyoshi's widow and son were trapped in Osaka Castle, not quite prisoners, but certainly not free. Ieyasu still paid perfunctory respect to them, but there was no doubt who the real ruler of Japan was. There was also no doubt that it was Ieyasu's intention to declare himself Shogun.

By tradition, only members of the Minamoto family, the same family that built the Tsurugaoka Shrine in Kamakura, dedicated to Hachiman, the God of War, could become Shogun. The Tokugawas had never been considered as Minamotos. Then, as Tokugawa Ieyasu's power increased and becoming Shogun became a possibility, he suddenly "discovered" that his lineage was actually connected to the Minamotos, although no such link had been claimed before. So now Ieyasu was suddenly qualified to take the title of Shogun, and people loyal to the Toyotomi, such as Kaze, found themselves penniless. At the same time, people like Hishigawa, who had seen the trend in the new Japan and had capitalized on it, were able to wander the countryside with pushcarts holding a chest full of gold.

"You must love your wife very much," Kaze said.

"It goes beyond love," Hishigawa said. "It goes beyond passion and it goes beyond need. This woman is my life and my existence."

A poetic song from a mud frog, Kaze thought. Love can do amazing things. "You've been married a long time?"

"No. Less than a year."

The newness of the marriage could explain the merchant's infatuation, but Kaze was still surprised. It was not often that a Japanese man would find passion in his marriage. That's what concubines, or perhaps young boys, were for.

From the way Hishigawa was talking, it sounded like his marriage was one of those bonding of souls that sometimes occurs in life. This happened much less often in the warrior class than in other classes, because in the warrior class marriages were arranged according to economic and military advantage, with no regard for the feelings of the people actually involved.

Kaze's own marriage had been arranged this way—a dry alliance between Kaze's family and the family of his bride. Although his marriage had been proper and respectful, it was not filled with love or passion. He did love the two children the marriage produced, and he grieved for their death much as he grieved for the loss of the Lady.

◆ ◆ ◆

Kaze had actually only seen his wife once before their wedding. The negotiations between his family and her family were handled by a go-between, and consideration was given to the political and economic consequences of the union, but scant attention was given to the state of Kaze's heart, save for the fact that he found his new wife acceptable in appearance.

After the marriage, he went through the process of adjustment and sexual accommodation with her, but it was not a relationship that grew to great affection and depth of spirit or passion. He had two children with her and his marriage was normal for a person of his station, with the exception that Kaze never took a concubine or male page for a lover. His taking a lover would have been perfectly acceptable to his wife, but Kaze didn't choose to, keeping the reason in the secret recesses of his heart.

All in all, his was an extremely proper samurai marriage. So proper that when the castle that he lived in fell in the immediate aftermath of the climactic battle of Sekigahara, Kaze's wife killed her own children before taking a dagger and shoving it into her own throat to kill herself. This was done to spare the children and herself from humiliation and torture if they were captured alive.

The Lady, the wife of Kaze's Lord, did not kill her daughter when her castle fell. Kaze never asked her why, but he knew it was because she loved her daughter too dearly and could not bring herself to do what samurai tradition expected of her. She also didn't kill herself, and Kaze knew this was also related to her daughter. If her daughter was alive, the Lady would also want to be alive, not for her own sake, but so she could fight for and try to protect her daughter. Kaze knew the Lady would not refuse to take her own life out of cowardice. He had seen enough examples of her courage to know that she would not hesitate to do what was required of her. But the love of her daughter changed the requirements of what was proper.

It seemed strange to Kaze that the heart of this aging merchant should be so captivated by a new wife. Still, the Taiko himself, Toyo-tomi Hideyoshi, had found satisfaction and passion with a new wife at the end of his life. And this new wife had given Hideyoshi a child. In fact, she had given Hideyoshi two children. When the first child died, a second was conceived and born—a son. Since Hideyoshi had a long-standing relationship with his first wife and at least a hundred concubines, there was endless speculation on how Yododono, the mother of the child, could have created such a miracle. The pious believed it was because Yododono had prayed to the proper gods. The cynical believed that Yododono had taken other means, or perhaps other men, to guarantee her conception. In either case, Hideyoshi believed the child to be his and tried to ensure his son would succeed him to the rulership of Japan.

Now the child and his mother ruled only Osaka Castle and there was speculation that they would not be ruling that for long. Ieyasu continued to give proper respect to the memory of Hideyoshi, but his forces were gathering the threads of power and weaving them into a mighty and enveloping tapestry.

Hishigawa remained quiet, perhaps still caught up in the memory of his wife. Soon Kaze heard snoring as the exhausted merchant fell into a deep sleep, despite the miserable conditions. Kaze focused on the sound of the falling raindrops hitting the cart and the ground around him, filtering out the man's snores.

Splat-splaaat-splat-splat-splaat. The rain was coming down harder now, hitting the earth in an irregular rhythm. It was a mesmerizing sound, and one that brought back memories that flooded Kaze's mind like the water washing down the hillside.

Kaze reflected on how strange it was that so many of his encounters with the Lady involved falling water.

CHAPTER 5

Falling water and
falling tears. Both can cleanse and
both can drown the soul.

His very first glimpse of the Lady was when he was ten. He had been with his Sensei, his teacher, for about two years. Every time Kaze had thought he had mastered something that the Sensei had to teach him, the old man would suddenly increase the difficulty of the lesson with an effortless grace, which always left Kaze frustrated that he would never truly learn anything, even the most rudimentary thing.

Once, when he expressed his feelings about this to his teacher, the old man had looked at him very seriously and said, "If you are going to follow the way of bushido, then you must learn throughout your entire life. After a while the mechanical things I can teach you will no longer be new, but in their application and feel they will always be new. The simplest parry with your sword—the very first one I taught you—will evolve through the years as you grow in skill and understanding. So even though the motions you make will be the same ones that you made when you were eight years old and started your lessons with me, throughout your entire life those motions will be ever changing, yet still the same. Thus it is with life—ever changing but still the same. Just as important, you must expand your circle of skills beyond the sword to art and literature and music. The true warrior is not just a killer. Remember the lesson of Yoshimori and the foxes."

Kaze looked puzzled.

"The great warrior Yoshimori had a suit of exceptionally fine armor commissioned," the Sensei continued. "Part of the process of creating this armor was the reinforcement of key points with fresh fox skin. The special glue used to attach these reinforcements took three days and nights of constant attention to prepare. Someone had to be stirring it continuously and minding the fire to make sure it did not get too hot. Three times the master armorer prepared this glue, but Yoshimori's vassals could not supply a freshly killed fox whose skin could be used to finish the armor, so each time days of effort were wasted and the glue had to be thrown away.

"In frustration the armorer complained to Yoshimori because he had to throw away three batches of glue after laboring over each of them for three days and three nights. Yoshimori immediately told the armorer to start another batch of glue because he was very anxious to have this new suit of armor. He said he would personally deliver a freshly killed fox to the armorer. He then took his bow and went alone into the hills above Kyoto hunting for foxes.

"He hunted all day, trudging up and down hills in the hot sun, using his keen instincts to try to find the lair of a fox. Despite his best efforts, he could not find a fox, even though the hills around Kyoto are usually teeming with them. He returned that night puzzled and discouraged, determined to do better the next day.

"The second day he went hunting again in a different area. Once again, after a hot day searching the hillsides, he could not find a fox. Yoshimori returned home empty-handed, and he knew that the special glue would be ready the next evening.

"The third day, Yoshimori was up before dawn and scouring the hills. As on the previous days, he could find no trace of foxes, and he grew increasingly frustrated and anxious. As the sun dipped low on the horizon, he thought about how humiliated he would be if he did not make good on his promise to deliver a fresh fox skin to the armorer. Just as he was about to return home, a flash of brown caught his eye. Fitting an arrow to his bow, he stealthily crept toward where he had seen what he thought to be a glimpse of a fox's fur.

"Suddenly, he came upon a family of foxes trapped and cowering under a rock. It was a male, a female, and a young kit. Yoshimori was pleased, because he would be able to have his pick of foxes now and have his armor completed. He would not suffer embarrassment because he could make good on his boast to provide a freshly killed fox skin to complete the armor. As he drew back his bow, he noticed that the male and female fox did not run away. Instead, they pressed in close to their tiny baby, protecting it from Yoshimori's arrow.

"As he saw this scene, he was moved to pity, for he thought that even these dumb creatures were acting with bravery, ready to sacrifice their own lives to protect their child. He lowered his bow and vowed to tell the armorer that he could not kill a fox on his hunting expedition, even though it would cost him great embarrassment to make such an admission. The armorer was so angry that he vowed not to finish the armor for Yoshimori, an unprecedented insult for a samurai to suffer at the hands of a tradesman.

"Yet, despite the embarrassment, Yoshimori did the proper thing. He was not a wanton killer, but a complete warrior. He understood the difference between killing and murder. It is the warrior's duty to kill or be killed, but only the outlaw or brute commits wanton murder, even of a simple creature like a fox. As you grow and mature you must strive to be a complete warrior, too. The natural result of our art, our *gei*, is death—either your death or your opponent's. Yet this death must always be honorable and never simple murder. Do you understand what I'm telling you?" the Sensei asked.

"I think so," Kaze answered.

"Good. I want you to meditate on that, but I want you to learn how to meditate while suffering distractions." Saying that, the Sensei took him from where they had been talking to the foot of Dragonfly Falls.

Dragonfly Falls was a small but beautiful waterfall near the Sensei's hut in Kaze's home prefecture. The waterfall tumbled the height of three men in a steady silver stream. It was framed by black volcanic rocks in a rugged cliff. Lush green ferns and trees surrounded the picturesque setting. The sound of the falling water made a refreshing music that eased the soul. It was a favorite diversion to pass by the waterfall when any traveler was in the neighborhood, and this diversion was shared by intense orange and bright blue dragonflies, who gave the falls its name. The insects seemed to share the pleasure of humans in loitering near the beauty of the falls.

"At this time of year the water of the falls will be cold from snow runoff," the Sensei said. "I want you to stand under the waterfall and meditate on the lesson of Yoshimori. I want you to reflect on what it means to kill and not be a murderer."

After two years, Kaze had learned not to hesitate at the Sensei's orders. He shrugged off his kimono, leaving him standing only in his *fundoshi* loincloth.

"Do you know why I want you to do this reflection while standing under this waterfall?"

"Yes, Sensei, you want to see if I'm tough enough to withstand the icy water."

"*Baka!* Fool!"

Kaze cringed, and the Sensei sighed. In a gentler voice he said, "There are ways to toughen you up without being cruel. The purpose of this exercise is not to mortify the flesh, but to learn to focus. Just as a Zen priest will sit under a waterfall to meditate, now you must meditate. I will leave you here, and when you've truly focused and thought about what we've talked about today, then you can come back to the hut."

"Yes, Sensei," Kaze said.

Without another word of instruction the Sensei turned and left.

Kaze stepped into the cold water of the pool at the bottom of the falls and immediately felt the truth of the Sensei's prediction of how icy the water would be. He waded out to the tumbling waterfall, feeling the drops hitting his skin like crystals in an ice storm. Taking a deep breath to steel himself against the cold, he stepped under the stream of water coming down Dragonfly Falls and turned to face outward. He put his hands together, closed his eyes, and tried to concentrate as the water from the falls pummeled his head and shoulders and made his body shake from its frigid embrace.

It was hard to do what the Sensei instructed him to, but he tried to turn his thoughts and feelings inward, thinking about the lesson of Yoshimori. His powers of concentration were not strong enough and the noise of the falling water and the cold bothered him sufficiently so that he had a hard time focusing. He squeezed his eyes tighter and tried to think even more single-mindedly about the story he had been told.

Then he heard a sound that disturbed him much more than the falling water and noise and frostiness of his surroundings. It was the sound of a young girl giggling.

Because of the popularity of Dragonfly Falls and its beauty, it was not unexpected that someone else might come by. But it annoyed him that some young girl found his attempts to meditate under the tumbling water an excuse for laughter. In moments the young girl's laughter was joined by the sound of three or four men, and Kaze opened his eyes to see what was going on.

In front of him was a bamboo palanquin held by two *kago* porters. To the front and back of the kago were two samurai acting as guards. Sitting in the kago, the protective bamboo strip curtains raised so she could see the view, was the most beautiful girl Kaze had ever seen. Her face was oval with high cheekbones and a small pointed chin. Her large, expressive eyes were sparkling with some forbidden merriment. She held her hand to her mouth as she giggled uncontrollably. The porters and samurai guards had joined her in laughter, but theirs was a hearty guffaw.

When the girl removed her hand to suck in some air, Kaze could see a small mouth, perfectly formed with even white teeth. The smoothly arched eyebrows that accented her eyes looked natural rather than painted on. Her long black hair was in a casual style suitable for traveling, and her robes were extremely rich, including a kimono with a pattern that showed *botan,* peonies, scattered across a large brown branch.

Kaze was stunned by her exquisite beauty, but this beauty also heightened his discomfort about her laughing at him. Kaze closed his eyes and tried to concentrate even harder, to squeeze out the distraction that this rude group of people was causing him.

"Hey, boy," a male voice called to him.

Kaze was determined to ignore the summons.

"Boy!"

Kaze concentrated even harder.

"Please cover yourself, boy," the man said.

Kaze was puzzled by what the man meant, and, reluctantly, he opened his eyes again and stared out at the group. The water streaming down his face blurred his vision, but he could see that one of the samurai guards was lowering the kago's protective bamboo curtain on the young girl, while the other, the man who had shouted at Kaze, was pointing down toward Kaze's groin.

At first Kaze did not understand what the man was doing. Then he understood that he meant Kaze should check himself. Looking down, Kaze saw to his astonishment that the strength of the water coming down the waterfall had actually loosened his loincloth. Kaze was so numb from the cold that he hadn't noticed. And although the fundoshi was still on Kaze, the cloth had pushed to one side, exposing him. His young manhood was shrunken and shriveled by the cold water, but it was still plainly visible for all to see.

Normally Kaze was very comfortable with his body, but discovering why the beautiful young girl was laughing at him caused him to blush so hotly that, at least on his face, it momentarily blanked out the cold of the water.

Mortified, Kaze immediately turned his back to the group on the bank and the girl who had found his manhood a source of amusement. It was a long time before Kaze could concentrate on the tale of Yoshimori and foxes, as ordered. It was so long he almost froze.

◆   ◆   ◆

More than a decade later, Kaze was a rising star in his Lord's service. He had left the Sensei's training years ago, yet he often thought about the old man and the lessons he had learned.

After returning to his family from the Sensei, Kaze was married. After marriage, he got a post at his Lord's castle. The strength of his character and martial skills soon earned him a rapid string of advancements.

One day the Lord's castle was in a frenzy of excitement and anticipation because the Lord's bride was arriving at the castle for the first time. As with Kaze's marriage, this union was made on the basis of political, financial, and military considerations, but rumors circulated that the young Lord was also getting a woman of remarkable beauty.

Kaze was chosen to lead the escort that was to meet the future Lady of the domain at the border and escort her to the Lord's castle. He sat in his best battle armor, astride his favorite horse, with the *ashigaru,* the foot troops, selected for the rest of the honor guard, waiting for the bride's party to arrive at the border.

Before the Lady arrived, the martial display was literally and figuratively dampened by the start of a driving rainstorm. It beat down on the assembled troops, making them drenched and miserable, but it also made their helmets and armor glisten. The line of men formed a serpentine cordon, the wet scales of their leather *do,* or chest protectors, blending together to create the illusion of a dragon's body, with Kaze at its head. Kaze wore his best armor, including a metal *kabuto,* or helmet. Some kabuto for generals had enormous crests on them, to allow them to be identified on the battlefield, but Kaze's helmet just had a modest copper crescent on its front.

Kaze was thinking about getting his troops out of the rain when the vanguard of the Lady's entourage was spotted. Kaze gave an order in a voice trained to rise above the din of battle, and the men snapped to attention, holding their spears smartly to their sides. Kaze had trained these men, and he was proud of their appearance and discipline.

In a few minutes, four samurai on horseback, the advanced guard of the bride's party, reached Kaze's position. Then the palanquins of the Lady and two of her companions came by, followed by an oxcart full of luggage. The palanquins carrying the Lady's companions were simple bamboo kago, but the Lady was in a fancy *norimono*. The lacquer work and polished brass fittings of the norimono broadcast the wealth of the Lady's background, and the painted family crest on the folding door of the norimono proclaimed her lineage. Because it had this crest, instead of the three plum blossom crest of the Lord, Kaze knew this norimono would be returned to the Lady's family after the wedding.

The companions in the kago had chosen to follow the Lady to ease her loneliness at being sent to a new family to live. The Lady's new family, the family she was marrying into, would be expected to arrange suitable marriages for these companions in exile when the proper time came.

The remaining troops escorting the Lady marched past Kaze's guard, their heads bent into the rain. They stood opposite Kaze's troops, forming a corridor of honor for the Lady's palanquin. Walking with the bowlegged gait of palanquin porters, two men carried the small covered platform hanging from a thick lacquered beam between the two rows of troops. The palanquins of the companions were put on the wet ground a proper distance from the changing of the escorts ceremony.

The rain had been reduced to a steady curtain, so Kaze decided to greet the Lady. He jumped off his horse. The wooden, C-shaped stirrups allowed him to ride in sandals, the front of his sandaled foot fitting into the open end of the C. The leader of the Lady's escort came forward and announced his lineage and his assignment of escorting the Lady to the border. Kaze also announced his name and lineage and declared that his assignment was to escort the Lady from the border to the Lord's main castle, a half-day's journey away. Both men bowed to each other, each carefully bending at precisely the same angle to show they were equals. Now the responsibility for the Lady's safety had been passed to Kaze.

He walked forward and saluted, kneeling on one knee and bowing his head. After announcing his name, Kaze said, "I have the honor of escorting you to our Lord's castle. Despite the weather, I hope you will have a marvelous nuptial ceremony and that your life in our domain will be a happy one. There's a teahouse less than half a *ri* down the road. We can rest there if you want, or we can continue to the Lord's castle."

Kaze expected the Lady to express her wishes through the closed door of the palanquin. Instead, the hinged door opened. One of the guards ran up with an oiled paper umbrella to keep stray drops off the Lady.

Kaze had his head bowed, looking at the earth before him. He didn't immediately see the Lady, but he heard a soft, melodious voice saying, "That's very kind of you, Captain. My party is soaked by the rain, and I think they'd like a chance to dry out before proceeding to the Lord's castle."

Kaze looked up at the speaker and his breath caught in his throat. Large brown eyes framed by expressive brows looked at him. Her face was serene, with high cheekbones and a small mouth. If she was discomforted by the heavy rain, she didn't show it. Her gaze was steady and seemed to drink in tranquilly every detail of the scene before her.

Kaze tried to talk and found his voice catching. He cleared his throat and finally managed to say, "Of course, my Lady, your comfort and safety are my primary concerns."

She laughed. It was the same tinkling laugh as at the waterfall, and Kaze was sure it was the girl, now grown into an incredibly beautiful woman. "I'm not discomforted," she said. "Falling water never bothered me, although it might bother others. I simply suggested we stop at the teahouse so my escort can dry out. You and your men look soaked, too. I'm sure you'd all like to warm yourself by a nice *hibachi*."

Kaze hesitated a moment, not sure if her remark about falling water was directed at him. Could she have remembered and recognized him after all these years? If she did, she gave no further sign and simply closed the door of the palanquin without additional conversation.

Mounting his horse, Kaze led the procession to the teahouse, his mind racing.

The next day, Kaze safely brought the bride to the Lord's castle, and within a week the Lord and Lady were married. If the Lady recognized him as the boy at Dragonfly Falls, she never mentioned it during their time together.

A few years later, Kaze won a fencing exhibition in front of the Taiko, Toyotomi Hideyoshi himself. The combatants used *bokken,* wooden practice swords, but every entrant made a maximum effort to win for the honor of their clan in front of the ruler of Japan. As a result, several injuries and one death occurred during the competition, because the carved oak swords could be as deadly as any made of steel.

Kaze made it to the finals of the competition, his heart secretly glad that his opponent in the final round would be his boyhood nemesis, Okubo. The latter was not Lord of his clan yet, although his father's age made it a certainty that he would be shortly. Kaze had known Okubo since childhood, because he had spent time as a hostage with Kaze's clan after Okubo's father had lost a bid to conquer Kaze's clan in a war. Okubo's period as a hostage was intended to guarantee his father's good behavior, lest he lose his son and heir.

This period as a hostage had planted a deep-seated enmity and rivalry toward Kaze's clan in Okubo's heart, and Kaze relished the chance to defeat Okubo in the final match of the tournament. Right before the match, Kaze was approached with inducements to lose the match to Okubo. Kaze was so outraged by this attempt to guarantee a win for Okubo that he didn't just defeat Okubo, he destroyed him. Okubo now carried a limp in his left leg to remind him of that match and Kaze's reaction to the attempt to bribe him.

As a reward, Kaze was given command of a key castle on the border of his Lord's domain. It was an unusual honor for one so young, but it was an honor that evoked no jealousy or comment from elder members of the clan. Kaze's performance before the tournament and the glory that his victory brought to the clan made the promotion seem just and proper.

Right before Kaze left to take command of his new castle, his wife went to pay a good-bye call to the Lady.

"She's so nice and so generous," Kaze's wife said, returning from the courtesy visit.

"Why do you say that?" Kaze asked.

"Well, look what she gave me as a farewell gift," his wife said. "I really didn't want to take it, but she absolutely insisted. She said it was most appropriate for me."

"What did she give you?" Kaze asked, puzzled.

"Why, this piece of jewelry." Kaze's wife pulled a hairpin from her kimono sleeve. It was a long brass pin, with a silver decoration adorning the head of the pin. The decoration was a silver dragonfly.

CHAPTER 6

A fluttering leaf.
The transient moments are
sad and beautiful.

Falling water, in the form of rain, was also involved the last time Kaze saw the Lady alive. It was the day he pledged to the Lady that he would find her daughter and rescue her.

Memories of that time entered Kaze's mind. He shook his head, as if sending the drops of water clinging to his hair and face flying would also cast away the bitter memories of the day the Lady died. Sometimes memory can be like a bronze razor, Kaze reflected, lacerating the soul and shredding the heart, cutting deeply into the core of who we are and what motivates us. Kaze squeezed his eyes shut to block out thoughts of the past.

He sighed as he realized that there was also falling water involved the time he had seen the Lady's obake. That time the water was in the form of tears. The skin on his arms wrinkled into bumps and Kaze told himself it was simply a reaction to the cold rain and not to his encounter with a ghost on a mountain pathway—a ghost that had no face, but that he still knew to be the dead Lady.

Next to him, Hishigawa woke and immediately started his grumbling about how uncomfortable he was, how wet he was, and how cold he was. It seemed that the litany of complaints from the merchant formed a kind of mantra, reminding Kaze of the miserable existence of man and how the petty complaints and suffering of one man could seem more important to that man than the anguish, pain, and death of others. There were three guards and four bandits lying dead where Kaze first met the merchant. They would have been happy for a chance to feel the discomfort of the rain.

"I think it's letting up a little bit," the merchant said abruptly.

Kaze just grunted. The merchant was right, it was letting up.

"Maybe by morning things will dry out enough for us to push this cart," Kaze said. "Stop talking and try to sleep." Then Kaze wrapped his kimono closer about him, closed his eyes, and also tried to sleep.

The next morning, Kaze awoke to the sound of the merchant snoring loudly. The rain had stopped during the night, but the earth was still wet and muddy. Kaze crawled out from under the cart without disturbing the merchant and walked into the woods.

The pine scent was crisp and vibrant, a tart, bracing smell that you could almost taste on your tongue. Kaze came to a stream swollen by the heavy rains and watched the different shades of silver blinking at him. He took off his mud-smeared kimono and rinsed it in the steam. Walking to a place where the water was eddying a bit slower near a curve in the streambed, he stepped into the water to wash the mud off himself.

The water was cold. It seemed even colder than the icy spray of Dragonfly Falls. He told himself to be strong and wondered if, at thirty-one, he was already starting to get soft. Still, age didn't have much to do with toughness. The Sensei had been at least twice as old as Kaze was now, and he had been like a stone whose surface had been made smoother and harder by the passage of years. Although the body couldn't help but age, it was the spirit that got old, buffeted by too much pain, too many bitter memories, and too many disappointments. Kaze took a scoop of cold water and washed his face.

Getting out of the stream and donning his wet kimono, Kaze walked until he found an open space. A large cryptomeria was growing at the edge of the space, an infrequent procession of water drops dripping off a low limb. Kaze braced himself, his hand on his sword, and waited.

A tiny drop formed at the end of the limb, swelling until finally it released its bond with the branch and started falling to the ground. Kaze drew his katana and cut at the drop in one smooth motion. The polished blade made a flat arc, meeting the drop in midflight. The drop exploded into a constellation of minute stars that flew outward from the contact point of the sword and the water.

The borrowed sword had stuck slightly in the scabbard. Kaze made a note to use more force next time. He returned the sword to the scabbard and waited. When the next drop fell he repeated the act, cleanly meeting the drop before it hit the ground. He waited and did it again. And again.

Then he stopped and looked around the periphery of the space until his eyes finally settled on a young bush. He scrutinized the bush and picked off a tiny budding leaf, smaller than his thumbnail. He put his hand on the sword handle and threw the leaf in the air. The leaf caught a light breeze, and its irregular shape caused it to tumble about in the air, following an erratic path. Kaze drew his sword and sliced at the leaf.

He bent down and picked up the leaf, looking at it closely. He had missed it completely. He picked off a second leaf and threw that in the air. Once again he sliced at the leaf. Again he missed it. The normal swing of the katana was too long to catch the flitting leaf as it made its erratic way through the air. The dropping water was predictable, but a standard draw and swing on an erratically moving object was useless. Something like a small tumbling leaf required a different technique.

Kaze kept the sword in his hand and threw the leaf in the air. This time he used a sharp, flicking motion with his wrist instead of a normal cut. It was a motion that wouldn't generate enough power to deliver a mortal blow to a man, but it allowed the tip of Kaze's sword to move with blinding speed and catch the fluttering leaf.

This time when he picked up the leaf, he noticed he had sliced off a tiny section of it. He picked out other leaves and threw them in the air, repeating the process again and again and again until he was picking up two pieces of each leaf cut neatly in half. It was an unorthodox move with a sword, but Kaze practiced it as diligently as he practiced any move.

The purpose of practice, his Sensei would tell him, was to transcend technique and take his motions with the sword into the realm of expression and art.

By repeating the motions over and over again, you could reach a point where the mind and muscles no longer had to coordinate consciously. When that point was reached, the sword movement became a part of your body's existence, like breathing or the beating of your heart—a natural movement of your body that required no thought to execute.

Kaze still strove to learn his art and to perfect it. But despite the fact that he had great skill, he always considered himself a pupil who had to strive to learn just one more technique or movement. In the hands of a master like the Sensei, the way of the sword was an art, but it was one that could have unfortunate consequences.

Kaze had thought that great good would come from his skill at one time, when he was much younger. But he understood the capriciousness of fate and that the movement of forces greater than one man often held the key to our lives. One swordsman, no matter how good, could not fight the changes transforming Japan.

Kaze came out of the woods and returned to the pushcart to find the merchant had found some dry wood and had a small fire going. On the fire was a black metal pot; in it was water boiling for tea.

"It's probably best not to light a fire," Kaze said as he walked up to the merchant.

"Where were you?" the merchant said quickly. "I was worried you might have left me."

"No, I simply went into the woods."

The merchant just grunted his understanding, thinking that Kaze was simply answering a call of nature.

"The bandits might see the smoke," Kaze continued.

"I don't care," Hishigawa replied petulantly. "I have to get dried off and warmed up or else I'll die."

Kaze shrugged. "Unless we get some help," he said, "we will not be able to push that cart through these muddy pathways."

"Where can we get some help?" Hishigawa said.

"A pathway always goes somewhere," Kaze answered. "You simply follow it until you come to a village or farmhouse. There, we might be able to recruit some help to allow us to get this pushcart from here to the barrier."

"When do you think I should do that?" the merchant asked.

"Right now," Kaze answered. "If you go to a village or farmhouse, you'll probably find a hot breakfast."

The merchant looked over at the pushcart. "But what about the cart?"

"I'll stay here and watch it," Kaze said.

"But . . . " The merchant let the word trail off.

Kaze smiled. "Don't worry, I can't push the cart by myself either. So your gold will be safe. If you can't recruit some help, we are going to be here two or three days, until the roads dry up."

Sighing, the merchant took one last, reluctant look at the water starting to boil in the kettle and said, "All right. I'll go get some people to help us push the cart."

He started off down the road in search of a farmhouse or village. As he left, Kaze looked at the cart. He stared at it for several minutes, thinking about the possibilities.

Hishigawa was tired, stiff, and cold. All these things drove the fear from his heart and replaced it with anger. He was used to ronin doing as they were told, not giving orders. In fact, he was used to most people doing as they were told.

He was raised as the only child of a wealthy merchant family. First-born sons of Japanese families were always special anyway, but being the only son of a rich household made him the object of constant attention and pampering.

His first nurse, Ando, was barely older than he, yet she insisted on carrying him about on her back, his legs around her waist and a wide piece of cloth strapping him in place. This continued until Hishigawa was almost as big as Ando, so Ando would stagger around with the burden, a burden she seemed to relish. Ando was still with him, and as a reward for her loyalty, Hishigawa had given her more responsibility than a servant and a woman usually had.

Hishigawa wished she was with him now, to tend to his comfort. Instead, he was being sent to scour the countryside for help while the strange ronin was supposed to be guarding his gold. Gold. Until he met Yuchan, his entire life was motivated by the need to acquire more and more wealth. Now his life had two driving objectives.

His father had given up the life of a samurai to enter commerce. Hishigawa still wore the swords of a samurai and claimed two names, maintaining the fiction that he was a samurai, but he had never received training in the use of swords and knew that technically he was not entitled to wear them. Still, the ability to wear the two swords was just one of the privileges that wealth brought, so he guarded his wealth closely, insisting on personal involvement when large amounts of it were at risk, such as during this transfer of gold from Kyoto.

His apprehension over what the ronin might be doing with that gold added quickness to his step. He ignored the aches that pushing the cart and a night in the rain had brought to him. Curse that ronin! Why couldn't he have let them find a nice temple or farmhouse to spend the night in, away from the rain?

Goro and Hanzo were arguing. That was the natural condition for the two men. They lived in the same small farmhouse and shared a farm that was currently too muddy to work, so instead of bickering in the fields, they bickered in the home.

"Those must have been soldiers," Goro said.

"They didn't look like soldiers. They looked like bandits," Hanzo answered.

"What do bandits look like? You've never really seen a bandit because you have nothing worth stealing!"

"I have seen what soldiers look like, and they didn't look like them. And, if I had a better partner in this farm, I'd have plenty worth stealing."

"I'm the one that does all the work!"

"If you did all the work—"

"*Oi!* You! Is someone home in there?" Hearing the abrupt greeting "oi" rather than the polite "sumimasen," both Goro and Hanzo froze. Despite their bluster, they had been scared by the group of armed men who had stopped at their hut the night before, searching for a party with a pushcart.

"Do you think they're back?" Goro whispered, a quaver in his voice.

"I don't know. I don't recognize the voice," Hanzo whispered back.

"What should we do?"

"I don't know. Should we open the door?"

"I don't know, either. If we don't open the door, they can break it down."

"I think we better open it."

"Okay," Goro said. He looked around and grabbed a rake leaning against the wall, holding it like a weapon. "You go ahead and open it."

"I don't want to open it!"

"We just said we should open it. If you—"

"Oi!" The voice was more insistent and angry. "I hear you whispering in there. Open the door!"

The two peasants looked at each other. Hanzo finally went to the door, removed the stick that functioned as a lock, and slid the wooden farmhouse door back. Standing before them was a potbellied middle-aged man, dressed like a merchant but wearing two swords. He was bedraggled and smeared with mud from head to foot. It spotted his hair, streaked his kimono, daubed his legs, and encrusted his sandals. He looked like he was half clay and half flesh. His filthy appearance made a comic counterpoint to his bearing. He was standing with a hand on the hilt of his katana, his weight on one foot, staring down his nose at them like he was the greatest *daimyo* in the land. Relieved, the two peasants burst out in laughter.

Hishigawa couldn't understand what the two louts were laughing at and shouted "*Yakamashii!* Shut up!" at them. The two peasants sobered up at the command, and Hishigawa invited himself into the relative warmth of the crude farmhouse, demanding that they serve him breakfast.

"Please come in, Samurai-sama," Goro said, bowing low. He went to the cook fire in the hut to stir the breakfast soup, where he was joined by Hanzo.

"Do you think we should have let him in?" Hanzo whispered.

"What choice do we have? He's wearing the two swords."

"Yes, but he's covered in mud. He doesn't look like any samurai I've ever seen. He looks more like a merchant. In fact, I'm not even sure he's human. He might be a *kappa*. He's covered with mud, like he just crawled out of a pond." Kappa were creatures who lived under bridges and in ponds who drowned children.

"What are you whispering about?" Hishigawa shouted. "Where is my breakfast!"

"Coming, coming, Samurai-sama," Goro said soothingly. Then, whispering to Hanzo, he said, "How can we tell if he's human or kappa?"

"Kappa have little saucers of water in the top of their heads. They have to be near water or they grow weak, so they always carry water with them. If we knock him down so the water spills out, he'll be helpless."

"A saucer in his head?"

"Yes. Made of flesh."

"I'll check," Goro said.

He took the bowl of *miso* soup and walked over to Hishigawa.

Hishigawa reached up for the bowl, but Goro, intent on peering at the top of Hishigawa's head, kept moving the bowl as Hishigawa reached for it. The merchant made a couple of ineffective grabs for the soup bowl, but Goro unintentionally moved it each time as he shuffled to the side to get a better view, just to make sure a fleshy saucer of water wasn't hidden in the man's thinning hair.

Finally, in exasperation, Hishigawa shouted, "What is wrong with you?"

Snapping to attention, Goro said, "Oh, nothing, nothing, Samurai-sama. *Gomen nasai,* excuse me. Here is the breakfast soup. It is humble, but please enjoy it." He gave the bowl to Hishigawa and scurried back to the fire and Hanzo.

"Well?"

"He's going bald, but I didn't see any saucer on his head. He doesn't have lice," Goro added helpfully.

Hishigawa drained the soup and held out the bowl for another helping. Goro gave it to him, scraping the bottom of the pot in the process. When he had finished the second bowl, Hishigawa asked, "Is there a village near here?"

"About two ri away, Samurai-sama."

Hishigawa moaned. That was too far to walk. "Are there porters or samurai at the village?"

"No, Samurai-sama. It's just a small village. Nothing but poor farmers."

Hishigawa sighed. "I have need of porters and fighting men." He looked the two scrawny peasants over and decided they were better than nothing. "How about you two? Do you want to earn some money? I'll give you four coppers to go to Kamakura."

"Kamakura?"

"Yes. I have a pushcart that I need moved to Kamakura. With this mud, I need help."

The mention of a pushcart raised alarm bells in the two peasants. The men who came by the night before were searching for a party with a pushcart.

"But we have our farm to tend. In a few days the fields will be dry enough for us to work them."

"All right, six coppers," Hishigawa said.

Normally six coppers would have gotten their cooperation, but the memory of the men made the peasants hesitate. "But all the way to Kamakura! We've never been to Kamakura," Hanzo said.

Hishigawa glowered at the peasants. Peasants were shrewd, but these two wouldn't know the value of making a dangerous journey. "Ten coppers, my final offer," Hishigawa said sternly.

"I'll take it," Goro said hastily.

"That's for both of you," Hishigawa added.

"What about it, Hanzo? Let's go to Kamakura. When we get there, we'll have money to spend," Goro said.

Hanzo hesitated a second, still not sure that the gruff, mud-covered man was completely human, but the wheedling of his friend finally got him to agree. The thoughts of the searching men were driven from his mind by the thought of more money than their little farm could earn in a year.

CHAPTER 7

Two chickens on a
branch. The clucking sounds of
meaningless discourse.

A few hours later, Kaze saw the merchant returning with two other figures. Kaze was in the midst of packing mud into the end of one of the large bamboo poles that formed the rails of the cart. The bamboo was almost as thick around as a man's arm, and it took several scoops of mud to block off the end. Then Kaze bent down and washed his hands in a puddle of rainwater.

Kaze's brows furrowed into a V at the sight of the merchant's recruits. Both were short and skinny. That wasn't necessarily a sign of a lack of strength for pushing the cart, because peasants were notoriously wiry and full of stamina. What caused Kaze to frown was that both seemed to be engaged in some kind of dispute, gesturing wildly and shaking their fists at each other.

Hishigawa, leading the quarreling pair, had a grim look to his face, his jaw set and a clear look of displeasure painted across his visage. As the trio approached, Kaze was able to pick up the substance of the argument.

"We should split it evenly," one of the peasants said. He was wearing a filthy gray kimono.

"No, I am the one who agreed to this job, then I asked you. Therefore, you are working for me. I should have two coins for every one you get. In fact, you should call me Boss Goro for the rest of the journey!" He was wearing a pair of traveling pants and a jacket. His bald pate was topped by a headband of twisted cloth.

"Ridiculous!"

"It's ridiculous that you think it's ridiculous!"

"Yes? Well, it's ridiculous that you think my saying it's ridiculous is ridiculous!"

Goro had his mouth working like a *fugu*, a blowfish, as he sorted through his companion's retort, trying to understand what his response should be. He gave up and hit Hanzo on the forehead with an open hand. The blow made a sharp slapping sound.

"*Itai!* Ouch! What gives you the right to hit me like that?"

"Because I'm the boss."

"You're not the boss! What makes you the boss?"

"I told you it was my idea to take this job."

"You don't speak for me. When you asked me, I was the one who said I would take the job."

"See! See! You admit I asked you. That makes me the boss."

"It doesn't."

"It does!"

"Ridiculous!"

"Ridiculous yourself!"

Slap.

"I said that hurts! You better stop that before I get mad and hurt you, too. But I won't just give you a slap on the head. I'll smash you!" Hanzo shook a fist at Goro.

Slap.

"Oh! Now you've really hurt me!" Tears formed in Hanzo's eyes. He grabbed his forehead and moaned.

"There, there. I didn't mean to really hurt you. I see I've gone too far. We'll split the money evenly. I promise you. You don't have to call me Boss." Then, in a low mutter, he said, "But I'm still the boss!"

Kaze cocked his head to one side and looked at Hishigawa. "This is the best you could do?" he asked dryly.

"Of course it's the best I could do," Hishigawa said with a tight jaw. "They've been arguing like this ever since we left their farmhouse. They won't stop!"

"What are you called?" Kaze asked the peasants.

The two were a bit surprised that a samurai would bother to ask their names.

"I'm Goro," the man with the headband said.

"I'm Hanzo," said the one in the filthy gray kimono.

"What were you told about what we want you to do?"

Goro pointed to Hishigawa. "He promised us ten coppers if we'd help him push a cart to Kamakura."

"You'll get gold," Kaze said.

"Gold!"

"What are you promising?" Hishigawa said.

"Now listen carefully," Kaze said to the peasants. "There will be danger."

"Why are you telling them—"

Kaze looked at Hishigawa, silencing the angry merchant. "I'm telling them because they should know. Their lives will be in danger, as ours have been."

Returning his attention to the peasants, he said, "That chest tied to the pushcart has gold in it. There are men who want that gold. Perhaps by now there are many men. They've already killed the three guards who were assigned to protect that gold, and they will kill us, if they can. We must get that cart to the barrier, where additional guards can be hired to protect us for the rest of the journey to Kamakura. Until then, we will be in great danger. Do you understand that?"

As Kaze spoke, the eyes of the two peasants grew in size. They looked at each other, then at Kaze, and said, "Hai! Yes!"

"And do you still want to help?"

Once again the two peasants looked at each other, then at Kaze. But this time they looked at each other a second time before answering.

"What do you think, Hanzo?"

"What do you think?"

"I think these men must be the ones who those other men were looking for. Still, this samurai has been honest with us, and he's promised us gold. I think we should help."

"What other men?" Kaze asked.

"Last night a group of men came by our hut, looking for a party with a pushcart. I suppose that's you."

"How many men?"

"I don't know. A lot."

"More than four?"

"Yes, quite a few more than four."

"Yes, they are looking for us," Kaze said. "They want that gold. We still need your help, and there might be the chance that those men will find us. Will you still help us?"

Goro looked at Kaze. "We're not fighters," he said.

Kaze smiled. "I don't expect you to be. We just need men who will push the cart. If there's any fighting to be done, I'll handle it."

There was a moment's hesitation as the two peasants looked at each other.

"Gold for us?" Hanzo asked.

"Gold," Kaze confirmed.

"Then we'll do it."

"Good! There's no better time than now to start. *Yosh!* Let's go! Give us a hand getting the cart back on the road."

Goro and Hanzo took a position behind the cart to push it, and Kaze took one of the bamboo rails of the cart, with Hishigawa on the other. As they got the cart back on the road, Hishigawa groaned, "It seems even heavier than yesterday."

"It's the mud slowing us down, and you're tired from yesterday," Kaze said.

Hishigawa grunted a reply and the four men moved the cart down the road. Unlike Hishigawa and Kaze, Goro and Hanzo were not silent. They bickered constantly as they pushed. Kaze noticed that they pushed much better when they were arguing with each other, so he let them. Hishigawa tried to silence them a couple of times, and his harsh words and glowering gaze did silence them for a moment, but within minutes they would find some new cause of dispute between them and the arguments would start again.

Late in the morning they came to a fork in the road, with paths traveling both left and right.

"What path do we take?" Kaze asked.

"We take the left path," Hanzo replied.

"No, we should take the right path," Goro said.

"The left path is flat and the shortest way to the barrier."

"We know bandits are looking for the cart. They'll surely be waiting along the left path."

"But the right path is much longer. You have to circle the entire mountain before you get to the barrier. Along the left path, we'd be at the barrier late today or early tomorrow. The right path will be at least another day of hard travel."

"But—"

"Yakamashii! Shut up!" Hishigawa screamed. "You two bicker like an old married couple. It is intolerable!"

"Perhaps intolerable, but in this case interesting," Kaze said. "We have a choice to make."

"The faster path," Hishigawa said. "The faster we get to the barrier, the faster we will all be safe, along with my gold."

"All right," Kaze said, "the left path. But we should remain alert, because if the bandits know anything about the paths in this district, they will surely set an ambush before we get to the barrier."

The men started moving the cart down the left branch of the trail, and within minutes Hanzo and Goro were arguing about some past dispute. Kaze sighed but continued pulling on the cart, while Hishigawa ground his teeth.

For most of their journey, the path went between wooded patches punctuated by open meadows. The tree branches converged over the path, providing the illusion of shelter and safety and highlighting how exposed the group was in the open areas. As they came to each meadow, Kaze stopped the cart and advanced to reconnoiter the territory. Hishigawa protested the first stop, calling it an unnecessary delay, but Kaze's look was enough to silence him.

After several hours the path left the woods, went down a long slope, and passed into a marshy valley filled with tall reeds. At the fringe of the remaining woods, Kaze stopped the cart and told the three to wait. Hishigawa opened his mouth as if to protest again but closed it without voicing his frustration over the delays.

Kaze started down into the valley. Soon the reeds were above his head. It was the perfect place for an ambush, because the reeds could conceal any number of men. He didn't like the looks of this part of the journey and returned to the edge of the woods and the pushcart.

"Well?" Hishigawa demanded. "Can we finally continue our journey? We could have been at the barrier by now if it weren't for these constant delays."

"I don't like the feel of what's ahead."

"Feel? Feel? That's no reason to stop us!"

Kaze made no response. Instead he stood looking at the valley, searching for some clue of what was ahead. The valley stretched before him like a sea of green and brown. In a slight breeze, the reed stalks swayed with the grace of a *Noh* performer. The brown heads of the reeds rippled as the wind caressed them, revealing the green stalks below. A soft rustling sound emerged from the waving sea of stalks. At the end of the valley, Kaze saw a flight of birds ascend into the blue sky, startled by something. In a few seconds, Kaze saw another group of birds leaving the safety of the reeds, just a short distance from the first.

"There are men in there," Kaze said.

"Where?" Hishigawa asked.

"Moving. Watch the far side of the valley."

As he talked, a third group of birds flew up from the reeds.

"There," he said.

"I don't see any men," Hishigawa said.

"Neither do I," Goro said.

"Me, neither," Hanzo echoed.

"You don't see the wind, but you can see its results on the reeds. You can't see the men, but you can see the results of their progress through the reed field. When Minamoto Yoshiie led an expedition against Kiyohara Takehira, he was able to detect an ambush from geese taking flight from reeds, disturbed by men getting into position. Here three groups of birds have also escaped from the reeds, fleeing the approach of men."

"They could be fleeing the approach of a badger or *tanuki*," Hishigawa said.

"Are you willing to take that chance?" Before Hishigawa could answer, Kaze added, "If you die, you will not see your wife, Yuchan, again."

That seemed to convince Hishigawa. "What should we do?" he asked.

"We don't know how many men are there, so there may be too many to fight. Also, it's likely they haven't seen us yet because they're among the reeds, so their view is blocked. I think we should return to the fork in the road and take the mountain path."

"But it will take hours to get back to that path, and we won't reach the barrier today," Hishigawa protested.

"Is your life worth a few hours of travel?"

Hishigawa sighed. "All right."

"When we go back, try to keep the cart in the same ruts. Perhaps we can fool them if they get tired of hiding in the reeds and come down this path looking for us."

Kaze went into the bushes and cut a branch from a bush and a stave from a small sapling. When he returned to the road, the three men had turned the cart around and were already moving it down the path, following Kaze's instructions to try to keep the cart in the same ruts.

Kaze used the branch to smooth out the soft mud of the path, erasing the evidence of the cart having been turned around. Then he used the sapling as a staff, gouging out false ruts in the dirt road to make it look as if the cart had been taken off the road and into the woods. This was the same technique Kaze had used to fool the bandit who had been following them earlier, making it look as if the cart had gone off the path and miraculously been able to pass through a tree.

Kaze continued making the false ruts into the woods. When he reached ground rocky enough to stop the creation of the ruts, he threw the staff away. Now it would look as if the cart had been taken off the road again.

Come on, fools," Hishigawa said.

Hanzo stopped pushing and motioned to Goro to do the same.

"You shouldn't call us fools," he protested.

"What are you talking about?" Hishigawa snapped.

"I think you're really a merchant, not a samurai. You don't act like that other samurai, Matsuyama-san. If you're not a samurai, you shouldn't be calling us such rude things." By rights, peasants actually ranked higher on the social scale than merchants, right under nobles and samurai.

"My family is a samurai family," Hishigawa said.

"But you're not a samurai, are you? You've given it up to become a merchant. Isn't that true?"

"Why, you little—"

"You really should control your temper," a voice said.

Hishigawa, Hanzo, and Goro looked about them.

"Up here."

They looked up and saw Kaze sitting on the branch of a tree above their heads. He was balanced in the lotus position, completely at ease at a height twice that of a man. He had circled ahead of them and had been waiting.

"We need the help and hard work of Hanzo and Goro," Kaze said reasonably. "It's not much to show politeness. When dealing with customers, you must do it all the time, even when you don't feel like doing it."

"I . . . " the merchant started, then thought a bit about what he was about to say. "You're right," Hishigawa said to the samurai. "There's no reason for us to fight," the merchant said with forced affability to Hanzo and Goro. "We all want to get out of here."

Goro looked up at Kaze. "Do you think the bandits are gone now?" he asked.

The samurai shook his head. "They won't rest until they get that chest of gold. I laid a false trail for quite a distance. Eventually they'll figure out that the cart didn't go through the woods. Then they'll come back to the point where we took the cart off the road and start searching."

Kaze put his hands on the tree limb to steady himself and unfolded his legs from the lotus position. Then, with the lightness of a child, he swung downward from the limb, hanging from his arms briefly before he dropped to the earth.

Picking himself up as quickly as he had dropped, Kaze said, "Come on. Let's get back to the path that leads toward the mountain."

CHAPTER 8

*Swirling water is
deep and murky. I claw to
the surface and gasp.*

Before they came to the mountain path's branch, they came across an old peasant trudging down the path with a load of firewood on his back. Seeing there was a samurai in the group, the old man bowed his head and stood to one side of the path.

"Do you have any coppers?" Kaze asked Hishigawa.

"Why?"

"I need a few."

"For what?"

Kaze held out his hand, and, reluctantly, Hishigawa put three coppers into it.

Kaze walked over to the old peasant and said, "Hello, Grandfather. Are you traveling a long way?"

The peasant, startled that a samurai was talking to him, bowed his head even further and mumbled, "All the way to the barrier, Samurai-sama."

"Then you will be going through the valley of the reeds."

"Yes, Samurai-sama. To get to the barrier, one must travel through that valley."

"I would like you to do a service for us, Grandfather."

The peasant, who had seen Kaze get the coppers from Hishigawa, looked up and eyed Kaze shrewdly. "What service is that, Samurai-sama?"

"When you go through the valley of the reeds, or perhaps before then, you may be stopped by some men. If you are, they will ask you if you have seen two men with a pushcart. All you have to do is say no. As you can see, we are four men with a pushcart, so you won't even have to lie. Can you do that?"

"Hai. Yes, Samurai-sama."

Kaze held out the coppers, and the peasant reached forward with both hands cupped together. Kaze dropped the coppers into the old man's hands. The peasant put his hands together and brought them up to his forehead in a sign of gratitude. "Rest assured, Samurai-sama, I shall say nothing."

"Good."

Kaze rejoined the group and started moving the pushcart down the path.

"You should have killed him," Hishigawa said. As a samurai, Kaze had the right to kill any peasant for any reason.

"Perhaps," Kaze observed mildly, "but so many men have already died on this journey, and there is no need to add another. Besides, I don't like to use a dead man's sword to kill another."

Darkness fell before the men reached the mountain path branch, so they pulled the cart off the path and fell down around it, exhausted. Hishigawa told Hanzo to get the iron pot from the cart and make some tea.

"It's all muddy," Hanzo said.

"Nonsense," Hishigawa said. "Only tea water is boiled in that pot."

"Well, it appears—"

"Don't bother," Kaze said. "We shouldn't make a fire tonight anyway. If we stay quiet and the bandits come down the trail tonight, they'll miss us in the dark. If we make a fire, they'll certainly see us.

After some grumbling by Hishigawa, Kaze prevailed, and the men made a meager supper of some cold brown rice that Hanzo and Goro had brought with them.

The next morning, Goro was up first. He looked about him in the half-light of dawn and saw that all the others were still sleeping soundly. Stealthily, he got up and crept to the pushcart. He looked at the strongbox on the cart, reached out with one hand, and speculatively fingered the rope tying the treasure chest to the cart.

"Even if you took some, I'd find you."

Goro jumped in surprise, spinning around to find the ronin standing behind him, watching him.

"You scared me, Samurai-sama!" Goro said. "I was, ah, I was . . . "

"I promised you gold," Kaze said, "but you must earn it."

"I wasn't thinking about stealing!"

"Of course not. Now come with me into the woods so we can gather some roots for breakfast."

Early in the morning the men returned to the branch in the path and turned onto the road to the mountain. Soon the path grew stonier and started rising in elevation, which made moving the pushcart harder. The men were pushing the cart up a path cut into the lower slope of a volcanic mountain. The gray rock was pierced with sparse outcroppings of the most tenacious plants, but otherwise it was bare and forbidding. The desolate nature of the surroundings silenced even Goro and Hanzo; the only sound was the grunting of the men, the creaking of the cart wheels, and the rush of a river, down the slope from the path.

Hot and thirsty, the men stopped the cart. Goro picked up the water jug from the cart and peered inside. "It's almost empty," he said.

Kaze pointed down to the river, rushing at the foot of the path. "There's an unlimited supply of fresh water," he said.

Goro and Hanzo made their way down the long incline to the river with the jug to fetch fresh water. All the way down the slope, the two men were arguing.

"When we get paid for this job, I think we should pool our money and start a business," Hanzo said.

"Well, I want to keep my money and enjoy myself. We'll be in Kamakura and can have a lot of fun. If we have enough, I might want to go and see the new capital, Edo."

"Wasting money on pleasure is not the way to wealth. We should save it for a business."

"What business?"

"How should I know? We'll decide that after we see how much money we get. The samurai said gold."

"The samurai didn't even have copper. He had to get the money for the old peasant from the merchant. The merchant said copper."

They reached the river. It was full from the recent rains and flowing swiftly. Goro got on a large rock, bent down, and dipped the jug into the swiftly flowing current to fill it. Standing up, he said, "Regardless of whether it's gold or copper, I want to have a good time with it."

"You're stupid," Hanzo said. "A business is the right thing to do with it."

"You don't even know what business to be in. You're the one who's stupid!"

"I am not!"

"You are too!"

His face red with anger, Hanzo gave Goro a push. Goro, off balance because he was holding a heavy jug, staggered backward, slipping off the rock and into the rushing river. He was instantly swept up by the river's current, moving downstream at a rapid rate.

"Help!" Hanzo screamed. He looked up the slope at Kaze and Hishigawa. "Please help! Goro can't swim, and neither can I!"

Kaze handed his sword to Hishigawa and started running down the road, following Goro's progress in the river. When he caught up with the hapless peasant, he plunged down the steep slope to the river, keeping to his feet with amazing balance.

"Try to hold on to a rock," Kaze shouted to Goro.

The peasant heard the command and tried to flail out and secure himself to a rock. He wasn't able to, but his efforts slowed him down as Kaze leapt from rock to rock in an effort to reach the peasant. Finally, seeing that he was as close as he was going to get by acting like a mountain goat, Kaze plunged into the foaming river.

Swimming with the current, Kaze avoided being thrown against the rocks that studded the stream. Right before he reached Goro, the peasant disappeared under the water. Hanzo, who could still see the two bobbing heads moving ever farther away, gave a great groan when he saw his friend disappear under the swirling water.

Kaze reached the spot where Goro had vanished and dove under the water, frantically searching for the peasant. He realized that he could be dashed against a rock or drowned himself, but he focused on trying to save the quarrelsome peasant and put such considerations out of his mind. He looked about underwater, but the water was too turbulent and murky. He surfaced to see if Goro had made his way to the top again, didn't see him, took a quick breath, and dove under the surface once more. Reaching out into the swirling water, his hand brushed against a piece of cloth. Propelling himself forward with a powerful kick, he grabbed the cloth with his strong grip and held on to it with tenacity.

Breaking the surface of the water, he hauled the peasant, gasping and coughing, back into the sweet air.

Kaze swam to a quiet eddy in the river and dragged the peasant onto the shore. Goro continued to cough, spitting up water.

Hanzo, who had made his way downstream, rushed to the side of his friend, holding him in his arms. "Goro, Goro! Please forgive me! It was stupid of me to push you. Please say you forgive me."

Goro looked up into Hanzo's face, then spit up a mouthful of water into it.

"You idiot!" Hanzo said.

"You were the one who just said he was an idiot."

"I said I was stupid to push you. That's not the same thing as being an idiot."

"Well, then you're stupid."

"If I'm stupid, then you're an idiot."

Kaze shook his head and started making his way back up the stream to the place where Hishigawa was waiting with the pushcart. He was sitting on the money chest, resting his feet as Kaze came up the slope.

"I can see the peasant didn't drown," Hishigawa said casually, pointing to Goro and Hanzo, also making their way up stream and still arguing. "This has been a terrible waste of time."

Kaze said nothing but took back the sword from Hishigawa and also sat on the cart to rest. Goro and Hanzo made their way up the slope, miraculously stopping their bickering. They came up to the cart and dropped to their knees in front of Kaze. They bent down with their hands on either side of their heads and touched their foreheads to the ground in a deep kowtow.

"Thank you for saving me, Samurai-sama," Goro said. "I will be eternally grateful."

"Thank you for saving my friend," Hanzo said. "I am sorry my foolish act caused you so much trouble."

"Get up," Kaze said gruffly. "I didn't want Goro's dead body stinking up the river, so I had to save him before he drowned."

Surprised, the two peasants looked up. When they saw the small smile on Kaze's face, they both started laughing.

Kaze's kimono was barely dry when they pushed the cart around a corner and were confronted by a half dozen armed men waiting a good distance up the narrow road. At the sight of the pushcart, the men started advancing, swords and spears at the ready.

"That old man must have betrayed us," Hishigawa said. "He told them we were heading back to the mountain path."

"Probably," Kaze said. "Wait here." He walked behind the cart a short distance until he could get a clear view of the twisting road behind them. Coming up the mountain path were four men. They were armed with swords and spears, too.

They were trapped.

Kaze approached the cart. "There are men coming up the path, too."

Hishigawa looked at the narrow path, with the mountain on one side and the steep slope down to the river on the other. There was no place to move the cart, except either up or down the path. Looking at the samurai with terror in his eyes, he asked, "What should we do?"

"Hurry," Kaze said, "we only have a few minutes."

"What is it?"

"With the men coming up the trail and the six ahead of us, there are ten men to fight."

"You'll fight ten men?" the merchant said, incredulous.

"If I must. I hope not to." He took out his sword.

"Are we going to fight, too?" Hanzo said, with a quiver to his voice. "I said we weren't fighters."

"No, you're not going to fight. Just keep out of the way. I have an idea. Perhaps none of us will have to fight."

"What is it?" Hishigawa asked.

"Just watch."

Kaze walked to the cart and used his sword to cut the ropes holding the strongbox to the cart. As he finished, the two groups of men coming up and down the path saw each other, the cart trapped between them.

"Help me," Kaze said urgently. He grabbed one end of the heavy strongbox. Hanzo, still not understanding Kaze's plan, rushed to take the other end.

"Now, what, Samurai-sama?" he asked.

"Help me move it away from the cart."

"What are you doing?" Hishigawa said, a touch of alarm in his voice.

"Just watch," Kaze answered.

Kaze and Hanzo staggered to the edge of the road just as the two groups of men converged on the cart.

"Give us the gold," one of the bandits shouted.

"If you want the gold, you must work for it," Kaze said.

Kaze suddenly took his end of the box and dropped it over the edge of the road. Hanzo, who was unable to hold the box on his own, gave a cry and almost dove off the road to try to catch the box. Kaze grabbed him by the collar of his kimono and shouted to the bandits,"You better go after it before the gold gets washed away in the river."

Hishigawa gave a cry of pain, and Goro stood horrified as the box tumbled down the mountainside, end over end, making its long way down to the bottom of the mountain and into the river with a splash. The bandits stood mesmerized as the box somersaulted its way down the slope. The men formed a frozen tableau, watching the gold receding from their grasp. Suddenly, all the bandits started scrambling down the slope, some slipping in the loose dirt, one actually falling and sliding down the slope on his face.

"My gold!" Hishigawa sobbed.

"Samurai-sama, why did you do that?" Hanzo cried.

Kaze, seeing the road ahead was clear, said, "Quick, let's get out of here."

He reached over and grabbed one of the shafts of the pushcart.

"Why are you taking the cart?" Hishigawa said. "It's worthless now that you've gotten rid of the gold."

Kaze commanded, "Do as I tell you. Take the cart. Come on, let's go!"

Looking bewildered, Goro and Hanzo resumed their positions behind the cart pushing, but Hishigawa refused to grab on the cart's shaft to pull.

"It's still heavy," Goro grunted.

"But not as heavy as when that strongbox was on the cart," Kaze said. "Come on, let's hurry."

CHAPTER 9

*Part the curtain and
disclose the trick. The magic
of revelation.*

It's the barrier!" Hanzo cried out.

For centuries Japanese roads had barriers across them. They acted as checkpoints, taxing stations, and helped to regulate commerce. Since the Tokugawa victory at Sekigahara, the Tokugawa forces had manned the barriers on the Tokaido Road and other major highways. As a result, Kaze usually cut across country to avoid the barriers. Now he had no choice but to go through the barrier. He wondered if one of the warriors at the barrier would recognize him from the days when he fought against the Tokugawas.

The barrier was a sturdy fence of large bamboo that stretched for a long distance on both sides of the road. In the middle of the barrier, straddling the road, was a pair of large bamboo gates. Next to the gate were a guard barracks, an area for doing business, a teahouse, stands selling refreshments, and a stable where horses were kept for the Tokugawa messenger service. The messenger service used relays of horses and riders to speed messages from Edo to all points on the main island of Honshu.

As they approached the barrier, Kaze said to the disconsolate Hishigawa, "You should report the bandits. Then we should get an armed escort that will take us to Kamakura. You can continue on to Edo later."

Hishigawa looked at Kaze, his eyes flashing with anger, "What for? You threw the gold off the cart and down to the river below! By now the bandits would have retrieved it. All is lost."

Kaze sighed. "Stop the cart for a few moments," he said to Goro and Hanzo. The two peasants stopped pushing, glad to have a short breather while the samurai and the merchant seemed to be settling something. For once, others were fighting instead of them.

"What good is getting guards now?" Hishigawa screamed, his fury rising.

Kaze stopped for a minute and looked at the merchant. Seeing the steady set of Kaze's eyes, the merchant stifled his anger. When the merchant had himself under control, Kaze said, "Good. Now watch."

He pulled the dead man's sword from his scabbard in a smooth fluid motion. Without using his full force, he brought the blade down on the edge of the large bamboo rail that made up the framework of the cart. The blade cut into the bamboo, knocking out the mud plug that filled the end of the hollow shaft.

Hishigawa, Hanzo, and Goro watched Kaze's actions with puzzled looks on their faces, uncertain as to what the samurai was doing. Kaze took the blade of his sword and twisted it, splitting the bamboo and opening a gap to reveal what was inside.

"There's your gold," Kaze said.

Hishigawa walked to the split rail of the cart and looked into the gap. There, at the core of the bamboo, was a long plug of mud holding together large clumps of oblong *oban* gold coins.

"What?" Hishigawa asked, stunned.

"There's your gold," Kaze repeated.

"How?" Hishigawa said, shaking his head in befuddlement.

"When you went to get Goro and Hanzo, I opened your strongbox. Then I cored out this bamboo and dropped the gold coins from the strongbox down the bamboo. I used your pot for tea water to pour mud into the shaft so the coins wouldn't move around or make noise. Most of your gold is in this shaft, but the other shaft also has some. I put rocks in the strongbox so it would be heavy and tied it up again."

Hishigawa fell to his knees and reached up with a trembling hand to touch the bamboo shaft of the cart.

"It's all there?" he asked in wonder.

"Yes."

"My gold."

"I thought it would be a shame to lose the gold, but, if necessary, I knew it would be so much easier to give the bandits the strongbox. The fact that I was able to give them the strongbox in a way that caused them great effort to retrieve it was just a gift from the Gods."

"My gold," Hishigawa repeated, still stunned by the sudden reversal of fortunes.

"Come on," Kaze said, "let's get down to the barrier."

As Hishigawa went into the guardhouse to report the bandits and arrange for an armed escort into Kamakura, Kaze took Goro and Hanzo to one of the nearby stands that served refreshments. These were simple structures made of bamboo lashed together into a crude framework, with a rough thatched roof and wooden benches that served as both seats and table for weary travelers. In one corner of this stand was a stove made of mud, where tea water was heated and food was cooked.

As he entered the stand, Kaze asked the proprietor, a wizened man with a face like old leather from working outdoors in the summer sun and winter cold, if he had seen a trio of travelers consisting of an old woman, a youth, and an old, thin servant.

"An obaasan, a grandmother, with a headband? On the headband the kanji for 'revenge'?" the old man said.

"The same!"

"Yes. They went through here a few days ago. That was one tough old granny!" The man cackled. "I thought she was going to run me through with that spear she carries when I wouldn't give her a discount. Argued with me for the longest time, then finally took her business next door. Heard her arguing over there, too. She was something."

Having been so lucky, Kaze took a chance. "Is there a nine-year-old girl around here? She would have come within the past two years, possibly sold as a servant."

The old man scratched his head. "No, sorry, Samurai, there's nobody like that in these parts."

Hiding his disappointment, Kaze thanked the old man for the information, sat on a bench, and ordered hot tea and roasted gingko nuts on tiny bamboo skewers. Goro and Hanzo, not used to partaking of the amenities of the world, sat together on a bench. They were curious about Kaze's inquiries but so uncomfortable about being in the snack stand that they remained silent. The meager earnings from their farm made spending money on tea and service an unthinkable luxury.

Kaze was handed a brown earthenware cup, and then a woman with a coarse red face came by with a large copper teakettle that she used to fill it with steaming green tea. She went to serve Goro and Hanzo as Kaze lifted the cup to his face, content to drink the hot bitter liquid. He was happy he was going in the right direction to track down the trio and had decided to let his karma take him where it willed, even if it meant being recognized by the Tokugawa guards at the barrier. His mind was clear and he was unafraid.

He was in the midst of taking a second drink when he felt two men behind him. He put the cup down, stood, and turned before the men could get within a sword's length of him.

"It's the man who's kind to flies," one of the men said.

Kaze smiled. They were the two drunken samurai from the teahouse a few days before.

Since the barrier acted as a choke point for commerce, Kaze was not surprised to see fellow travelers he had met before. The chances were high that people would meet and sometimes meet again while traveling the Tokaido. Kaze relaxed his guard slightly, reaching down to pick up his teacup again. He gave a brief nod to the two samurai.

"Did you really believe that you could cut a fly?" one of the two samurai said rudely, not addressing Kaze properly or introducing himself.

Kaze cocked his head to one side.

"Cutting a fly with a sword, it really can't be done," his companion said.

Kaze put down his teacup. He looked about him and saw several flies buzzing lazily near the refreshment stand. Then he looked at the two samurai and again back at the flies. He was tempted but heard the voice of his Sensei. *When you play with fools, you act like a fool. When you act like a fool, you are one.*

Calling attention to oneself was never good. Doing it in this circumstance, while at a barrier checkpoint with Tokugawa guards, was especially foolish. Kaze picked up his cup of tea and smiled at the samurai, just as he would at a simpleminded child. "You might be right," he said.

Kamakura is in such a beautiful setting that it surely must be loved by the Gods, Kaze thought. This love manifests itself in the fact that many Gods, spirits, and holy people have touched various spots there, dotting its hills with countless temples, nunneries, and sacred places.

Kamakura is tucked into a deep green fold in the steep hills that ring the clear waters of Sagami Bay. It is reachable by a road that branches off the Tokaido. The Tokaido Road continued to Edo, but Kaze was pleased to be able to avoid the new capital of Japan, the stronghold of his enemies, the Tokugawas.

This was the second time Kaze had visited Kamakura. The first time was when he was eleven, when he had come to the city with his Sensei. Even when Kaze was eleven, he had a sense of *furyu*, that aesthetic and religious love of nature that samurai strove to develop lest they be considered barbaric and uncultured.

As he walked through the narrow mountain pass that opened the way to Kamakura and caught sight of the city, Kaze recalled the first time he had seen it. That time and this time, his reaction was exactly the same. His breath caught in his throat and he paused to drink in the vista.

The city spread across the narrow valley below, with the blue sea to the south and the steep hills to the north. Fuji-san could be seen in the distance beyond the hills, its majestic, snow-covered slopes dominating the horizon. With the steep hills and narrow passes leading to the city, Kaze immediately saw the military possibilities of the location as well as its beauty and understood why it had once been a military stronghold. Nitta Yoshisada had conquered Kamakura centuries before, but it had required intervention by the Gods.

The central part of Kamakura was laid out like a grid, in the Chinese style. Another former capital, Kyoto, was also laid out in such a grid. The rigid sense of orderliness imposed by a grid almost offended Kaze's Japanese sense of geometry, which liked some small degree of variation, much like the variations found in nature. Unlike that of Kyoto, the grid portion of Kamakura was relatively compact. It was organized along a main central avenue, *Wakamiya Oji*. At the head of this avenue, high on a hill, was the Tsurugaoka Shrine.

The Tsurugaoka Shrine was devoted to Hachiman, the God of War. It was the creation of the Minamotos, who ruled Japan briefly from Kamakura almost four hundred years before Kaze's time, adopting the fiction that the palaces and villas found on the beautiful rolling hills were like a military camp. They called their government a *bakufu* ("government of the tent"), as if this name would indicate that they had not strayed far from their military roots. One of their number, Yoritomo, became the first Minamoto Shogun, the "barbarian-conquering general."

Once away from the central grid, the streets and paths of Kamakura took a more Japanese twist, following the contours of the land and snaking about the countryside. Tall trees grew up and down the hillsides and blue and gray tile roofs dotted the landscape. Kaze knew from his previous trip that after a rain some of these roofs would capture the image of Fuji-san, a picture of glory reflected in a humble roof.

The sound of a temple bell filled the air, and Kaze let the deep, rolling sound of the bronze *kane* wash over him. Temples were everywhere in Kamakura, as well as sites important to Zen, Nichiren, and most other sects of Buddhism. Kaze watched the procession of hired samurai, Hishigawa, Goro, Hanzo, and the gold-filled pushcart pass before him and start down a side path, apparently to Hishigawa's home. Hishigawa had hired ten samurai at the barrier, and the trip from there to Kamakura had been made without incident.

Kaze thought briefly of simply continuing into town, but he was still a bit curious about the rich merchant and decided to go to his house to see what would develop. As he started off to catch up with Hishigawa's party, he noticed that Hishigawa seemed to be increasing his speed, until he was leading the procession.

CHAPTER 10

*The road can be a
prelude to the gates of hell.
Home is a heaven.*

Hishigawa walked along the familiar road to his villa. He often went down this road, either on foot or riding in a palanquin, so he knew each of the bends in the road and all of the trees growing alongside it. As he drew near to his home, his heart quickened. Yuchan. Yuchan. Yuchan. The name of his wife was like a mantra, driving him to see her. He forgot about the hardship and danger of the past few days and his mind became focused on one thing and one thing only: Yuchan. His steps quickened and it was as if he drew increasing strength from his growing proximity to her.

He didn't see the strange ronin stop at the top of the hill to look down on Kamakura. He didn't notice the surprised looks on the faces of the samurai escort he had hired as his quickening pace allowed him to take the lead of the group and eventually to start to pull ahead of them. The escorts looked at each other, unsure whether they should keep up with the man who was paying them or stay with the pushcart that seemed so important to him. The pushcart, which had its rails covered with fresh mud by the time the escort samurai saw it, seemed perfectly ordinary to them, but the merchant had made a great fuss about them guarding it.

Even before they reached Kamakura, Kaze had noticed a strange transformation in Hishigawa. After they reached the barrier, Hishigawa had seemed to grow in confidence and stature. A strange metamorphosis had started to occur, made all the stranger by its quick unfolding.

Hishigawa was no longer a weak and bent merchant cowering from bandits along the road. His spine straightened, his step lengthened, and his face slowly took on haughty lines, as if he was not some humble merchant but, in fact, some noble or high official. His assertiveness and power grew with each step toward his home.

Kaze had often seen men adopt the surroundings they found themselves in, especially in the merchant class. One moment they would appear weak and obsequious, fawning over a rich customer. Other times they'd be hard and cruel, punishing some miscreant clerk or an unfortunate servant who might have drawn their ire. Every creature feels more secure in its own den or home, but to Kaze, who had no home, it was interesting to watch how this merchant reacted as their journey neared an end.

Kaze wondered if Hishigawa was drawing his strength simply because they were near his space of power or because he was nearing his wife, for whom Hishigawa held an obvious affection.

The road they were on soon led to a gentle valley. There, in the valley, was a large villa surrounded by a high, whitewashed wall. Kaze looked at the villa in surprise, wondering how much wealth the merchant had managed to acquire to be able to afford a house as large and grand as any wellborn noble's.

In the distance, Kaze could see a guard lounging near the front gate, something unusual for a merchant's house. Upon seeing Hishigawa, the guard snapped to attention and called out to the house. Kaze saw several servants rushing out upon the guard's cry. They stood in a line as Hishigawa made his way through the front gate and into the compound. Then they waited for the rest of the party to arrive.

Hishigawa had rushed so far ahead that it was several minutes before Kaze arrived with the pushcart and the rest of the party. Three women and the gate guard were still standing in line when they arrived. Two of the women were pretty young maids, looking at the ground as was proper when guests arrived, but the third was a sturdy, middle-aged woman in a gray kimono. She was watching the approaching party with hard eyes.

"I am Ando," the woman said, addressing herself to the lead samurai in the group. "I am the Master's head of household."

This declaration was a surprise to Kaze. Normally Hishigawa's mother would be the head of household and, if she were gone, then Hishigawa's wife would serve this function. Kaze didn't know Ando's relationship to Hishigawa, but her position was obviously unusual.

The samurai Ando had addressed looked to Kaze, and Ando realized she had addressed the wrong man. Smoothly covering up her mistake, she gave a low bow and turned to Kaze. "Welcome to my Master's home," she said.

"I am Matsuyama Kaze," he replied. "I accompanied your Master for part of the journey from Kyoto to here."

Ando bowed again. "Thank you for bringing my Master home safely. If you'll excuse him, he will be with you shortly. It is my Master's custom to always visit his wife immediately upon returning from a trip."

Kaze nodded. He felt his understanding of Hishigawa's character unfolding the way a lotus unfolds in the cool of the evening. It was hard to picture a colorless merchant being infused with such passion for a new bride, but the evidence was before him, in Hishigawa's actions.

A man could have a passion for a fine blade or a beautiful horse or even for some aesthetic thing like the tea ceremony and display it openly. But openly displaying such passion for one's wife was unprecedented in Kaze's experience. One could have passion for another being, but it was to be held close to your heart, not flaunted before strangers.

"Please come in and let us serve you some refreshments. You must be fatigued after such a long journey." Ando's words were proper and gracious, but her manner was not. Her shoulders were tense and her hands were clenched. She looked at Kaze with small eyes that reminded him of a ferret scanning for prey. It was plain that she was annoyed to have an unexpected guest, especially a ronin.

Ando turned to one of the maids, and Kaze saw the young girl flinch, as if she expected to be struck. "Hurry! Get some tea and something to eat for the samurai while they wait for the Master."

The girl rushed off, and a bowing Ando motioned for the group to enter Hishigawa's estate.

When Kaze walked through the gate, the household staff took over the gold cart, leading the cart, Goro, and Hanzo to the side of the villa. "Please make sure the two peasants get refreshments, too," Kaze said to Ando. He could see the woman tighten her jaw again, and Kaze realized that the Hishigawa house was not one that normally gave peasants hospitality, but Ando said, "Of course, Samurai-san."

The courtyard between the gate and the front of Hishigawa's mansion was filled with white sand. Strips of wood outlined rectangles in the sand; the rectangles were filled with small stones, forming a walkway leading from the gate to the entrance. As the men walked along the path, the stones made a pleasant crunching sound under their feet.

"Your Master's love for his wife is unusually strong," Kaze observed.

Ando thought about this remark and pondered her response. Her family had served the Hishigawas for three generations, going back to the time when the Hishigawas were samurai. Hishigawa's father had given up that position to follow the way of the merchant, abandoning the path of honor for the path of gold. This took the House of Hishigawa and tumbled it, in the eyes of his fellow samurai, from a high position in society to one of the lowest. Despite this change in position, Ando's family had remained loyal to the Hishigawas. Although this ronin seemed to have been of service, she was unwilling to provide details about her Master's life and passions. So she said blandly, "My Lord loves his wife very much. Would you like a bath, Samurai-san? My Master may be a while before he can attend to more business."

The change in subject was a clear signal that Kaze had veered onto a topic the woman was unwilling to expand on. Acting as if he didn't notice this signal, Kaze simply said, "Of course. A bath would be most welcome."

The samurai guards were left in a room near the entryway while Kaze was taken into the cool darkness of the house. The paper walls filtered the light, producing serenity and a feeling of coolness even when the weather was hot.

As Kaze penetrated the depths of the house, additional layers of paper filtering made the light darker and darker. Almost all large Japanese houses shared this characteristic. For that reason, decorative objects, such as the designs on the tops of boxes, were often done in mother-of-pearl, silver, and gold. Sometimes these materials formed a design that looked garish in the sunlight, but it was absolutely perfect in the twilight that pervaded the depths of a Japanese home.

To air out the house and provide light, large panels or removable screens simply slid apart, eliminating the barriers between the inside and the outside. Each room in the house was made to a multiple of a standard-size rectangular tatami mat, the size of the rooms being expressed in terms of the number of tatami mats it would take to cover the floor.

Kaze was led to the back of the house, to the bathhouse, where a large wooden *ofuro* tub was. As he walked to the bathhouse, he noticed two plastered structures in the back of the house. These were the treasure-houses, where things of value were kept safely away from the threat of fire that hung over every Japanese wood and paper house. This was something expected, especially for the house of a merchant, but he also saw something that surprised him.

The back of the estate was much more sizable than he would have thought. He was learning that Hishigawa's ability to buy material goods was probably on a par with a minor lord rather than a merchant. In this backyard was a small lake and in the center of the lake was an island. On the island was a sizable palace with a green tile roof. The palace was so large that a midlevel samurai would have been happy to have it as his residence. A Chinese-style arched drum bridge connected the island to the rest of the estate. The bridge was in the shape of a perfect half circle, with stairs going up the steep sides of the bridge and an arched wooden causeway spanning the water. A railing lacquered red in the Chinese style added color to the bridge. A guard was standing on the island side.

"What is that?" Kaze asked Ando.

"That's the Jade Palace," Ando said, "the home of my master's wife."

It was not uncommon for husbands and wives to have separate quarters in the main house. It was less common for a wife to have her own palace to live in.

Kaze said nothing but noted that in some ways Hishigawa's wife seemed to have a status unlike any wife that Kaze had yet met. She was treated more like the Empress, who had her own wing in the Imperial Palace in Kyoto.

At the bath Kaze relaxed in the steaming hot water. Before he had entered, a pretty, young serving girl scrubbed the dirt off him. Kaze noted that almost all of the female servants he had seen in the house, except Ando, were young and pretty. This was another unusual aspect of Hishigawa's most unusual household. In most households, there was a mixture of servants, with a range of ages and appearances.

"Have you been in Hishigawa's household long?" Kaze asked the girl tending the fire that heated the bathwater.

"No, Samurai-san."

"How did you come to be in service at Hishigawa-san's house?"

There was a pause. "My parents sold me into the service of this family," the girl finally said.

This statement seemed to cause the girl so much pain that Kaze didn't pursue it. Instead he submerged himself in the hot water, letting the tiredness of the journey seep into the surrounding heat.

When Kaze had refreshed himself and put on a clean kimono lent to him by Ando, he was called in to meet with Hishigawa.

Kaze walked into the reception room of Hishigawa's house. It was a large room measuring eighteen mats, similar to the kind of reception room found in the palaces and manors of nobles.

Hishigawa sat at the back of the room on a raised dais. Behind him was a large screen painted on four panels. The picture was of herons stepping their way into an iris pond, all on a gilt background. It was obviously expensive, but Kaze judged it vulgar. It was the kind of art done for newly rich merchants who had not yet developed an eye for the use of color and the mastery of the brush that marked a true artist.

Flanking Hishigawa were two rows of retainers, facing inward, six in each row. Eleven of these retainers were men; Kaze was surprised to note that Ando was the twelfth. Sitting between the rows were the samurai hired at the barrier. The arrangement was impressive and confirmed Hishigawa's true wealth.

Hishigawa was dressed in a brown kimono with a white bamboo pattern. He sat easily, a man comfortable and assured in familiar surroundings. His elbow rested on a lacquered armrest that sat on the floor like a small piece of furniture. With a practiced eye, Kaze quickly looked over the men in the room. Most were of no consequence, but his eyes lingered on one man.

He was tall and thin, with the shaved pate of a samurai. He sat comfortably, with his hands on his knees. His two swords were impeccably placed, and he was looking back at Kaze with the same studied gaze that Kaze was using on him. Just as two creatures of the same species will always recognize each other, these two men knew from one another's bearing, sharp eye, and stance that each was a master swordsman.

Kaze approached Hishigawa and sat down by the barrier samurai, giving Hishigawa a shallow bow. A small cloud passed over Hishigawa's face . It was obvious that he was not satisfied with the depth of the bow. In the comfort of his own house, he was transformed from the pleading merchant Kaze had found on the Tokaido Road to an undeclared noble holding court. Kaze found it interesting that a merchant should be taking on airs simply because he was wealthy.

"This is the samurai I told you about," Hishigawa said to the assembled group of retainers. He pointed with his chin at Kaze. "This man was not only able to save my life, he was also able to bring me and the gold safely to Kamakura. No thanks to the men assigned to me as bodyguards by my head of guards."

At this Hishigawa glared at the swordsman who had caught Kaze's eye. The swordsman looked back at Hishigawa coolly, meeting his glare with a measured stare that was hard and full of power. The two men looked at each other for several seconds, until finally Hishigawa broke away. Glancing downward, he said, "Well, it's no matter. I'm here. In fact, Matsuyama-san, I would like to introduce you to my head of guards. This is Enomoto-san." Hishigawa again pointed with his chin, this time to the swordsman.

Kaze looked at Enomoto, pivoting slightly.

"Enomoto Katataka," the swordsman said.

"Matsuyama Kaze."

Kaze put his hands on the mat and gave a polite bow. Enomoto returned the bow in exactly the same manner and at exactly the same depth. To the other men in the room it was a formal polite greeting, but to the two men involved it seemed like the punctuation to something else. They had already greeted each other when both took measure as Kaze walked into the room.

"You have already met Ando-san, the head of my household. The rest of these men are my retainers. They work for Enomoto-san or Ando-san."

Kaze gave a polite bow to all in the room.

"First, there is the payment for the good samurai who escorted me from the barrier." Hishigawa gave a nod and a man slid forward and placed a paper-wrapped stack of coins before the samurai. Much to Kaze's disgust, the head of the group scooped up the money as any merchant would and put it in his sleeve. He gave a deep, formal bow of thanks.

"And for you, Matsuyama-san, I promised enough to buy the finest sword in Kamakura." Hishigawa gave another nod, and the servant slid forward and placed another paper-wrapped stack of coins in front of Kaze. Kaze acted as if they weren't there, but he did give Hishigawa a thank-you bow.

"Good," Hishigawa said, "now we have some business to discuss. I want you to become my yojimbo, my bodyguard," Hishigawa said to Kaze.

"Aren't you happy with the security I provide you," Enomoto asked, his face darkening at Hishigawa's suggestion.

"No. It's not that," Hishigawa said quickly. "I simply feel the need for some additional personal protection. There have been attempts on my life lately, and I need someone to protect me."

Kaze was surprised at Hishigawa's suggestion and bowed deeply. Hishigawa interpreted this as gratitude and an acknowledgment that Kaze was joining his household. Instead Kaze said, "I appreciate the generous offer to join your household, but I have other duties and tasks I must perform."

"Duties?" Hishigawa said. "But you are a ronin."

"Sometimes wandering is a duty, Hishigawa-san."

Hishigawa looked as if he was going to try to argue with Kaze, but Kaze gave a short bow and stood up.

"Thank you for your hospitality and generosity," Kaze said. "I would like to stay with you a few days, until I obtain a new sword, but then I must be leaving." Kaze walked out of the room. He left the money behind.

CHAPTER 11

*Eagles spot other
eagles from a long distance.
Like gathers with like.*

A half hour later, Kaze was in a smaller room talking to Enomoto and sipping warm sakè.

"Hishigawa-san has told me how strong you are as a swordsman," Enomoto said. "If what Hishigawa-san says is accurate, you attacked the bandits when it was seven to one. Hishigawa-san also said you were able to save his gold as well as get him to the barrier. I'm glad I have a chance to drink with you. It's rare to come across a man of your quality."

Kaze gave a curt nod to acknowledge Enomoto's compliment.

"Are you sure you don't want to stay as a yojimbo?" Enomoto said. "If you don't want to work for Hishigawa you can work for me. I could always use another man with a sword like yours."

"I'm sorry. I have things I must do. I am looking for a young girl. She would be nine now. I noticed all your maids are very young, so perhaps you employ her or know something of her. I don't know what name she would be known as, but she might have come to your house with a kimono bearing a family crest of three plum blossoms. Do you know anything of such a child?"

"Ando-san likes young maids. She buys them from agents who scour the countryside for young farm girls. She likes to break them in so we can turn a profit by selling them into service elsewhere. Although we've had many young girls in this house during the time I've been here, there's nothing I can tell you about one with a plum blossom crest."

Kaze, who had made similar inquiries all over Japan, was neither surprised nor disappointed by Enomoto's answer.

"Is it true that the bandits were trying to kill Hishigawa-san?" Enomoto asked.

"It was very peculiar. Most hesitated after they had killed the guards and demanded Hishigawa-san's surrender, but at least one man, Ishibashi, had only the death of Hishigawa-san as his goal."

"Ishibashi?" Enomoto said.

"Yes. Hishigawa-san said he was the leader of the bandits."

Enomoto looked genuinely upset. "Disgusting," he said. "Hishigawa-san was robbed of gold less than a year ago. At that time they killed the guards with him, but they didn't hurt him. It's disturbing that they wanted to kill him this time."

"Why does Hishigawa-san transport gold from Kyoto anyway?" Kaze asked.

"Because his businesses get out of balance in terms of the amount of gold they have. He has to reallot gold among the three locations of Kamakura, Edo, and Kyoto periodically."

"I understand that," Kaze said. "I just don't know why he actually transfers the gold from each of his businesses."

"Do you know a way he could avoid that?" Enomoto said, surprised.

"I'm not a merchant," Kaze replied.

"Of course. Forgive me." Enomoto knew not to pursue talk of commerce, but he eyed Kaze speculatively. "Oh," he said. "Speaking of merchants, I apologize for Hishigawa-san's rudeness with this." He took the stack of paper-wrapped coins from his sleeve and put it in front of Kaze with a bow. This time it was properly wrapped, in a folded sheet of fine paper, to hide the fact that it was a stack of money. "He wasn't trying to insult you. He thinks it's normal to hand money to samurai. You saw how the barrier guards snatched up their payment."

Kaze waved his hand, as if dismissing Hishigawa's breach of etiquette in handing Kaze the payment so crassly. Kaze took the payment from Enomoto and put it in his sleeve.

"With so many samurai wandering the roads it's difficult to get employment, even for a man of your skills. Are you sure you won't change your mind and fight for me?"

"No. I can't work here," Kaze said.

"Why not?"

Kaze paused for a minute, then said, "As I told you, I have other obligations that I must fulfill. Besides, I think Hishigawa-san may be a bad man. If he's not a bad man, then he's certainly a weak one, the way he's possessed by his wife, Yuchan."

Enomoto grinned. "What makes you think that I'm not a bad man, too?"

Kaze looked at Enomoto and said, "I've already considered that possibility."

Enomoto laughed. "Very good," he said, "just remember that I am a bad man. A very bad man. We're all bad here. Otherwise we wouldn't be in this household."

Kaze picked up his sakè cup and took a sip. "That's something I'll remember in my future dealings with you," he said.

Enomoto laughed again.

Kaze decided to explore Kamakura and left Hishigawa's villa to go into town. When he walked out of the villa, he saw Hanzo and Goro sitting by the manor's front gate looking miserable.

Kaze walked up to them and said, "What's the matter?"

Both held out their hands. They each had a few coppers. "We were promised gold," Hanzo said accusingly, "and this is what Hishigawa-san paid us. He didn't even give us the full ten coppers he said he would."

Kaze looked down at the meager copper coins in their hands.

He reached into his sleeve and took out the paper-wrapped coins. He opened the paper, then tore open the tissue that was wrapped around the coins. He took four of the oblong gold coins and dropped two each into the upturned palms of the surprised peasants.

"I'm the one who promised you gold," Kaze said.

He started down the path into the town of Kamakura. He had only taken a few strides when Goro and Hanzo came rushing up to him. They dropped to their knees and placed their foreheads on the grounds, their hands on either side of their heads, "Thank you, Samurai-sama! Thank you, thank you!" they said.

Kaze looked down at the two peasants. "Get up," he said. "Don't be disgusting. I gave you gold, not something of true value."

Leaving the puzzled peasants looking after him, Kaze continued his journey into the town.

Kaze went past the main street of Kamakura, which had a raised stone causeway running down its middle. When Kamakura had its bakufu government, a Shogun had built the causeway as a way of begging the Gods to ease the childbirth of his wife.

On each side of the main street were numerous shops filled with food, merchandise, and clothes. Kaze picked a shop that sold *katsuo-bushi*, dried bonito. The slabs of dried bonito looked like blocks of wood. A small plane was used to shave pieces off for flavoring in soups and other dishes. The dried bonito looked so much like wood that sometimes scoundrels would sell blocks of wood to unsuspecting housewives at what appeared to be a bargain price for bonito. Often the housewives were so embarrassed that they didn't report the fraud to the village authorities, allowing the scoundrels to move on to the next village.

The words "katsuo-bushi" could also be interpreted as "victorious samurai," so dried bonito was a popular and auspicious gift. Kaze decided to start with this shop because he thought that "victorious samurai" might bring him luck.

"Sumimasen, excuse me," he said.

The shopkeeper looked at Kaze and bowed. He was a mere gnome of a man, wearing a gray kimono. "Yes, Samurai-sama?" he said, using the "sama" honorific to show how exalted Kaze, or any customer, was.

"Do you know if anyone in the neighborhood has a nine-year-old girl as a servant? She might have come here when she was seven."

If the shopkeeper thought this was a strange question, he was too polite to show it. "No, Samurai-sama, there is no girl like that in this neighborhood. We are poor shopkeepers, so most do not have servants of any age."

Kaze had been searching for over two years, and the only real clue he had to the girl's whereabouts was the piece of cloth he had received from the trio he was also seeking, so he wasn't surprised by the shopkeeper's response.

"I am also seeking a trio," Kaze continued. "One is an elderly woman who is still sturdy and fit. She may be wearing a headband with the kanji for 'revenge' on it. She's accompanied by a young man, perhaps fifteen or sixteen, and an old servant who is unusually thin."

"I can help you with those people, Samurai-sama. They were in my shop just two days ago. If you'll excuse me for saying it, Samurai-sama, but the woman was rather . . . well, forceful is how I would describe her. But I mean no disrespect, especially if she is related to you, Samurai-sama!" the shopkeeper added quickly.

"I take no offense," Kaze assured him. "Did the trio say where they were staying in Kamakura?"

"No, Samurai-sama. The woman talked about what poor quality my bonito is and, ah, insisted on a discount, but they made no mention of where they were staying. I should imagine it is not at an inn, if she was cooking, but perhaps they wanted the bonito as a gift."

Kaze thanked the shopkeeper and went a few shops down the street, repeating his inquiry. The fact that the trio might be in Kamakura was a great help to Kaze, although he had no way of knowing if they were staying in Kamakura or if they had gone on to Enoshima Island to the south or Edo to the north. After asking at several shops, he learned that the woman had also purchased miso and some rice, all at a discount after criticizing the quality. Kaze was confident that they were staying somewhere in the Kamakura area. One wouldn't buy supplies like that if they were still on the road.

Kaze asked at temples and inns about the trio, with no luck. He continued methodically searching Kamakura until it was dark and the cheery glow of colored paper lanterns hung in front of drinking places and inns illuminated the street.

He was aware that people were following him long before the sun set, but he ignored them. There were three men. They were quite good, periodically changing the one who followed Kaze and sometimes walking on parallel streets so they weren't directly behind him. They were careful to keep hidden, so Kaze couldn't see their faces to discover if the three men were familiar. Kaze didn't lack for interest in who the men were and why he was being followed, but he assumed the reasons would eventually be revealed.

At the end of his search of inns, Kaze headed down an alleyway that ran between two secondary streets. The darkness of the alley was relieved only by the faint light of the stars, and Kaze wasn't too surprised that the three men took this opportunity to approach him. What did surprise him was that the men made no attempt to talk to him. Instead, he heard the hurried shuffle of sandaled feet behind him as the three men rushed him.

Kaze drew the dead man's sword, dropped his body slightly, and made a sweeping cut with the katana as he spun around. The deadly arc of steel had a dull shine to it as it caught the faint light of the heavens. The blade cut into the midsection of one the three men and caught a second in the forearm. Kaze continued his turn and straightened, ending up to the side of the three men as the one caught in the belly collapsed to the earth with a loud groan.

The other wounded man and his unhurt companion stood for an instant looking at Kaze, who was standing at the ready with his sword in the "aimed at the knee" position. The faces of the men were obscured by cloths, so Kaze couldn't see their features. It was obvious that they had intended to kill him. They weren't Tokugawa officials, so Kaze had no idea why these men would want him dead.

The man wounded in the forearm was holding his sword with only one hand. His other was clamped across the cut on his arm, stanching the flow of blood. Suddenly, he grunted to his companion the single word "Go!" Kaze thought the word was a signal for a coordinated attack, but instead the two men started running down the alleyway, leaving Kaze with their dying companion.

Instead of pursuing the two fleeing assassins, Kaze turned the dying man over. The man's breathing was labored because the blade had cut into his diaphragm, and he held his hands across the cut, as if his actions could stop his life from leaking out of the terrible slice.

Kaze removed the face cloth. It was someone unknown to him. The masks were intended to hide the men's faces from townspeople as they murdered Kaze.

"Why did you attack me?" Kaze asked.

The man groaned.

"Tell me why you attacked me," Kaze said.

The man looked up at Kaze. In the dim light of the alleyway it was impossible to see his eyes, but Kaze saw the man sag and cease breathing, and he knew the eyes would be lifeless and already starting to film.

Kaze sighed. He thought briefly of taking up the pursuit of the other two but decided it was hopeless. He wasn't frightened by the attempt on his life, but he was curious. If the men wanted him dead because of who he was before he became a ronin, they could kill him with the help of the law. He was fair game for a wide variety of enemies, including the entire Okubo clan.

If they had tried to kill him because of the gold he carried in his sleeve, that narrowed down the potential suspects to Hishigawa's household. No, Kaze thought, that wasn't all. The suspects included Hishigawa's household and the two peasants, Goro and Hanzo. Kaze had saved Goro's life, but Goro was also the one Kaze had caught contemplating a theft of the gold. Kaze didn't expect gratitude when men were blinded by the glint of gold. He had no feelings of anger at the thought that the two peasants might have arranged his assassination to get the rest of the gold he carried. It was a hard time, and men did hard things.

He wiped the dead man's blade on the kimono of the corpse, then held it before him with both hands and his head bowed.

"Thank you for the use of your blade, Ishibashi-san," Kaze said to the spirit of the man who had owned the sword. "I'm sorry to have used your katana to kill someone, but in this situation it can't be helped." Kaze looked up and carefully slid the blade back into the scabbard. The sooner he got his own blade and stopped the use of the dead man's sword, the better. Next time the spirit of Ishibashi might not be so generous in letting the man who killed him use his sword so successfully.

Old face and gray hair,
but a heart that beats strongly.
Fearsome grandmother!

K aze left the body of the assassin in the alleyway and continued walking back to Hishigawa's villa. He didn't carve a Kannon statue, but decided he would bring one back to the site the next morning to appease the soul of the dead assassin. Someone would find the corpse in the morning, and it was better if Kaze was not entangled with the Tokugawa authorities as they investigated the killing. He still had much of Kamakura to search for the girl, and he also had the trio to find.

The moon had not yet risen in the sky but, in the center of Kamakura, lantern light shone and people were still wandering the streets in its mellow glow.

As Kaze left the center of the town, the lights and people became fewer, until he was alone on the path to Hishigawa's villa. Kaze could hear the quiet chirping of insects as he made his way between the dark trunks of trees that lined the path. His footsteps were muffled by the dirt and pine needles on the trail. As he approached the villa, his acute senses detected something besides the insects. He slowed his progress, straining to hear something besides the natural rhythm of the night.

There. He heard it again. The crackling of small tree limbs and the movement of bodies through the trees that bordered the path. Kaze stopped and stared into the darkness, drawing his sword from its scabbard and waiting to see who or what was hiding by the side of the pathway. He wondered if this was the prelude to another assassination attempt.

Suddenly a shape came flying out of the night from the deep woods. It landed on the ground behind him, barely missing his side. It was a spear.

Moving instantly, Kaze dashed into the woods, blending into the darkness and using the tree trunks to shield him from another spear. He could hear the rustling of several bodies in the woods, fleeing. He increased his speed, dodging one dark tree trunk after another, constantly moving in the direction in which he could hear the others escaping.

Ahead he heard a cry and a crash, and he knew one of his assailants had fallen. With the agility of an acrobat, Kaze dodged tree limbs and tree trunks and in seconds came across a dark shape picking himself off the ground. Kaze kicked the shape, and it went flying to the earth again, crying out in pain. Then it started shouting, but shouting something that Kaze could never have imagined.

"Obaasan! Obaasan! Grandma! Grandma! Help me! He's got me. Grandma—"

Kaze walked up and put his foot on the shape, giving it a second shove before it could scramble to its feet.

"Grandma," the shape screamed, "please help!"

Suddenly there was a crash to his right, and two additional shapes emerged from the darkness of the forest.

"Let go of him or I'll kill you!" It was an older woman's voice, but as sharp and authoritative as any samurai's.

"I don't really want to let go of him," Kaze said. "In fact, I've been looking for all of you ever since the last time I saw you."

"Who are you?" the old woman snapped.

"I'm the samurai you met at the teahouse many days ago. The one who fought a duel."

"You!" the woman said.

Kaze nodded and realized that the woman couldn't see him in the dark, so he said, "Hai! Yes."

"Why are you after my grandson?" the woman demanded.

"Because your grandson plays dangerous games," Kaze answered.

Kaze let the young man scramble to his feet. "I got scared," the youngster admitted. "He knew we were hiding in the woods, so I threw my spear and ran."

"It doesn't do much good to hide when you make as much noise as you did," Kaze said. "Stealth requires silence as well as cloaking yourself in darkness."

"Thanks for the lesson," the old woman said with sarcastic gruffness. "What do you want?"

"Well, I suppose I could ask the same thing of you," Kaze said, "because apparently you are watching Hishigawa's villa."

"You're the one who said you've been looking for us for days," the old woman declared. "Now you tell us."

Kaze smiled. The old woman would have made a good field general.

"I am Matsuyama Kaze," he said, bowing, even though they couldn't see his gesture in the dark.

"And I am the Elder Grandma of the Cadet Branch of the Noguchi family," the woman said.

"When I first met you, you were on a vendetta," Kaze said. "Did you complete what you set out to do?"

"I don't think I should tell you," the woman said.

"Why not?"

"Because Hishigawa is the person we have a vendetta against."

They sat around a small fire burning on the dirt floor of an abandoned temple not too far from Hishigawa's villa, where the ragtag trio bent on revenge had made camp.

"So what is it you want?" Elder Grandma said. She was flanked by her young grandson, Nagatoki, a youth of about fifteen, and by her aged servant, Sadakatsu, who was tall and cadaverous. Neither of the two males said a word.

"I want information," Kaze said.

"What kind of information?" she asked.

Kaze reached into his sleeve and took out a scrape of cloth. He opened it up and held it so that it could be seen in the light of the fire.

"Do you see this crest?" he said, pointing to the design on the cloth. It was the three plum blossoms.

"Yes," Elder Grandma said, showing no surprise at Kaze's display of the cloth.

Kaze looked at her and thought that this was a frightening woman. She was as tough as any man and as shrewd in any negotiation as the wiliest of peasants.

"This is the crest of the family I used to serve before they were eliminated in the aftermath of Sekigahara. I obtained this cloth from your grandson. It was wrapped around some rice crackers."

She gave a quick glance to her young grandson, who seemed frightened at the mention of him.

"Were those from the supplies we brought, Nagatoki?" she asked.

"Yes, Elder Grandma," Nagatoki said. "I'm sorry, but—"

She cut him off. "Never mind. Don't speak unless I tell you to."

Turning to Kaze, she asked, "What is it you want to know about that cloth?"

"I want to know where the cloth came from and if, by some chance, it was associated with a young girl. The girl would be nine now, but she was seven when I lost track of her."

Elder Grandma sat back. She was sitting on her heels, her legs tucked under her. "I know where the cloth came from. And I will tell you. But you must do something for me."

"What?"

"Kill Hishigawa."

"I'm not a murderer," Kaze said.

"But you're a samurai."

"Yes, and as a samurai I kill. But I do not murder."

"What's the difference?" Elder Grandma said aggressively.

"Murder is unjust. If I kill, it may simply be the luck of battle or it may be because the world is better off with someone dead. Murdering Hishigawa to get you to tell me about a scrap of cloth is not just. You have a vendetta against him, but I do not. You may have a good reason to wish him dead, but I do not. You must kill him, because I will not."

Elder Grandma pointed to her headband, emblazoned with the kanji character for "revenge."

"Do you see this?"

"It's hard to miss."

"The Noguchi clan has an official vendetta against Hishigawa. He killed my son and stole one of his daughters. Hishigawa did business with my son before Sekigahara, providing weapons to our clan. He saw my son's daughter and became possessed by her. If it wasn't my own blood, I would have said she was a fox-maiden, because Hishigawa was so totally enamored of her that it was almost like a man who is seized by a fox-spirit who is masquerading as a woman.

"He sent an evil hag called Ando to act as his go-between, to arrange a marriage. My son refused. Despite Hishigawa's wealth, my family saw no profit in linking its long lineage with a grubby merchant like Hishigawa.

"Soon my son's house was attacked by Hishigawa's thugs. They killed my son and stole his daughter, giving us the basis for our official vendetta against Hishigawa. Weeks ago, my grandson, Mototane, went to enforce the vendetta against Hishigawa and to bring back my granddaughter, his cousin. He was a superb swordsman and a brave warrior, and he should have been able to kill Hishigawa. If he didn't have the chance to kill him, he should have been nearby waiting for that opportunity. Instead, I have seen no sign of him.

"If you won't kill Hishigawa, then I want you to find out what happened to Mototane. If you want to know about this scrap of cloth, you will tell me what happened to my grandson. The moment you tell me what happened to him, I shall tell you where I got that cloth and what I know about it."

Kaze didn't bother trying to argue with Elder Grandma. He knew it would be useless to bargain with her. Instead he asked, "And what will you do?"

"We will wait to see if we have a chance to kill Hishigawa and rescue my granddaughter, Yuchan."

"Yuchan!" Kaze said.

"You've seen her?"

"No, but I've heard Hishigawa talk about her. She's his wife. He adores her and is still possessed by her. He even has a special palace for her inside his villa. She seems to be living in luxury."

"Then I want you to get us information about Yuchan, too."

"No," Kaze said. "You said you wanted information about Mototane. If I find information about Yuchan, I will also tell you, but I won't expand the bargain."

"All right," Elder Grandma said. "Done!"

It would take luck to discover the fate of Noguchi Mototane, but Kaze believed you sometimes made your own luck through work and preparation. It was like the story of Oda Nobunaga and the coins. Nobunaga was the predecessor of Hideyoshi, the man who recognized Hideyoshi's unique talents and raised him from a common *ashigaru* foot soldier to a general.

Early in his career, Nobunaga and his troops, although outnumbered twelve to one, were marching to Okehazama to have a decisive battle with the powerful *daimyo* Imagawa Yoshimoto. Imagawa was invading Nobunaga's territory, determined to crush him. He was launching a bid to march on Kyoto to claim control of all of Japan, and Nobunaga's small domain was in the way. Imagawa had already destroyed a frontier fortress of Nobunaga's and the Imagawa army was camped in the narrow and rugged gorge of Okehazama as they prepared to move on Nobunaga's main castle.

On the way to battle the Imagawa army, Nobunaga stopped at the Atsuta Shrine to offer a prayer for victory. The Imagawa forces were far greater than Nobunaga's, yet the headstrong Nobunaga chose to go on the offense instead of cowering in his castle. His troops felt that it would take divine intervention to come back alive, much less victorious.

While at the shrine, Nobunaga made an offering of several gold coins. Holding the coins in his hand, he looked at his retainers and announced, "If the Gods want us to win the upcoming battle, then all the coins I now offer will show their heads, to symbolize the heads of the enemy we will soon be taking." Nobunaga then threw the coins toward the altar. They all landed with their heads showing.

His retainers were amazed and heartened by this sign of divine support, and they soon spread the word to Nobunaga's troops. Under the cover of a furious thunderstorm, Nobunaga attacked the Imagawa army when they were still exhausted from their march. Imagawa, supremely confident, had not expected to be attacked by the smaller forces of Nobunaga. When he first heard the sounds of battle above the din of the thunderstorm, he thought a brawl had broken out among his own men. Without armor, Imagawa went to quell the brawl. Within minutes, he had lost his head. His troops, completely demoralized and routed, were defeated in a short, violent battle.

This victory marked the rise of Nobunaga. A year later Tokugawa Ieyasu, the same Ieyasu who later first allied himself with Hideyoshi and eventually conquered Hideyoshi's family at Sekigahara, was Nobunaga's ally.

The sign of divine favor shown Nobunaga at Atsuta Shrine was marred when it was later discovered that the coins that Nobunaga had used were doctored. They had heads on both sides.

After returning to Hishigawa's villa, Kaze ate and then quietly slipped out of his room. In the dark, he made his way toward the drum bridge and climbed a tree. Ever since he was a child, Kaze had had an affinity for trees, seeing them as stairways to heaven, a way to separate his body from the earth both physically and metaphorically. Relaxing on a tree limb in the lotus position, he watched the island silently, curious about Yuchan's lifestyle and convinced that Noguchi Mototane's disappearance and possible death were linked to her.

Presently, he saw Ando scurrying to the bridge, carrying two nested lacquer food trays. He couldn't see the contents of the bottom tray, but the top tray looked like it was full of delicacies, much finer than the supper Kaze had eaten. Kaze wondered if Yuchan was enjoying a special dinner. Yuchan seemed to live in cloistered elegance, like a member of the imperial family, her every whim and need catered to. Kaze was a bit surprised that a maid wasn't taking Yuchan's food to her, but apparently Hishigawa's wife received very special treatment from all in the household, including Ando. Kaze mused that this must be a strange life, so much like that of a pampered prisoner. Was the loss of freedom compensated for by the granting of luxury?

Later, Ando returned to the main villa, but a few minutes later she and Hishigawa appeared. They passed the man guarding the drum bridge and crossed over to the island, entering the Jade Palace. What Kaze found interesting was that several hours later they returned to the villa together. Kaze would have expected Hishigawa to spend the night with Yuchan.

The next morning, the maid found Kaze sleeping soundly in his *futon*, as if he had been in his room the entire night.

CHAPTER 13

A thin strip of steel,
holding a noble spirit
and a master's skill.

After a breakfast of miso soup and rice, Kaze went back into Kamakura. During his previous day's visit, he had asked about the forge of Kannemori, the swordsmith, and learned that it was in the hills in the opposite direction from Hishigawa's villa.

Kaze had met Kannemori during his first visit to Kamakura with his Sensei. Kaze was impressed by the Sensei's respect and affection for Kannemori, which had prompted Kaze to refer to Kannemori as a Sensei, in this case meaning a master of his craft instead of a teacher.

Kannemori's forge was tucked into a small valley high above Kamakura. The narrow mountain path to the forge gave Kaze an ideal opportunity to make sure he wasn't being followed by the assassins of the previous night. He had not yet decided why these assassins had been hired, but he knew that once he discovered why they were hired, he would know who had hired them.

Before Kaze saw the forge, he heard it. A rhythmic *clang-clang-clang-clang* sound of hammers striking hot metal drifted up from the valley.

During his first visit, Kaze had been allowed to witness part of the forging process for a katana. This was a rare honor, because each swordsmith jealously guarded the way he formed a sword, sometimes by drastic means.

Kaze knew the story of the master swordsmith Masamune, who had once been tempering a blade in the presence of another swordsmith. This involved taking the heated blade and plunging it into a vat of water. The blade was usually heated to a degree that matched the color of the moon when it started its nightly journey in June or July. The water was described as the temperature of water in February or August. In fact, blades were often dated February or August, regardless of the month they were actually manufactured.

Masamune's blades were of such superior quality that other smiths were convinced that he had some secret in their manufacture that he was hiding. The visiting smith surreptitiously stuck his hand into the water to see the exact temperature Masamune used when tempering his blades. Without hesitation, Masamune took the red-hot blade, still unfinished and held with pincers, and used it to strike off the offending hand of the visiting swordsmith.

Mindful of this and similar stories, the young Kaze kept his hands carefully in his lap as he sat silently next to the Sensei, watching Kannemori Sensei work on a blade.

Some blades were mass-produced for common soldiers and samurai, but Kannemori's blades were made for samurai who treasured fine swords. It could take weeks or even months to finish a particular blade, and many craftsmen became involved before the sword was completed. A special artisan created and fitted the tsuba, the sword guard. Another created the *tsuka*, or hilt, a complex assembly of wood, ray skin, pommel and hilt decorations, and silk, leather, or cotton tapes and cords. Another artisan created and custom-fitted the *saya*, or scabbard, to each individual blade.

At the heart of all this effort was the blade itself, the creation of the swordsmith and an object heavy with mystical, religious, and practical significance. The sword was one of the great symbols of Shinto, and the religious significance of the blade was marked by the ritual the smith went through before working on the sword.

As the young Kaze watched, Kannemori sat on a mat in his fundoshi and poured a bucket of water over himself in a ritual act of purification. Assisted by his *sakite*, his aides, Kannemori donned ceremonial dress, including a small, black lacquered hat that was tied under his chin with cord. He then prayed to the shrine shelf, dedicated to the God of the forge, which occupied a corner of his workshop.

His spirit in the proper mode, Kannemori then commenced to work on the sword, first heating bits of iron on a metal spatula. The iron was repeatedly heated and pounded until it fused into one piece, with Kannemori's assistants handling the heavy metal mallets as the master manipulated the iron using pincers. When the metal was one piece of the proper consistency, the process of folding and refolding the hot metal began. Care was taken to assure that no air or impurities were between the layers of metal, because this weakened the final product. Over and over again the metal was heated, folded, and pounded together, forming layer upon layer of fused steel. It was hard for Kaze to sit through this repetitious process, but he drew strength from the presence of the Sensei, who seemed to have an inexhaustible wellspring of patience.

The entire sword could not be constructed in one day, but Kannemori showed Kaze the grooved block of copper he used to correct the curvature of the blade, as well as the special files he used to shape it. He also showed Kaze the clay used to cover the blade before tempering. To Kaze, the clay looked like any clay, but Kannemori rubbed a bit between his fingers and even placed a tiny bit on his tongue to taste it, pronouncing it exceptionally suitable for the exacting work of sword creation.

Kaze marveled at the degree of subtlety in touch, sight, sensitivity, and even taste that the swordsmith must develop to help him properly gauge all the materials used in his art.

Now, two decades later, Kaze had not been invited to watch Kannemori at work, so he knew to hang back and not approach the forge while he was working. A master might be willing to reveal secrets to a young boy that he would keep hidden from a grown man. Kaze found a convenient tree limb and sat on it, balancing himself in the lotus position. He thought about the secrets of a master and the last long conversation he had had with his Sensei.

Kaze had been with his Sensei for several years, training hard and trying earnestly to learn. One day his Sensei said to him, "Have you heard that a master keeps one secret, one important secret, away from his pupils?"

"Yes, Sensei, I have."

"Do you think that's true?"

Kaze thought a moment. "I suppose it might be, or how could a master stay superior to his student?"

Sensei sighed. "What do you think is the supreme joy for a true master?" he asked.

Kaze shook his head. "I don't know, Sensei."

"The supreme joy for a true master is to have a pupil who surpasses him, so a true master would not withhold an important secret from a pupil. What do you think would be the effect of doing this? If a master did withhold a key secret from each generation of pupils?"

"Then I suppose, over time, that school of swordsmanship would get weaker and weaker as each succeeding generation of pupils knew less and less of the true essence of the art of the sword."

"Precisely," the Sensei said. "But now I think it is time for me to tell you the final secret in the art of the sword and, indeed, in the art of life."

"What is that, Sensei?" Kaze said eagerly.

"The secret is, there is no secret."

Kaze looked puzzled.

"The final secret is that after you've learned all the techniques, there is still something else that will make a difference. That thing will allow a pupil to excel beyond his master, and it is something within the pupil."

"What is that thing, Sensei?"

The Sensei smiled. It was one of the rare times that Kaze had seen the Sensei smile.

"That's the secret that is not a secret. I don't know what it is. It is some quality within yourself that may allow you to surpass me in some way and in some dimension. Now you have been with me several years. Despite your stupidity and slowness, you have learned the techniques of my school of the sword. In fact, you are now at the point where you are very close to being a novice."

Kaze was confused. He knew he had made progress with the sword. "Why do you compare me with a novice?" Kaze asked, slightly hurt.

"Because being close to a novice is being close to perfection in the use of a sword."

"What do you mean by that, Sensei?"

"When you were totally without knowledge of the sword and you picked it up, you might not have even been holding it in the proper grip. But if someone attacked you, you would instinctively parry their thrusts and try to use the sword to defend yourself. You would do this even if you knew no technique and had not been initiated into the secrets of the sword. In this, you would be using the sword in a Zen manner.

"Zen says there must be no space between thought and action. A space so much as to allow a hair is not desirable. It is the same with a flint and steel. When the flint strikes the steel, there is no hesitation before the production of the spark. The same is true in the use of the sword. When you are a complete novice, there is no thought or hesitation in how you instinctively use the weapon.

"As you start learning the technique of the sword, you start practicing. At first you are very clumsy and have a hard time putting together combinations of moves so that you can both defend yourself and then attack your opponent. As your skill with the sword increases, you become increasingly confident in your abilities, and you no longer have to think about each of the movements, so they can be executed smoothly and correctly in turn.

"Eventually you can get to the point where you no longer have to think about technique at all. You are simply imbued with a sense of Zen so that you are instinctively on the alert at all times, in the state of mind we call *zanshin*. When you are attacked, you parry and defend and eventually attack your opponent without thinking about which technique you use or hesitating between each movement.

"In other words, when you have achieved mastery of the sword, you are using the sword much like a total novice uses a sword, based truly on instinct and not based on conscious thought of one move with the sword or the next. That's why, when I say you are close to being a novice with the sword, it is, in fact, high praise. It means you've come the full circle from someone very inexperienced to someone whose mastery of the weapon now rivals mine."

"But Sensei, how can I achieve this last step? This use of something inside me to gain more skills?"

"Perhaps you can't achieve this step. Most people go through all their lives without understanding what is inside themselves—that core, that essence that makes them themselves. Some few achieve this consciousness late in life, as their years of study and meditation bear fruit. You had something from the first time I met you that let me know that you had an inner core wtih great possibilities."

"But Sensei, you're always criticizing me!"

"Yes. I am. And those criticisms are always true. But that doesn't mean that the greatness is not still inside you. It simply means that my expectation for you is merely perfection. When you're not achieving perfection, that's when I'm criticizing.

"Let me explain to you the final secret of the *Yagyu* school of fencing. After a student has mastered all its secrets, he is told one final secret and asked to meditate on its meaning. The student is asked the meaning of 'the moon in the water.' Do you know its meaning?"

"That the moon is so lofty that we can only capture a watery image of it here on Earth?"

The Sensei shook his head and sighed. "Perhaps I was wrong about your progress. That answer is neither Zen nor accurate."

Kaze thought furiously and said, "It means that it is the nature of water to reflect the image of the moon, just as it is the nature of the moon to be reflected. All bodies of water have this ability to reflect in their nature, from the great sea to a lowly mud puddle. Yet the water has no conscious desire to reflect the moon. It is simply inherent in every body of water. By the same token, the moon has no desire to be reflected by countless bodies of water, it is simply inherent in its nature, too. Thus it is with men. Some are destined to be reflected, and others have it in their nature to reflect."

The Sensei nodded. "You always surprise me, which is why you are my favorite pupil. A teacher is always happy to be pleasantly surprised by a student. That is the proper answer and, if you were a Yagyu student, you would receive a fancy piece of paper attesting to your skill and the completion of your training. As my student, you will receive no such paper. Instead, your life will be the testament of the training you have received from me. It's time to leave me and return to your parents."

"But, Sensei!" Kaze protested. "I still have so much to learn from you! Surely my training could not be finished."

"*Baka!* Fool! I don't know why I've bothered with you all these years. You are so exasperating! *Urusai!*"

Kaze cringed but was determined to stand his ground. He didn't want to leave the Sensei.

More kindly, the Sensei said, "There is really no more I can teach you. It is time for you to teach yourself. Your life with me was just a temporary dream, just as all of life is an ephemeral moment. It's now time for you to leave this dreamlike existence and return to your life and your karma. You must go down from our mountain retreat and enter the world of men and women again. You're still young, and it is time for you to see what kind of man you will become."

Kaze was heartbroken and thought of a thousand stratagems to stay. But the Sensei was insistent, and Kaze knew he must follow his orders. He had to return to his family and the life that was laid out for him.

The next day, as Kaze was about to go, the Sensei stood, his eyes watery as he fought to control his emotions. The Sensei's white mane framed his weathered face. His back was as straight as a fine spear's shaft, and he refused to let his thick shoulders sag, despite the emotional burden they were bearing. The power of the Sensei's suppressed emotions washed over Kaze. Despite the lack of outward reaction, it made Kaze realize the bond he had with this old man who had been educating him for many years and the debt he owed him. Kaze gave one final, formal bow to his beloved teacher.

"Go!" the old man said, his voice husky. "And look only forward. Look neither to the side nor behind. Simply advance, as I have taught you to do."

Kaze turned on his heels and did exactly that.

The clanging from the forge stopped. Kaze hopped off the tree limb with graceful agility and made his way to the swordsmith's domain. The forge was in a wooden structure open on three sides. Kannemori was talking to one of his assistants. Although the swordsmith had aged, he was still a small bull of a man, with thick muscles in his neck and shoulders, a bald head, and a quick smile at all times, except when he was working on a sword. Then he was the picture of concentration and seriousness.

Kannemori looked up at the sight of a ronin approaching the forge. The man was of average height but very muscular about the arms and shoulders. He walked like a swordsman. Each step maintained a centered balance so that, if he were suddenly attacked, he could immediately take a defensive or offensive posture. He did not shave his pate, and his long hair was gathered at the back of his head in a topknot. He was handsome, and Kannemori judged the man to be in his early thirties. There was something about the set of his squared jaw and the sharp glance of his dark brown eyes that evoked a memory from long ago.

Then the swordsmith remembered. The Sensei's young pupil. The one who had come to Kamakura over two decades ago. The promising young man that the Sensei called, out of the hearing of the young lad, his most promising student. Kannemori told an assistant to take away the blade he was working on. He would finish it tomorrow. Kannemori gave a quick bow to the shrine and then walked out to meet the man, wiping the perspiration from his face with a white cloth.

He said, "Is it you? The Sensei's pupil?" He gave a wide grin.

The man looked surprised. "Yes, it is, Kannemori Sensei. But now I'm known as Matsuyama Kaze, not by my former name."

Kannemori considered that and knew the reason instantly. "Are the Tokugawa looking for you?"

"Yes. Especially Lord Okubo."

"Lord Okubo," Kannemori said thoughtfully. "That is a bad enemy to have."

"Nonetheless, he is the enemy I have."

"And how can I help you, Mr. Wind on Pine Mountain? Do you need lodging or help in some other way?"

"I need a sword."

Kannemori eyed the sword in Kaze's scabbard. It was a fine, but not exquisite, sword with a tsuba with a falling cherry blossom design. His expert eye could see that the sword was not the mate to the scabbard. It was clearly a stopgap measure. "What happened to your sword?"

"It broke during a duel with the owner of the sword I now carry."

"Broke?"

"Yes, Kannemori Sensei. I don't know why. It was a fine Kiyohara blade, and it had served me faithfully from the day it was first presented to me by my former Lord."

Kannemori rubbed his chin. "It broke. . . . " His voice trailed off as he contemplated the meaning of this event. Swords sometimes did break, but they were invariably inferior weapons, katana forged by worthless swordsmiths, usually to equip common foot soldiers. A fine blade like a Kiyohara would not break, except for a reason. "Who was the man you were fighting when it broke?"

"A bandit chief. He was intent on killing a merchant I came across on the Tokaido Road. Even after my sword broke, I was able to kill him."

"And now you carry his sword?"

"Yes. A dead man's sword. I would like to replace it with one of your blades, if you would sell one to me."

"For the Sensei's pupil, I will always have a blade. Always."

Kaze gave the master craftsman a deep, formal bow, keeping his back straight. "Thank you, Kannemori Sensei."

Kannemori returned the bow, but not quite as deeply. "Come, let us go to my house. I want a bath, and then we shall share some sakè."

CHAPTER 14

Evil buzz and a
habit of tormenting me.
Die, pernicious fly!

As the two men walked to the swordsmith's house, which was located a respectful distance from the holy ground of the forge, Kannemori listened to Kaze's story of his search for the daughter of his former Lord and Lady. The fact that Kaze had been searching for almost three years didn't surprise him. Kannemori took it for granted that a pupil of the Sensei's would exert any effort to fulfill a pledge.

As he approached his house, Kannemori was greeted by his wife, who immediately took charge of his guest. She led Kaze to a sitting room to give him food and tea while the swordsmith took a bath. In the bathhouse, his assistants had already stoked the fire and prepared the ofuro. It was strange, but even on the hottest day of summer, when he had been laboring diligently in front of a blazing fire, he craved a hot bath instead of a cold one. The hot bath seemed to cool him off much more than a cool one would.

His assistants dutifully scrubbed his back, as they did every working day. Kannemori had not been blessed by sons, but in the three daughters that had survived childhood, he had found all the joy that a man could expect. His daughters had been married long ago, all to swordsmiths in Kamakura, and taken into other households, but the visits from his grandchildren were now the supreme moments of his life, second only to forging an exceptionally fine blade. He knew, of course, which katana would go to the Sensei's pupil.

His assistants rinsed him off before he entered the bath. After the master was done, the assistants would get to bathe and then, finally, the women of the house, starting with his wife. The scalding hot water of the bath eased his aching muscles. He knew that he would soon have to appoint one of his assistants his successor, adopting him as a son and grooming the chosen assistant to replace him at his craft. The adopted son would take the name Kannemori, to continue a line that had been unbroken for five generations. Kannemori sighed. He was getting old. Such was the wheel of life—the old replaced by the young. He stretched as the hot water washed away his aches. Perhaps that replacement would not be quite yet. Still, the demand for weapons had slackened considerably since Sekigahara and the coming of peace. Maybe it would be a good time to retire.

Kannemori got out of the bath and dried himself with a small damp towel. The hot water did not have to be absorbed by the towel. It dried off when the excess was taken up. An assistant helped him into a more formal kimono than he would normally wear because of his guest.

Asking his assistant to fetch the key, Kannemori went to the plaster treasure storage located behind the main house. Opening the door, he entered by himself and immediately went toward a *hinoki* wood chest at the back of the cramped treasure room. Opening it, he took out a bundle wrapped in a purple cloth and left to join his guest, leaving the assistant to lock up.

He found the Sensei's pupil in the formal sitting room, enjoying some *gomoku* rice. His wife gave him a small smile and immediately leaned over to pick up an iron kettle filled with sakè that had been sitting in a pot of hot water to warm it. Kannemori put the bundle on the floor and sat down across from the samurai. He was pleased that the samurai had the good manners to ignore the bundle, even though he must have known what was in it and must have been curious to see them.

As the guest, the samurai was served first, a splash of sakè poured into a small porcelain saucer. The samurai then insisted on taking the kettle from Kannemori's wife and serving the swordsmith himself. The two men toasted. "To the Sensei and happier times," Kannemori said.

Seeing the two men were intent on serious talk, Kannemori's wife left them to start preparing supper.

Kannemori reached over and poured another drink for the samurai. The samurai took the kettle and repeated the act for the swordsmith.

"*Oishi!* Good!" Kannemori said, smacking his lips after draining his saucer.

"Yes, it is," agreed the samurai.

"Do you still sit in trees?" Kannemori asked suddenly.

"I was a young man then," Kaze said, a bit embarrassed. It was unseemly for a full grown man to indulge in childish things.

"But . . . " Kannemori prompted.

"But I still do it, Kannemori Sensei."

Kannemori laughed and said, "I asked not because I wanted to embarrass you, but because of something the Sensei and I used to speculate about when you were a lad."

"What's that, Kannemori Sensei?"

"Have you ever been to the temple Kenchoji?"

"No, Kannemori Sensei."

"Kenchoji has the first garden laid out in Zen style, and by the lake in the garden was *Yogo no Matsu,* the shadow pine, an especially lovely tree. On one occasion the priests of the temple were gathered in a room overlooking the garden when they saw a branch on this beautiful tree suddenly dip toward the ground. Lord Abbot Doryu immediately started a conversation with someone sitting on the branch that no one else could see. The Abbot said he was a man in costly court robes and asked where he came from. The man said 'Tsurugaoka,' the hill of cranes."

"Where the Hachiman Shrine is?" Kaze asked.

"The same. Today that tree is called Reisho, the Cold Pine, and the monks swear that the stranger on the branch was the God Hachiman, the God of War himself. When you were a boy, the Sensei and I talked about your love of sitting on tree limbs, and we speculated about whether this was related to your precocious skill with the sword. I thought it might be a sign that Hachiman himself had touched you."

"And the Sensei?"

"The Sensei said I had spent too much time near a clanging forge and that my senses were addled!" Kannemori laughed. "Still," Kannemori said thoughtfully, "even an addled fool can sometimes see something a wise man cannot."

The two men poured drinks for each other again.

"I suppose Tokugawa will declare himself Shogun soon," Kaze said, wanting to change from a subject that made him uncomfortable. He left off the "san" or "sama" honorific normally used with Tokugawa's name.

Kannemori looked surprised. "Haven't you heard? Tokugawa-sama declared himself Shogun months ago."

Kaze was stunned. "I've been wandering the mountains and had not heard the news. I knew Tokugawa was thinking of declaring himself Shogun when he claimed descent from the Minamoto. I'm still surprised he dared to do it."

"He received the imperial decrees earlier this year," Kannemori said. The reception of imperial appointments, including one as great as Shogun, the supreme military dictator of Japan, was almost an anticlimactic affair. The official decrees appointing Ieyasu would be sent from Kyoto, probably written in the emperor's own hand. Each decree would be in a separate box. Ieyasu would receive the imperial delegation in his reception room, sitting on a dais. A box would be handed to an assistant, who would take it out of the room. The box would be opened and the decree, often consisting of only a line or two, would be read to see what honor was bestowed. Then the decree would be replaced by a bag of gold and the box would be returned to the delegation. Ieyasu would then be told what honor had been assigned. No doubt, in addition to Shogun, Ieyasu had received decrees granting many other old Court titles, such as Minister of the Right, which made him the military commander of Kyoto. The more titles granted, the more bags of gold flowing into the imperial coffers.

"After being appointed Shogun, Tokugawa-sama went to Kyoto to celebrate," Kannemori continued, "and he's just returned to Edo to check on the progress of his new castle and to see how the town is being rebuilt after the great fire last year. Edo is now a bustling place, full of growth."

"And also full of charlatans, cheats, and enemies. Men like the Tokugawas," Kaze said. "There was a Shogun who ruled for only thirteen days. Tokugawa's rule will not be that short, but he may not enjoy a long dynasty. I truly need a new sword now."

"I will give you my finest sword. However, I wish you would reconsider your feelings about the Tokugawas. A sword is not just an instrument for killing. It should be an instrument of righteousness. Do you know the story of the blade of Okazaki Masamune and that of his pupil, Muramasa?"

"No, Kannemori Sensei, I don't."

"As you know, Okazaki Masamune-san was a master swordsmith who worked in Kamakura several hundred years ago. His forge was just in the next valley, as a matter of fact. I consider Masamune-san to be one of the finest swordsmiths ever. Today his blades are valued above all others as reflections of the swordsmith's art. What isn't commonly known is that his pupil, Muramasa, was perhaps an even finer craftsman, looking at his blades from a purely technical standpoint.

"One day a Lord who owned both a Masamune-san blade and a blade by his pupil, Muramasa, decided to test them. Now, the standard way to test a blade is to use it to execute a condemned prisoner or to cut at the body of an already killed prisoner. This Lord, however, decided to try a new kind of test.

"He took the two blades to a swiftly moving stream and thrust the pupil Muramasa's blade into the rapidly flowing water. It was the month of no Gods, and in the water were many fallen leaves. As the leaves touched the edge of the Muramasa blade, the edge was so keen that the leaves were all cut in two, just from their contact with the sword. The Lord was then curious to see if Masamune-san's blade was as sharp, so he removed the pupil's blade from the water and replaced it with the master's blade."

"And was it as sharp?" Kaze asked.

"The Lord never found out," Kannemori answered. "When he put Masamune-san's blade in the water, he was amazed to see that the leaves in the water avoided the blade, keeping away from the sharp edge. You see, the pupil's sword was a wonderful weapon, with as keen an edge as can be imagined. But this weapon was just a weapon. Masamune-san's blade was more than a weapon. It was an expression of Masamune-san's spirit, a spirit intent on righteousness, not just killing. The result was that even the leaves wanted to avoid the sharp edge of the sword."

Kannemori reached over and moved the purple bundle between himself and the samurai. He slowly unwrapped the bundle, revealing a katana and a wakizashi, the long and short swords of the samurai. The swords were in plain black-lacquer scabbards. The tsuba had a pattern of swirling water curled into a wave, the foaming edges of the wave picked out in silver. This tsuba was appropriate for a ronin samurai, for ronin meant "wave man."

"These are the weapons I have chosen for you," Kannemori said. "They are the finest swords I have ever made. I've never been able to repeat their quality, although I've tried many times. I have kept them for many years, waiting for the proper owner to appear. You are that owner. If you put them into a stream, unfortunately you will find that the leaves will not avoid them. When they touch the edge, however, the leaves will be cut in two. With this sword I captured the technical prowess of Muramasa, but I lack the spirit of Masamune-san. I'm hopeful that you will be able to endow these weapons with some of your spirit. I know that spirit is strong, or the Sensei would not have had the affection he had for you." Kannemori bowed, then slid the bundle toward Kaze.

Kaze also bowed, then picked up the wakizashi and placed it in front of Kannemori. "I'm sorry, Kannemori Sensei, but I can only accept the katana. When I accepted the task of finding the Lady's daughter, she took my wakizashi, the samurai's keeper of honor, and said my honor belonged to her until I finished my task."

Kannemori accepted the short sword back. "I understand," he said. "I'll keep this, and when you redeem your honor, you can come and get it from me. In the meantime, it will remind me of who has my masterwork."

"Thank you, Kannemori Sensei."

"Do you want to see how the katana feels?" Kannemori asked.

"I'm sure it's fine."

"Nonsense! Please don't be shy. Take it outside and try it for feel and balance."

Kaze did as he was directed, and the swordsmith followed him outside. In front of the house, Kaze removed the blade from the scabbard, noting with satisfaction that the scabbard had a ko-gatana knife embedded in it.

The blade felt marvelously light and lively as Kaze tried different grips and positions. The highly polished blade caught the late-afternoon sun, reflecting fiery flashes across the gray wooden walls of the house. Suddenly, Kaze saw a large fly buzzing by. With a quick flick of his wrist, the blade snaked out and the fly was cut in two.

Kannemori gave a cry of surprise and bent down to retrieve the pieces of the fly. Looking at his palm, he could see the fly was sliced cleanly in half. "Well, that little trick has named your sword. It didn't have a name before, but now I think it shall be called Fly Cutter! Prince Yamatotakeru had a sword called *Kusanagi no Tsurugi*, the Grass-Cutting Sword, because he used it to mow down grass and escape when rebels set fire to a field. It's fitting that you have a similar name for your weapon, after such a display."

"Tell me," Kannemori said, giving Kaze a big grin, "was that skill or practice?"

"Merely practice," Kaze acknowledged.

"Still," Kannemori said, looking at the two insect pieces in his hand, "that is an incredible way to test this blade."

CHAPTER 15

Happy warrior!
So favored by the war Gods
that seas will recede.

Kaze walked down the pathway, lighting his way with a paper lantern Kannemori had given him. The lantern was at the end of a stick of wood, allowing Kaze to lower the lantern close to his feet to illuminate the path with the pale yellow light that filtered through its square paper sides. There was a full moon, but the lantern was a welcome aid as Kaze walked paths not completely familiar to him. He passed Gokurakuji, or the Temple of Paradise, and he knew he was coming up to Inamuragasaki Point. To the eyes of the people who named it, this point resembled the stacks of rice straw seen at harvest time all over Japan.

He had enjoyed a delicious dinner at the swordsmith's and left with his new weapon. He had discreetly given the remaining gold coins he got from Hishigawa to Kannemori's wife right before he left, not wanting to insult the master swordsmith by engaging in commerce with him.

Taking the lantern Kannemori had given him to illuminate his journey home, Kaze had headed toward the sea instead of back toward Hishigawa's villa.

Kaze walked to the edge of the cliff at Inamuragasaki Point and stopped. Looking down at the rolling black water that surrounded the base of the cliff, he stood for a moment, gaining a sense of the place and a feeling for its history and importance.

Looking out at Sagami Bay, he took out the cherry blossom sword that had been stuck in his sash along with his new sword, the Fly Cutter. He held Ishibashi's sword in both hands for a few minutes and, overcome by the place and its past, he recited some of the story of Nitta Yoshisada.

"*Nitta ascended to the summit of the cliff, the pale moonlight casting dark shadows on the rocks and crannies that gave him precarious purchase for his hands and feet. At the summit he looked down and saw the enemy encampment. To the far north the kiridoshi, or pass, leading into Kamakura was steep and forbidding. A dark fortress stood brooding over this gateway to the city, and, from the fires of the encampment near the fortress, he could see that warriors numbering in the tens of thousands were waiting for his army to act foolishly and attack.*

"*Below him the salty sea lapped at the base of the cliffs. On the narrow strip of sand that acted as the buffer between earth and water, a barricade had been constructed. And in the deep water just off the cliffs, countless warships filled with archers were ready. To make an assault along the beach in order to breach the defenses of Kamakura and take the town would be as suicidal as an assault from the north, through the pass.*

"*Nitta stood and saw his future in his hands. To the north was impenetrable. To the south was the sea with the barricades and warships. And waiting by the shore, waiting silently, waiting cunningly, was his army—waiting for Nitta's leadership, waiting for him to give the signal to attack. Waiting, ever waiting, for its chance at victory.*

"*Nitta took his gold sword from its scabbard and held it in his hands. He fixed his gaze beyond the edges of the waiting warcraft and closed his eyes in sincere supplication to the Sea God. Then, with the strength of a hero, he flung his gold sword into the sea, crying out that his prayers be answered.*

"*The sword flew past the waiting warcraft and was swallowed greedily by the dark waves of the bay, as if the Sea God were accepting this sin-*

cere offering from the supplicant. And lo! The waters receded, forcing the warships farther and farther from the point, until finally they were out of arrow range. Nitta's army saw before it a broad and sandy highway, as wide as seven ri, *aimed straight into the heart of the city of Kamakura. Crying his thanks to the Sea God, Nitta descended from the cliff, mounted his horse, and led his army across the sandy highway into the city, earning victory!"*

As the last echoes of the word "victory" were swept up by the sea wind, Kaze reached back and hurled the cherry blossom sword far into the air. In the pale moonlight he saw it twirl lazily against the background of stars as it sank its way toward the water below. It hit with a small splash that formed a silver circle for a brief moment, and then Ishibashi's sword was gone.

"Thank you for letting me use your sword, Ishibashi-san," Kaze said to the spirit of the dead man. "And thank you for letting the sword defend me from the three assassins who attacked me."

Kaze prayed that the spirit of Ishibashi would be appeased and at rest, ready to be reincarnated into its next life. He also prayed to the Sea God, just as Nitta had done. He looked to the sea to see if there was some sign that his prayer, like Nitta's, would be answered. His prayer was that he would find the young girl he was seeking. Though he stood at the cliff side for several minutes, there seemed no change in the ocean, land, or stars that would act as a sign that the Gods had heard his prayer and would grant it. Only the lapping of the eternal waves hitting the cliff below punctured the silence.

Sighing, he started walking back. Then, on a whim, Kaze walked to Yukiaigawa bridge. Kaze followed Zen, the religion of the warrior, so he was not a Nichiren Buddhist, but he thought that if a sacrifice with a sword was to generate any divine intervention, then the most likely place for this to manifest itself would be at Yukiaigawa, the River of Meeting.

More than three hundred years before, Nichiren had almost been executed here. The priest was old then and had converted many disciples to his style of Buddhism. But he had angered the authorities and was condemned to death.

As Nichiren knelt with his neck extended to have his head lopped off, the executioner raised his sword high before bringing it down with the same sudden swiftness and fatal result as the hawk descending on the mouse. When the blade was at its acme, a divine show of force occurred: A lightning bolt came down from the sky, striking the sword blade and breaking it into three pieces, leaving the executioner stunned and senseless on the ground.

The local authorities were frightened and amazed by this display of heaven's divine favor to Nichiren. The breaking of the sword was a clear sign that its use to execute the saint was unjust. The authorities sent a messenger to the Regent to recount what had happened and ask for instructions. At Yukiaigawa, the messenger from the local authorities met another messenger coming from the other direction. This messenger had been sent by the Regent, who the night before had been visited by a heavenly apparition in his dream, warning him not to slay the holy Nichiren. The two messengers met at the river and, after exchanging messages, each was in awe of what had happened.

Surely, Kaze thought, there could be no better place than the River of Meeting to meet someone who could give him information about the girl, or perhaps even to meet the girl herself.

But as Kaze reached the bank of the stream, watching the black river water in its constant flow to the sea, he reflected that perhaps it was his karma not to have this task made easier by an intervention of heaven.

He walked along the riverbank to the bridge where the two messengers met. As he made his way, his lantern illuminated the pathway before him just a few steps ahead. His life was like the glow from the lantern. He could see only one or two steps ahead of him, yet his faith in the future kept him moving forward, sure that he would complete his task if allowed to live. He could hear the sound of the water in the river, brittle and cold in the night air. Above him the night sky formed a black canopy pierced by tiny points of shimmering light, the round moon hanging over his shoulder.

As Kaze approached the bridge, the sound of water faded away and around him darkness started gathering, as if a black fog were rolling over him and darkening the heavens. The stars above grew dim and the moon became obscured, as if behind a cloud. His steps slowed and eventually halted. From the bridge, he heard a sound that he had both feared and anticipated. It was the crying of a woman.

This had happened to Kaze once before when he was on a mountain path walking through the mist. He took a deep breath, but the air was stale and lifeless. He walked forward slowly.

There, sitting in the middle of the bridge, he could see the woman. She was dressed in a kimono of white, the color of death and mourning. Her long black hair hung loosely against the kimono, looking like the stroke of a calligraphy brush against snowlike paper. Kaze stared at the figure but could not bring the edges of the apparition into sharp focus. Looking within his soul, Kaze recited a piece of the *Heart Sutra*. I have no doubt and therefore no fear. No doubt and therefore no fear. No doubt and no fear.

Repeating the phrase over and over to himself like a mantra, he approached the figure and stopped a short distance away.

He got to his knees and bowed deeply. When he was done, he looked up at the figure. The figure's head was bent down in sadness, her hands across her face. Through her fingers he could see the teardrops falling like steady drops of rain. They hit her white kimono, staining the cloth with spreading points of wetness.

"I am here, my Lady," he said almost inaudibly. He knew the ghostly figure before him would hear him, no matter how softly he spoke. She straightened at the sound of his voice and took her hands away from her face. Even though Kaze had steeled himself for what he was about to see, he still felt a cold shiver gripping his body, shaking him with an icy firmness that penetrated to his very soul.

The figure had no face. It had no eyes, no mouth, and no nose, yet it could still cry piteously.

Kaze made another bow. "I suppose you want news on how my search for your daughter goes," he said. The sound of sobbing lessened.

Kaze reached into his sleeve and brought out the scrap of cloth with the three plum blossoms, the crest of the Lady.

"This is what has led me to Kamakura, Lady. First down the Tokaido Road and now to this place. I must find a secret. People who might have information about your daughter will not give it to me until I perform a service in return, which is to find out what happened to their family member. When I find out what happened to their relative, they will tell me more about your daughter's location. Because you are visiting me, I know that your daughter is still alive. If she were with you in another world, between life and rebirth, then I assume you would not be coming to me."

The figure waved a ghostly arm in a wide sweep, moving slowly, like a piece of wood bobbing on the ocean. Kaze took the wave of the arm as confirmation that the child was still alive.

"I have not forgotten my promise to you. I've not lessened my dedication to find your child. I'll do my best to find her." He bowed once again. In the midst of this bow, he could suddenly hear the river rushing beneath him, flowing swiftly past the wooden boards and bamboo that made up the bridge. He knew from that, even before looking up, that the ghost of the lady would be gone. And she was.

Kaze stood and felt his legs weak and trembling under him. He lurched slightly and grabbed the guardrail of the bridge. He held himself upright until the strength returned to his limbs. He looked about him and saw the lantern sitting on the ground. Its candle was still flickering. He reached out to grab the lantern stick and noticed that his hand was trembling slightly. He took a deep breath and closed his eyes for a moment to center himself. When he opened his eyes, his outstretched hand was no longer trembling. He picked up the lantern and, by its pale light, made his way back to Hishigawa's villa.

◆　◆　◆

The next morning, Kaze started walking about the grounds of the villa. Elder Grandma's grandson was a samurai, and a merchant killing a samurai was a serious matter. A samurai could kill a peasant for any reason. But for a merchant to kill a samurai, or to have one killed, would result in severe punishment if it were discovered.

Because of this, Kaze looked for fresh earth and signs of a new grave as he wandered within the walls of the villa. His eyes were those of the experienced hunter, so he was sure he could detect the aftermath of the crime if Hishigawa had had the grandson killed and buried within the villa's walls.

His search uncovered an interesting area, although it didn't look like a fresh burial. It also uncovered another interesting sight. As he was walking around the lake that surrounded the Jade Palace, he saw some young girls sitting on the veranda of the palace, on the side facing away from the main house. The palace was as large as a house in its own right, so it was natural that Yuchan would have attendants and maids with her. These girls were richly dressed in expensive kimono, however, much more opulently than any maid would ever be.

As Kaze walked by on the shore, the girls stopped talking. Kaze glanced their way and noticed they were not looking downward modestly, as would be proper for young ladies in the presence of a strange man. Instead, they were looking at Kaze boldly, even speculatively. Kaze stopped and rudely stared back at them. They didn't flinch from his gaze and instead met it.

Kaze broke into a grin. Then he stuck his tongue out at the girls. They burst into a fit of giggling. Kaze turned and continued his search of the villa grounds, but now he also contemplated the meaning of this encounter with richly dressed, bold, and pretty girls at the Jade Palace.

The interesting area was one he wanted to examine in darkness, so he decided he would try to talk to the various guards stationed around the villa to see if he could gather more information. These men viewed him with suspicion, and none would talk to him, except for the barest words required by politeness. Instead of being frustrated by their taciturn response to his overtures, Kaze was impressed by the level of discipline that Enomoto had managed to instill in his men.

Enomoto gave every indication of being a true swordsman. His men gave every indication of being good, also. Like the young girls at the Jade Palace, this was another element out of place, as nagging as a misplaced flower in an *ikebana* arrangement. Kaze decided to seek out Enomoto.

He found him grooming his sword.

Enomoto sat with his katana held in one hand, and in the other he had a small piece of bamboo. The end of the bamboo bore a small cloth ball that had been dipped in powder. Enomoto was patiently hitting the ball lightly along the length of the katana blade, absorbing old oil on his weapon. Kaze looked at the blade of Enomoto and understood what Kannemori had been saying about the blades of Okazaki Masamune. To Kaze, swords were a thing of beauty and spirituality. Each blade reflected something of its maker and its owner. The blade in Enomoto's hand was a coldly efficient killing machine.

Enomoto looked up as Kaze approached and gave a nod of greeting. He returned his attention to his katana. Kaze sat down quietly, waiting politely for Enomoto to finish. When Enomoto had wiped off the powder with a piece of paper, he took a soft cloth and lightly oiled the blade.

"Here in Kamakura, we are so near the sea that one must oil his blade regularly or it will rust. I notice you have a new sword," he said without looking up. "It looks to be a fine one."

"I don't know. I hope so. I know it is well made, but I haven't tested it yet. Or I have tested it, but only on a fly."

"A fly?" Enomoto was surprised. Finished oiling his sword, he slid the blade smoothly into its scabbard.

Kaze waved his hand. "It's a silly thing, of no matter."

Enomoto politely let the subject drop.

"I have been talking to some of your men," Kaze said, "and I've been impressed by their caliber."

"Yes, they are good. You've also been wandering about the villa."

Kaze smiled. "I like to walk. After so many days on the road, it's in my blood. I simply took a walk around the villa grounds."

Again politely, Enomoto let this topic drop, too.

"I was surprised that men of such caliber were not able to protect Hishigawa better when he was attacked by bandits."

"I understand it was eight bandits to my three guards," Enomoto said.

"Yes, but the three were able to kill only one of the bandits before they were slain."

"Then perhaps they are not too good," Enomoto answered. "I've been thinking that lately."

"Perhaps," Kaze said. He looked at Enomoto speculatively, and Enomoto coolly returned his gaze. Enomoto was more closed than the first time Kaze had talked to him. He wondered why.

"Hishigawa mentioned that he's been robbed like that before."

"Yes, earlier this year."

"They killed his guards but didn't harm him?"

"Yes, they could see he was no threat to them. Despite his samurai ancestors, he barely knows how to hold a sword."

"Was he carrying a lot of gold that other time, too?"

"Yes, a lot. When he's moving an especially large amount, he likes to go along because he doesn't trust anyone. You said you had an idea that would save him from this bother. Have you told Hishigawa-san yet?"

"No. I'm waiting. If there's no need to tell Hishigawa, I won't."

Enomoto said nothing.

"Hishigawa mentioned that there was an attempt on his life. . . . " Kaze let the statement hang, but Enomoto did nothing to pluck it down.

Instead Enomoto said, "I suppose it's a dangerous time for everyone. You, for instance, seem to be doing a great deal of traveling, looking for this child. It's a strange story. Why would you be looking for this child?"

"Call it a whim."

"Few men put out great effort for a whim."

Kaze smiled. "Perhaps I am foolish." He returned to his agenda, trying to garner information about Mototane. "Has Hishigawa ever been attacked here, at the villa?" he asked. He didn't bother to use a casual tone, for he knew it wouldn't fool Enomoto.

"No," Enomoto said. "We have many guards here. It would require a large group of men or a fool to attack Hishigawa-san in this place."

Kaze wondered if Elder Grandma's missing grandson, Mototane, was such a fool.

CHAPTER 16

Soft skin, bright brown eyes,
a mother's gentle touch, and
a heart of evil.

Ando was going over the household accounts. Because she was a woman, she could not hold the title of Chief Steward or Chief Accountant. But the reality was that, except for the guards, she ran the business as well as the household.

All her life, Ando had been devoted to the Hishigawa family and the man she still thought of indulgently as the Young Master. She had first started serving Hishigawa when she was eight and Hishigawa was four. She could barely lift the chubby boy, strapping him to her back with a cloth like a Japanese grandmother. Hishigawa's mother found it cute that the young servant girl was so devoted to her son and let Ando dote on the child.

The Young Master had been shrewd in time of war, trading weapons and other goods in the years leading up to the climactic battle of Sekigahara. After Sekigahara, the trading was not quite as lucrative, but Hishigawa had adapted his business admirably to match the times and availability of merchandise and was still making much gold in his various enterprises.

Throughout his entire career, Hishigawa had shown a single-mindedness and tenacity that always got him what he wanted. Perhaps that was what made him a success, although Ando thought this same single-mindedness about Yuchan's love was sometimes a bother. Still, as a devoted servant, it was not Ando's role to question her master's whims. It was her role to help him achieve them.

Ando had also achieved some of her own goals. She was powerful and feared and wielded more authority than any other woman she knew. To reach this height, she had overcome many obstacles, starting with her husband.

As good masters, the Hishigawas had decided to arrange a marriage between their son's young nursemaid and the son of the Andos, another of their servants. To the bride, the marriage was a bother and a bore. She had focused her devotion on the Young Master and found the social and physical demands of marriage a tremendous distraction. She found no pleasure in the body of her husband and chafed under the numerous new restrictions on her as a married woman.

She knew her new husband would never have the drive and ambition to rise in the hierarchy of Hishigawa family servants, so she decided to do something about it. She started nagging her husband, urging him to devote more hours and show more initiative in his service to the Hishigawas. At first he complied, but as her nagging grew more strident, he started showing his annoyance by ignoring her and talking back. Finally, on the advice of his fellow males, he struck Ando during one particularly violent argument.

Ando stopped talking to him immediately after her husband slapped her face. She said nothing for the rest of the evening but seemed to welcome his sexual advances that night. Her husband congratulated himself, thinking he had subdued the shrew with his firmness.

The next morning, she went to the woods and searched out a certain mushroom. She knew about the various types of plants and fungi used in cooking, which things to eat and which things to avoid. She was looking for a mushroom that was normally one to avoid and she found it.

That night, her husband ate *oden*, a vegetable stew Ando had prepared. He complained that it had a bitter taste. By midnight, Ando's husband was retching into a wooden bucket while squatting over a privy with diarrhea.

The husband's distress continued through the night and into the next day. Ando made sure everyone knew of her husband's illness. He was in such misery that he moaned that he wished to die. But Ando knew he wouldn't die from the mushrooms. They were not mushrooms that killed. They only sickened and made one weak, which is exactly what Ando wanted. Had she wanted to kill, she would have used *neko-irazu*, literally "cat not needed," a deadly rat poison. No, physical weakness in her husband was exactly what she wanted.

That afternoon, with her exhausted husband lying asleep on his futon, Ando took a basin of water, a cloth, and a thick piece of paper to the side of her spouse. She took the paper and soaked it in the water, making sure it was soft and pliable. When the paper was soaked to Ando's satisfaction, she removed it from the water and placed it on the cloth.

She took the cloth and paper and flipped them over so the wet paper was on the bottom. Then, holding the cloth and paper with both hands, she brought them down on her husband's face.

The soaked paper molded itself to her husband's face. The water-logged paper cut off all air to the sick man, and the cloth allowed Ando to press it down hard without leaving marks.

With his air supply cut off, her husband immediately roused himself from sleep and tried to throw off the suffocating presence on his face. His cries were muffled by the paper and the cloth. He reached up and grasped Ando's wrists. He tried to pry her hands away, but the sickness caused by the mushrooms had weakened him so much that he didn't have the strength to dislodge her.

Ando felt the weakness of her husband's grip, and she knew that the mushrooms had worked exactly as she had planned. She would be the victor, and it would come at her own hands. She liked seeing his body thrash about in distress and found she enjoyed the sensation of his grip weakening on her wrist as his life ebbed away. She thought of releasing the cloth, not to save her husband's life but simply to toy with the dying man. She wanted to revive him just enough to pull him back from the edge of death. Then she would press down again, so she could feel his life slipping away under her hands. Before she could put this plan into action, however, her husband released her wrists and his hands fell limply to the futon.

Disappointed, Ando removed the cloth and paper and watched intently to see if her husband would revive. If he did revive, she intended to smother him again, but his spirit had departed. He lay there limp and lifeless.

Ando used the edge of the cloth to wipe the dampness from her husband's face. Then, after removing the cloth, paper, and basin of water, she set to wailing in a manner that she thought would be suitable for a new widow.

Afterward, it was easy to prey on the Hishigawas' sympathies to regain her old position as the Young Master's protector. She was able to indulge the young man's every whim and nurtured him to grow up thinking he was a merchant prince and not just a grubby trader. If she had been asked, she would have gladly shared the young man's bed, giving her body to please him, although she found no pleasure in the act. She would often slip into his bed on cold winter nights to warm the futon before the Young Master got in. But as the boy turned into the man, he expressed no inclination to use his nursemaid in this fashion, even though she was only a few years older.

Since she could not sacrifice her body for her Master, she took a hand in arranging a series of accommodating concubines for Hishigawa. Intent on growing his business after his father and mother died, he seemed content with this arrangement and passed up several chances at marriage. Then he met Yuchan.

Hishigawa came back from a business trip obsessed with this woman. He was in a fever to have her and wanted desperately for her to love him with the same passion and need he had for her. This last part, that she love him, was as important to the Young Master as having her.

Ando volunteered to act as a go-between to arrange a match. She secretly thought that perhaps she could actually arrange to have the girl come as another of the Young Master's concubines. But, if necessary, she would even arrange a marriage if that would get the young girl for the Master.

When she first saw Yuchan, Ando had to admit she was pretty enough. She had a certain grace that came from the training in flower-arranging, dance, and the other indulgences that rich samurai could afford for their children. How such a creature was able to raise the lust and desire of a superior man like the Young Master was something Ando could not fathom. Ando thought that surely she must be a witch.

To Ando's surprise, Yuchan's father was cold to the idea of a match between his daughter and Hishigawa. Ando talked about Hishigawa's wealth and success, while the old fool rambled on about his daughter's happiness. Despite being offered a tremendous sum, a price that would have bought a dozen girls prettier than Yuchan, her father rejected the offer. Although he talked of Yuchan's desires in the matter, Ando was convinced that the rejection was based on the fact that the Noguchis were samurai and Hishigawa was a merchant.

Ando could see that this man was unreasonable and perfectly capable of thwarting the Young Master's happiness to indulge his little daughter, so she decided to take drastic action.

With the help of a half dozen of Enomoto's men, Ando kidnapped Yuchan. Being a bit impatient, she had had to kill the father and a servant during the abduction, and now the Noguchis had obtained an official vendetta against the Young Master. Fortunately, most of the Noguchi men had been killed fighting in the great battles between the Tokugawas and the forces loyal to Hideyoshi's heir, so there was little danger that they could get past the Young Master's yojimbo to carry out the vendetta.

They had brought the willful child to the villa and installed her in the Jade Palace, which had been constructed for another purpose. They had found a rogue priest to marry the Young Master to the witch, and Ando was sure it was only a matter of time before the girl thought as she and the Young Master wished. In fact, like the smothering of her husband, Ando found she quite liked training the willful girl to be a good wife to the Young Master.

She looked up and saw the new ronin approaching her. She was grateful to this man for saving the Young Master and his gold, but she also had an instinctual wariness about him. Enomoto seemed to hold him in high regard, but there was something about this ronin that made Ando uneasy. Perhaps it was because she could not understand him. Enomoto she could understand. He could be bought with money, and therefore his loyalty to the Young Master could be assured with an adequate supply of it. The samurai the master hired, all of them ronin, were much the same. But this new ronin was different, and this difference made her see him as a threat. If he became too much of a threat, perhaps it would be time to go picking mushrooms again. Ando had killed before in the service of the Young Master. It would be no great trick to kill again.

"Hello, Ando," the ronin said. Ando was used to being called "san" by the ronin at the villa, but this one was too new to know her real power, so she let the slight pass.

"Hello, Matsuyama," she said, purposely dropping the "san" herself.

If the ronin noticed, he gave no indication. Instead he said, "I'm a bit impressed by the love your master shows for his wife. I can't recall ever seeing a wife so pampered and treated like royalty as Yuchan is."

"My master is a man of strong emotions and deep sentiment," Ando said. "It is only natural that when he gives his heart, it results in the maximum expenditure of effort to make his love happy. I think it's an admirable thing."

"So do I," Kaze said. "But it is also an unusual one. How did he meet Yuchan?"

"It was a love match," Ando said. "From the time they first saw each other, they knew they were soul mates. I had the honor of being the go-between, to arrange the wedding. Naturally, with my master in the offing, Yuchan was anxious for the match, as was her family."

The ronin looked at Ando reflectively. It made a pretty story, Kaze thought, even if it was a false one.

"Well, he certainly treats her like a noble," Kaze said.

"Oh, yes. She even has special food. Often we have delicacies brought from the best restaurants in Kamakura. We also cook food for her here. I personally supervise the cooking for her. My master wants nothing but the best for his wife."

"Since he's so much in love, it must greatly bother Hishigawa-san that he is in such danger."

"Danger?" Ando showed genuine alarm.

"Yes. You heard about the danger he had on the Tokaido Road, and apparently he has been in danger here at the villa. . . . " Kaze left the last word hanging, hoping to induce Ando into telling more about the attempts on Hishigawa's life. This could bring information about the fate of Mototane.

"Those are affairs of men," Ando said, pursing her lips. She looked down at her work. "Now, Samurai, if you'll excuse me, I have to return to my household accounts."

Not so easily dismissed, Kaze stood staring at Ando. She kept her head down, studiously looking at the books. Kaze smiled and then gave a short laugh that made Ando start but didn't make her look up. At the sound of his laughter, Ando's face reddened, but Kaze thought this was from anger, not embarrassment. He looked at the servant thoughtfully and wondered if she was capable of killing. It would be difficult for a woman to kill a samurai like Mototane, but a woman was capable of using a dagger or spear as well as a man. Besides, women sometimes had other, more deadly weapons to draw on.

CHAPTER 17

Wolves cross the highway.
Ducks, rabbits, and fat chickens.
Who warns the helpless?

Melons! Juicy, sweet melons!" the peasant called out. The old servant, thin as a skeleton, walked up to him and picked up a melon. He sniffed the stem to test its ripeness and hefted it to judge its weight. Satisfied with the quality of the merchandise, he then set to bargaining in earnest with the melon seller to effect the purchase of two of the melons. In the servant's hands were several bundles from other purchases in Kamakura's open-air market.

It only took a few exchanges before the two men were intently talking price. In the heat of bargaining, neither man saw the four ronin circling the marketplace. The ronin fancied that they had the look of wolves, but in fact they looked more like stray dogs. They were used to making mischief and converged on the two men because they looked weak and vulnerable.

"That's still too much for such inferior merchandise," the old servant said.

"But sir, these are superior melons! The finest in Kamakura. Juicy, sweet, and at the peak of ripeness. Just ask anyone. They know the quality of my melons." The peasant was quite enjoying the intense debate over price. Modern wives these days didn't seem to have time for a good argument over price. This servant knew how to bargain! He must have been trained by a master.

"They seem overripe to me. If I don't take two off your hands now, at half the price you want, then you'll just throw them away tomorrow."

"Overripe! Why sir, these melons . . ." The peasant's voice trailed off. He noticed that they were now surrounded by the four ronin. He licked his lips in apprehension and gave a polite bow of greeting.

"Good morning, Samurai-sama!" the peasant said with a forced heartiness. "Would you like some sweet melons today?"

The leader of the pack smiled. "Of course. I'm glad you're giving them to us."

"But Samurai-sama," the peasant said hastily, "I didn't—"

The leader gave the peasant a violent shove, pushing him away from his fruit. Then he put his hand on his sword, loosening it in the scabbard with an ominous click. "Are you taking back your offer to give us the melons?" the samurai said angrily.

The peasant regained his balance and looked at the four hard faces staring back at him. He licked his lips again. A tight knot of fear grew in his belly and moved up to constrict his throat. "Please excuse my stupidity," the peasant said hastily. "Of course you may take anything you wish. It was my fault entirely that I did not make myself clear. Please help yourself. Dozo! Please!"

The smile returned to the samurai's lips, and he motioned to the rest of the pack to pick up some fruit. Half the melons disappeared into their hands. Helplessly, the peasant looked at the depleted stock of melons left to him. He was depending on the money from selling the melons to feed his nine children. Still, better to have hungry children than a large family without a father. "I hope you enjoy them," the peasant said with forced pleasantry, while thinking he hoped the melons gave the thieves cramps.

"And what do you have to give us?" the leader of the pack said to the servant.

"Excuse me, Samurai-sama?"

"Are you deaf? I said, 'What do you have to give us?' This peasant has been generous with his melons. Surely you can be equally generous with some of your purchases."

"I'm sorry, but I can't, Samurai-sama. I am Sadakatsu, a servant of the cadet branch of the Noguchi family. My mistress would be very distressed if I did not return with all the supplies she sent me to get."

The leader looked at his three companions and snickered. "The cadet branch of the Noguchis. He's not even a servant to the main branch of the family!" He turned his attention back to the servant. "Perhaps I didn't make myself clear." He gave the servant a hard shove, and the old man staggered back into the arms of one of the other ronin. This ronin pushed the servant away from him and sent the old man sprawling in the dirt, his packages scattering about him. Looking down at him, the leader said, "Now have we made ourselves clear, or do we have to administer a few good kicks to further explain things to you?"

"I'm sorry, Samurai-sama, but my mistress would never approve of me giving away the food she has sent me to fetch." The old man looked up, defenseless but not frightened.

"This fellow is very dense," the leader said. "I think we'll have to administer a good beating to help clear his mind, so he'll know to be generous when given the opportunity."

"Melons," a voice said.

Startled, the ronin leader looked up to see another samurai standing next to him. He was in his early thirties and muscular in the shoulders and arms. From his looks, the newcomer was a ronin, too.

The newcomer reached over and took a melon out of the hands of the leader. "Hey!" the leader said, but the newcomer ignored him. He took his sword out of the scabbard in a smooth motion and the four ronin stepped back in surprise.

The newcomer took his sword and held it, cutting-edge down. He tossed the melon lightly onto the back of his sword. He caught the melon there and balanced it on the thin edge of steel. He tilted his sword up slightly and the melon rolled toward the tsuba. Then he tilted the sword downward and rolled the melon the other way. Finally, he leveled his sword and held the melon motionless on the back of his katana. He said, "Catch your half."

"What?" the leader said, still mesmerized by the display of control exhibited by the newcomer in balancing the melon on his sword.

The newcomer gave his sword a quick flick and sent the melon high into the air. In one smooth motion, he brought his sword around and sliced the fruit neatly in two while it was still in the air. With his other hand, he reached out and caught half of the fruit. The other half fell to the dirt because the ronin leader was too startled to make a grab for it.

"You let your half fall to the ground," Kaze observed. "That's too bad. It's a shame to waste good fruit." He looked at the other three. "Have you paid for your melons yet?"

"He, ah, the peasant, ah, gave them to us," one of the ronin said slowly, his eyes still glued on the half of the melon on the ground.

"He doesn't look like a rich man," Kaze said. "So we can't let him be foolish in his generosity. I know you'll put back what you can't pay for."

The four men looked at one another, and Kaze took a quick cut with his sword, slicing air and making the four ronin jump. Hastily, they put the stolen melons back on the pile in front of the peasant. Kaze smiled, and the four ronin started backing away as a group. They turned and hurriedly walked out of the marketplace, looking over their shoulders to make sure the man with the quick sword was not following them.

"Thank you, Samurai-sama!" the peasant said.

Kaze held up the half melon in his hand. "How much for this melon?"

"Nothing, Samurai-sama! This time it truly is a gift. I want you to have it!"

Kaze gave a small nod of his head to acknowledge the gift and reached down to help Sadakatsu up. When he got to his feet, the old man gave a low bow. "Thank you, Samurai-san. That was very kind of you. You saved me from a beating."

"Tell Elder Grandma that food shopping can be an adventure. Do you need help picking up your packages?"

The idea of a samurai helping a servant was so novel and strange that Sadakatsu could barely stammer a refusal.

"All right, then," Kaze said. He replaced his sword in its scabbard and took out the ko-gatana knife, slicing off a piece of melon and eating it with relish. He looked at the peasant and said, "Oishi! It's very tasty!"

"See," the peasant said triumphantly to Sadakatsu. "I told you my melons were good!"

Kaze left the two men to resume their bargaining. He was glad he didn't have to fight the four ronin over something as silly as stolen melons. Well, he thought, he supposed it would actually be a fight about something besides stolen melons.

There was a time when Kaze would have gladly fought over melons, or almost anything else. In fact, dueling just for the sake of fighting seemed to be a growing trend. But Kaze remembered what his Sensei had told him about fighting.

The Sensei had just finished a lesson on military strategy, and Kaze, full of youthful enthusiasm, had said, "I can't wait to go fighting. My father has taken me on some military campaigns, but I was left to guard the camp with the other boys while the men went off to fight. When I get done with this training, I'll be big enough to fight, too. Then I'll know the glory and beauty of war."

The Sensei fixed two steady eyes on him and said very softly, "Listen to me. There is no glory or beauty in war. There's beauty in the weapons of war and the brightly colored armor and helmets that we wear. There's beauty in columns of men marching off to war with banners flying and the tramp of hundreds or thousands of feet upon the road. There's even beauty as the first wave of men charges against the enemy, their swords and spears flashing in the sunlight.

"But once the men clash and the killing starts, there is no beauty—only death and destruction. The best swords are kept in their scabbards, and the best armies do not have to fight. Hideyoshi showed that time and time again when he was able to conquer and defeat enemies with his words or the threat of his army instead of actually spilling blood.

"As for glory, the only glory in war is doing your duty as a samurai. And that same glory can be found by diligently performing your work when you are doing something like inspecting a castle."

"But Sensei," Kaze blurted out, "if there is no glory or beauty in war, why do we fight?"

The Sensei sighed. "I was once crossing a bridge near Nara," he said, "and I looked down at the stream and saw a woman there. She had a huge pile of clothes to wash and she was scrubbing each piece of clothing in the river, beating it against a rock. She had already washed so many clothes that she was actually having trouble doing the washing, because her fingers were bleeding and she had to use great care not to get blood on the clothes she was washing. I looked at her, surprised to see the blood, and asked her, '*Obasan*, lady, why are you washing clothes when your fingers are bleeding?' The woman stopped washing for a moment and looked up at me silently, and then I felt foolish and ashamed."

The thought of the Sensei feeling foolish and ashamed was something outside the realm of Kaze's imagination, and he stood there speechless for several moments. Kaze did not understand the Sensei's story or why it should develop feelings that seemed alien to the Sensei's character. Finally, Kaze worked up his courage and said, "Sensei, I know I'm stupid, but I don't understand the story."

The Sensei looked at Kaze and said evenly, "It is never stupid to ask when you do not understand. The woman was washing the clothes because she had to. She may have been the servant of a cruel master. She may have had an unreasonable mother-in-law. Perhaps she made money by washing the clothes and had children to feed. But whatever the reason, she was washing the clothes until her fingers bled because she had to. And that is the same reason we study war and fight as samurai. It is our karma to fight, just as it is our karma to die. I sometimes think that all samurai must have been especially wicked in a former life to be brought back as warriors. No matter how haughty we are or how we try to dress up the trappings of war with talk of beauty and nobility, the fact is that we deal in death. There is nothing wrong with that, because all things must die, and that includes samurai. But you must not confuse the necessity of doing something with the joy of doing something. When the humblest potter creates a cup, he is doing more than what we accomplish, even if we kill a hundred men. The potter deals in the art of creation. We deal in the art of destruction."

Now Kaze was dealing with something that was neither creation nor destruction. He was supposed to find out what happened to Noguchi Mototane, a man he knew neither by appearance nor by character.

Elder Grandma was convinced that Mototane was dead because he had not killed Hishigawa and he wasn't in Kamakura. Yet, he was a man and therefore he could be diverted from his duty by drink or women. For all her fierceness, would Elder Grandma have the objective knowledge to see these flaws in her own blood?

Mototane's absence could also be explained by something as simple as a slip or fall. Perhaps he was laid up in some roadside teahouse waiting for a broken bone to heal. Perhaps he was dead. But also, perhaps his death had nothing to do with Hishigawa, and he was a victim of the countless brigands, bandits, and thieves who now inhabited Japan.

Enomoto had denied that Hishigawa had been attacked at the villa. Was that a lie? If Enomoto had killed Mototane under orders from Hishigawa, that would be a serious offense—a merchant ordering the death of a samurai. Yet Enomoto could also claim he had simply killed Mototane in a duel, and the authorities would think nothing of the event, except to record it officially. Kaze did not think it wise for him to deal with the Tokugawa officials. To check on this possibility, he would have Elder Grandma inquire with the Kamakura authorities.

Kaze had an interesting spot to look at in the villa grounds, but what if Hishigawa had had Mototane killed and buried somewhere outside the villa? The hills of Kamakura were full of secluded spots and caves, and it would be easy enough to hide a body. How could Kaze find such a spot? He had wandered Japan for almost three years looking for the Lady's daughter. Would he now have to wander the hills of Kamakura looking for the hidden grave of a man he did not know?

CHAPTER 18

There! Then quickly gone.
You blend with a cloudy day.
Elusive shadow!

Kaze walked through the streets of Kamakura methodically checking each neighborhood to see if there was a nine-year-old girl that fitted the circumstances of the Lady's daughter.

As he walked down a wide side street, a dozen men walked out of
an inn. They were wearing black armor, and several had banners in
their hands. The banners were black with a white diamond, surrounded by eight bent bamboo leaves. It looked more like a spider
than what it was supposed to represent—a square well surrounded by
a bamboo grove. They were Okubo's men.

Kaze stopped to look at the merchandise in front of a vegetable
stand, slouching his shoulders and trying to look like a henpecked
samurai husband shopping for dinner, a job usually done by the wife.
The stand had small purple eggplants, large white *daikon* radishes,
and green leafy vegetables of all types displayed in shallow wooden
trays. Kaze lifted a few vegetables to examine them, all the while keeping a watchful eye on the soldiers coming out of the inn. He was trying to blend into the background instead of calling attention to
himself.

The merchant came out of the shop, bowing obsequiously and
saying, "What can I get for you, Samurai-sama?"

Kaze pointed to a few small purple eggplants, then hunted in his sleeve for a copper coin. As he did this, the vegetable merchant took some rice straw and expertly tied it into a sling to hold the eggplants. Merchants had special ties to hold all sorts of vegetables, fruits, and produce. There were even special slings to hold one, two, three, or four eggs, all twisted from rice straw when the merchandise was selected.

As Kaze paid for the eggplants, more of Okubo's troops came out of the inn, including some officers. Catching a glimpse of the officers, Kaze realized he could no longer rely on playing a part to masquerade his identity. He turned and started walking away from the inn, negligently swinging the eggplants from one hand.

"You!" One of the officers was calling to him. Kaze didn't turn around. He kept walking, not increasing his pace, but not slowing down, either.

"Get him!" The officer commanded his men. The officer shouted Kaze's real name. He had been recognized.

Kaze started running down the streets of the neighborhood, keeping one hand on the hilt of his sword to steady it. Behind, he could hear the sound that came from men running in armor, the metal plates of the armor, sewn to a leather backing, banging against each other.

The street was narrow but straight because they were in a part of the city laid out in a grid. This made following Kaze easy for his pursuers and made it harder for him to elude them. He cut down a side street, then ducked into an alley. He ran behind a shop past a privy occupied by a man. Although the privy had only a half door, made of woven reeds in a bamboo frame, the man ignored Kaze, as if he weren't there, and Kaze did the same. Kaze briefly thought how convenient it would be if he could actually make himself as invisible as Japanese etiquette demanded people act they were when presented with potentially awkward situations.

Emerging from the alley, he continued down a street. He looked over his shoulder. Although he had outpaced the men chasing him, he had not lost them. He turned down another side street and had run half its length before he realized it was a dead end, terminating at the gate of a large cooper's yard instead of at another street.

Quickly glancing around, Kaze realized he would not have time to escape out of the cul-de-sac without being caught by Okubo's men.

The cooper's yard was large and bustling. At the gate was a large piece of wood with a picture of a painted barrel, a sign easily understood by both literate and illiterate customers. At the front of the yard, just inside the gate, several men were busy finishing large barrels for bulk sakè storage and manufacture. In the back of the yard, premade barrels of all sizes and shapes were stored, waiting for shipment or sale.

Kaze ran up to a large, burly man who seemed to have an air of command. The man looked at Kaze with a raised eyebrow, curious about a ronin bursting into the yard carrying eggplants.

Kaze said just one word. "Toyotomi."

It was a calculated gamble. Tokugawa Ieyasu had been ruler of Japan for less than three years, and he had been ruler of the Kanto area for only a dozen years. Ieyasu had been given the Kanto, the rich area around Edo, as a reward and ploy by Toyotomi Hideyoshi. Ieyasu's hereditary fief was Mikawa, the province of the three rivers. By offering him the richer Kanto, the wily Hideyoshi had simultaneously rewarded his most important ally and moved him to a new base of power, which would temporarily weaken him as he gained control of his new domain.

Although they had ruled the Kanto for a dozen years, Ieyasu's men still referred to themselves as *Mikawa-bushi*, Mikawa warriors. They lacked deep ties to the Kanto, and Kaze was gambling that the feeling was mutual. Toyotomi Hideyoshi, on the other hand, had a special place in the hearts of peasants because Hideyoshi had been a peasant himself. He had come from nowhere and ascended to command based on his intelligence and ability, not his family.

Hearing "Toyotomi," the man in charge of the cooper's yard understood the situation immediately.

◆ ◆ ◆

A few moments later, Okubo's men thundered up to the gates of the cooper's yard, panting from the exertion of running in armor. Sword drawn, the officer in charge walked into the yard and looked around. The men in the yard seemed to be going about their business, making barrels or tying them up for transport. The officer looked behind him and satisfied himself that the street was a trap. The man he was look-ing for, Lord Okubo's enemy, must be in the yard. Dreams of reward flitted into his head, blanking out the thought that this man, a renowned swordsman, would be dangerous when trapped.

"Who's in charge!" the officer shouted.

A burly man walked up to him and bowed.

"Where is he?" the officer demanded.

"He, Samurai-sama?"

The officer gave the lout a cuff with the back of his hand. The burly man staggered from the blow.

"The ronin," the officer shouted. "Where did the ronin go?"

Holding his cheek, the burly man pointed toward the back of the yard with his chin. "He went back there, Samurai-sama. I thought he was looking for a barrel to buy."

The officer snorted and motioned to his men to fan out and search. They took out their swords and formed a long line that cov-ered the yard from side to side. They moved forward cautiously, not sure if the quarry would bolt from behind a stack of barrels or attack in a desperate, suicidal attempt to evade capture. Their quarry's abil-ity with a sword was well known. All of them knew the story of how their Lord had been crippled with a wooden practice sword by this samurai.

Suddenly, one of the soldiers stopped by a large overturned barrel. At the foot of the barrel was a small purple eggplant. He waved to his comrades and his officer, putting his finger to his lips to demand si-lence.

The troops quietly gathered around the barrel, weapons at the ready. The officer approached, and the soldier pointed to the eggplant. The officer nodded his understanding.

He waited until his entire contingent of troops had surrounded the barrel. Looking at their faces, he saw anticipation, anxiety, and flashes of fear. The officer approached the large barrel as quietly as possible. He lifted one foot and placed it on the side of the barrel. Then, in a sudden move, he kicked the heavy barrel on its side, jumping back out of harm's way.

The barrel toppled over with a clatter, forcing the encircling troops on that side to leap back. There, on the ground under the barrel, was the straw sling and the rest of the eggplants.

A few streets away, two men were walking with the rolling gait of palanquin porters. The reason for this peculiar walk was a thick bamboo pole resting on their shoulders. Suspended from the center of the pole was a large covered barrel. The men turned into an alley and put the barrel down. After looking to see that they weren't being observed, they knocked on the top of the barrel. The top was shoved aside and Kaze popped up.

"Thank-you," Kaze said to the burly head of the cooper's yard. "Any trouble?"

"No. Once they thought you were hidden in the yard, they completely ignored us."

"Do you want to know why they were chasing me?"

"No. I just want to deliver this barrel."

Kaze smiled and got out of the barrel.

CHAPTER 19

Make your hidden plans.
Weave your nefarious web,
you silent spider.

The *ninja* carefully studied the floor plan using a tiny candle. Satisfied that he had the villa design committed to memory, he put out the candle to let his eyes adjust to the dark.

The ninja had started his training as a child. As with most Japanese occupations, the teaching of *ninjutsu*, the art of the ninja, was started young. Ninja had existed from the time of Prince Regent Shotoku, so the ninja followed a craft with a lineage of almost one thousand years. Engaging in assassination, espionage, and even pitched battles, the ninja were organized around clans, just as the samurai were. Unlike the samurai, the ninja clans were secret societies. When they were not on an assignment, ninja lived the lives of farmers, also like early samurai. While the samurai evolved into a professional warrior class, however, the ninja remained disguised as farmers, keeping their deadly talents away from the eyes of the authorities and others.

The villages of Iga and Koga were the best known centers of ninjutsu, but there were several others. It was well known the Tokugawa used the ninja of Koga for their dirty work and spying. This ninja's clan did not have patrons as powerful as the Tokugawas, but once they accepted a fee, always paid in advance, an agent was committed either to completing the contract or dying in the attempt. The contract was negotiated by the ninja clan leader, the *jonin*, and conveyed to him by his leader, the *chunin*. He was a simple agent, a *genin*, but a good one.

He was born to the profession, as were his father and his father before him. People almost never studied ninjutsu by choice, for they could not find a member of a ninja clan who would teach them. To reveal the secrets of the clan was an offense punishable by death.

The ninja was hiding in a closet normally used to store linens. The closet was specifically chosen because it abutted an outside wall of the villa. The ninja knew that the last few roof boards in a home, the ones nearest the outer wall, were not fastened down. They were only weighted with stones to keep them in place.

He stepped on a shelf in the closet and reached up, moving the ceiling boards to allow access to the attic. He did a last check to assure that his equipment was secured and wouldn't make a noise, then, using the closet shelves as a ladder, he crawled up into the attic of the villa.

In a farmhouse, the attic would be stuffed with everything from old tatami mats to food, but Hishigawa's villa had the luxury of space, so the area above the ceiling was occupied only by dust. Staying on the *taruki*, the cross beams, the ninja traversed most of the length of the villa before he started moving to his left, balancing from beam to beam. The attic space was washed with a faint light that leaked in from holes in the wooden lattice that covered openings in the crest of the roof. The lattice was designed to keep birds and other animals out of the attic, while allowing summer heat and smoke from winter hibachi to escape.

When he was in the proper spot, he stopped. He risked striking flint to steel to light his small candle again, and he was able to see the top of the ceiling of the room he was interested in.

The ceiling was supported by thin wooden sticks stretched from wall to wall. On top of these strips were thin slats of wood that formed the actual surface of the ceiling. Each slat lapped its neighbor, small bamboo pegs holding them in place. He used a knife to pry the pegs out of one slat. He put out his candle, then he lifted the slat to peek into the room below.

The ronin was sleeping on his back, his head resting on a wooden neck rest. The futon was pulled up under his neck, and he seemed to be sleeping comfortably.

The ninja returned the slat to its place. He did everything methodically and slowly. With the victim sleeping soundly, there was no need to hurry.

He crabbed his way across the ceiling until he was in the spot directly over the ronin's head. Once again he lit the candle and pried out the bamboo pegs holding the ceiling slat in place. Then he snuffed the candle and quietly lifted the slat to look down on the face of his victim.

From a pouch around his neck, the ninja took a coil of silk string, a piece of cloth, and a small bottle. He carefully lowered the string down from the ceiling, holding it with the cloth. The gossamer thread inched downward until it was just a few inches above Kaze's mouth. Then the ninja stopped.

The stopper on the bottle was specially shaped so it could be removed by gripping it with the teeth, but with a wide guard so none of the bottle's contents would touch the ninja's lips. Such an event would be fatal. Using a steady hand, the ninja placed the mouth of the bottle next to the thread and slowly poured the contents onto the thread.

A thin amber liquid clung to the thread and started sliding its way toward the floor. It oozed its way closer and closer to the end of the thread, which was hovering right over Kaze's mouth. There, the liquid would gather until a drop broke free and landed on Kaze's lips. This would be followed by a second and third drop until the victim, almost by reflex, would lick his lips. Then he would die.

The amber liquid slid down, and a drop started forming at the end of the thread. Suddenly, Kaze moved his head to the side, mumbling in his sleep. The ninja moved the thread away from Kaze's head and stopped pouring. He didn't want a drop to fall on Kaze's cheek, waking him but not killing him.

Suddenly, Kaze yawned and started to sit up. The ninja quickly pulled up the thread from the room, running it through the folded cloth to wipe it clean of the poison. Then he waited to see what the ronin would do.

Kaze stretched and scratched himself on the belly, smacking his lips contentedly. Then, taking up his sword from the bedding, he got up and sleepily stumbled to the door. The ninja decided that the ronin was answering a call of nature and placed the ceiling slat partially in place so he could peek into the room when the ronin returned. The ninja could be patient, and he would wait until his victim fell into a deep sleep once more.

As he settled down to wait, the ninja quieted his soul and listened to his own breathing. While he was in the midst of administering the poison, his hand had been steady but his heart was racing. He had been told that this man would be hard to kill. Now that his attempt at assassination had been aborted, he had to bring his heart and body in balance so when he made his next attempt, it would be done with a serene mind.

As he meditated, the ninja became aware of a sound in the attic space. His eyes opened and he stared into the murky darkness, which was relieved only by moonlight coming through the lattice in the crest. He heard another small sound. A man not as trained as he would not have detected it, but upon hearing it, he knew immediately what it meant. He was not alone in the attic.

He quickly capped the bottle of poison and put it, the cloth, and the silk string in his pouch. Then, trying to be as silent as the person who was in the attic with him, he started moving toward the lattice opening in the crest.

He kept near the edges of the roof as he made his way from rafter to rafter. If he went into the middle of the attic, he would provide the best target, silhouetted against the light from the lattice, so he avoided this space.

As he scrambled along, he caught glimpses of a dark shape also traversing the rafters of the villa's roof and also staying out of the faint light. The figure seemed agile and surefooted, and the ninja wondered if it was the sleepy samurai he had observed just minutes before. Then it struck him. If the samurai was answering a call of nature, why had he taken his sword with him? The ninja had chosen poison and the silk thread in recognition of the samurai's strength, and he wondered now if his quarry was trying to turn him into the hunted.

The ninja reached the end of the attic and moved to the center, just under the crest, and quickly stood up. Speed was now more important than stealth, and he yanked the wooden lattice out of place and quickly scrambled onto the tile roof. He carried a short, straight sword in a scabbard tied to his back. It was a Chinese-style sword, not curved like the swords favored by samurai.

He removed his sword from its scabbard and stood slightly behind and to the side of the opening in the roof crest. When his pursuer emerged from the opening he would be vulnerable. Then the ninja would strike.

Holding his sword above his head, ready to deliver a death blow, the ninja focused all his senses on the dark hole in the roof. He listened acutely for the smallest shuffling and his eyes strained to see the slightest difference in the blackness of the hole, which would indicate the emergence of his pursuer.

Time seemed to pass slowly, but from experience the ninja knew that when one was in a heightened state of awareness, time often did strange things. Sometimes it crawled like the turtle, inching its way forward in slow increments, forcing one to show increased patience while waiting for something to happen. On other occasions, time was lightning, striking forward with an alacrity that was truly frightening. On this occasion, time seemed to slow, and the ninja waited patiently for his pursuer to make it to the hole in the roof and his death.

Suddenly, with the sixth sense of all highly trained fighting men, the ninja knew that he had been fooled. He turned to see the ronin, bathed in moonlight and carrying an unsheathed sword, moving toward him across the tiles of the villa roof. The ronin had realized that the opening was a death trap and had crossed to the other end of the roof, removing the lattice there and emerging to come after his assassin.

The ronin was already too close, and the ninja could not drop his guard and throw a knife. Instead, he pivoted and rushed the ronin, determined to take the initiative. His Chinese sword struck the katana, and the clang of steel shattered the stillness of the night, sparks flying from the contact of the two blades.

The slope of the slippery tile roof made maneuver difficult. Kaze braced himself as best he could and watched the ninja closely.

The ninja pressed his attack, but Kaze was able to parry all his blows. The ninja, seeing his attack was ineffective, retreated a few paces. Kaze stepped forward, keeping the pressure on. He didn't want the ninja to have time to throw a knife or some other weapon, an art they were famous for.

"Oi! You! What are you doing up there?"

Attracted by the noise, the ineffective villa guard was finally drawn to the scene of battle, looking up at the two figures on the roof.

"Get more men," Kaze shouted. "There is an assassin here."

The ninja took the occasion of Kaze's speaking to press another attack, thinking the ronin would let his guard down slightly while he was talking. He was wrong. Kaze parried the blows of the ninja without having to give up ground. Kaze was interested in keeping the ninja alive because he wanted to find out who his employer was. He was curious about who would want him dead enough to pay for a ninja. Was it the same one who had paid for the other assassins? He knew it wasn't Okubo. If Okubo knew where he was staying, Okubo would simply surround the villa with his men and, if necessary, burn it down.

The ninja, realizing he would soon be surrounded, looked around for the best escape route. Kaze knew immediately why the ninja was looking around and pressed his attack. Moving forward, his foot stepped on a tile that had come loose from its mud base and slipped, throwing him off balance.

With a shout of triumph, the ninja surged forward to take advantage of the mishap. Instead of trying to recover, Kaze let himself fall forward. He brought his sword around as he fell, and it sliced deeply into the ninja's right leg, cutting the tendons of the knee to the bone. Then Kaze fell to the roof and rolled to its edge. He fell off, but with the agility of a cat he twisted himself around so he landed on his feet. His momentum carried him forward and he did a roll on the ground, springing to his feet as soon as the momentum dissipated.

Still holding his sword, Kaze looked up at the roof and the ninja. The ninja stood balanced on one leg, his other hanging uselessly, bleeding profusely. Hishigawa's guards were running from the house, and it was obvious that he would soon be surrounded and captured.

Without a word, the ninja reversed his sword and put it under his chin. Putting both hands on the handle, he brought it up and into his throat. He stood for a brief moment like some strange statue, standing on one leg, with the sword impaled in his neck. Then he collapsed, rolling off the roof and falling to the ground.

Kaze ran to the ninja and ripped the cloth from his face. As Kaze suspected, the ninja's features were unfamiliar to him. The dying man looked up into Kaze's face with no hate or animosity. Kaze didn't bother asking him who had hired him. A man who would commit suicide when he was about to be captured would not have the weakness of spirit to make a confession at the moment of death.

"I'll carve a Kannon for you," Kaze said.

A flicker of surprise crossed the ninja's face. Then the brightness left his eyes and he was dead.

CHAPTER 20

White testament to
a short life of troubled tears.
Bones fill a cold grave.

The four figures were huddled together in a deadly serious council.

"Why do you think the ninja was here?" Hishigawa said.

"It was an assassination attempt," Enomoto said.

"Yes," Kaze agreed blandly. "Apparently you have created some bitter enemies, Hishigawa-san."

Ando, the fourth figure, sucked her breath in at the assertion that the ninja was there to assassinate Hishigawa.

"How do you know the ninja was here to assassinate Hishigawa-san?" Enomoto asked.

"Who else? Hishigawa-san himself said there have been attempts on his life lately. That's why he offered me the job of yojimbo." Kaze looked at Hishigawa. "Can you tell me about these other attempts and who might have a grudge against you?"

"A man such as myself can make many enemies," Hishigawa said evasively.

"It's hard for me to help you if I don't know the facts," Kaze said reasonably.

"Well, there is—"

"Hishigawa-san," Enomoto interrupted. "Before we discuss past problems, I'd like to ask Matsuyama-san a few questions about this ninja."

"Dozo, please," Kaze said, masking his disappointment that Hishigawa had been interrupted.

"How did you come to discover the ninja, Matsuyama-san?"

"I was out to view the moon. It's in an especially beautiful phase now—almost full but with a delicate sliver still removed from it. When I looked up, I saw a figure on the roof."

"Why didn't you call the guard?"

"The guard wasn't near where I was. There was a handy tree next to the house, so I decided to go up and investigate for myself."

"Do you know why the ninja removed the lattice screens from both roof crests?"

Kaze smiled. "I imagine he took the wrong one off. He realized he was too far from Hishigawa-san's sleeping room, so he went to the other end of the villa and removed that screen."

"Do you really think he was trying to kill Hishigawa-san?" Ando broke in.

Kaze shrugged. "No one else here would be worth spending the money on a ninja. Don't you agree, Enomoto-san?"

"I suppose so," Enomoto said.

"Good," Kaze said. "Now, Hishigawa-san, you were going to tell me the details of the other attempts on your life."

"Before I left for Kyoto, we noticed a man watching the villa," Hishigawa said. "Enomoto-san's guards could never get close enough to him to question him, but he was interested in my movements. Once, when I went to Kamakura with just one guard, he attacked and killed my yojimbo. While he was doing that I managed to escape, but it forced me to move about with two or more guards."

"Why do you think he wanted to kill you?"

"It's a personal matter." Hishigawa looked like he was going to be stubborn. If the attempted killer was Noguchi Mototane, Hishigawa was not going to admit to the vendetta. It was acceptable for the object of a vendetta to defend himself, but for some reason Hishigawa didn't want to reveal the vendetta to Kaze.

"Did you eventually kill this assassin?"

"I didn't kill him. Nor did Enomoto-san or any of my men." Hishigawa said.

"You said there were many attempts on you life. What else happened?"

"Well, you saw one yourself, when Ishibashi tried to kill me."

"Any others?"

"Aren't three attempts to kill me in a few weeks enough?" Hishigawa said indignantly. "First a swordsman kills my yojimbo, then bandits kill my escort and their chief tries to kill me, and now a ninja tries to sneak into my house to assassinate me."

"I would say three attempts in a short period of time were obviously not enough, Hishigawa-san, because you have survived them all," Kaze said.

The excitement in the household had died down. Enomoto had doubled the guards patrolling outside the house and this presented a small annoyance, but not an obstacle, to Kaze's slipping away from the villa to go to the place on the grounds that he had spotted earlier.

He had taken the trouble to get a wooden spade from the shed where the gardener stored his tools, and in the pale moonlight it was easy to get back to the location he sought. He squatted for a moment, looking at the ground in the faint light with a hunter's eye. It was definitely disturbed, but its appearance troubled him because it didn't look fresh. He stood and stuck the spade in the ground.

The ground had settled, but it was relatively easy to dig. He had only gone down a few hand spans when the square nose of the spade struck something.

Kaze got to his knees and cleared away the dirt at the bottom of the hole with his hands. In the flat silver moonlight, gleaming white bones started emerging from the dark soil.

CHAPTER 21

Honor. Trust. Duty.
All are fragile soap bubbles,
popped too easily.

Enomoto stood before the straw practice dummy, focusing his energy on his blade. As a samurai, Enomoto had the right to commit "practice murder" or "sword-testing killing." He could cut down a *heimin*, a commoner, for the simple pleasure of trying his blade on a living body. In practice, a samurai who indulged this right too often soon got a bad reputation. Killing too many peasants could hurt rice production.

To avoid this, some samurai tested their blades on the corpses of criminals. Others indulged themselves only when some real or imagined slight gave them justification for cutting down a heimin, especially if they were away from their home prefecture. Still others, like Enomoto, used straw dummies to practice their cuts.

Enomoto brought the blade up over his head, then returned it to the point-at-the-eye position. The polished blade stretched before him, a slightly curved piece of steel less than three *shaku* long that represented all that Enomoto still believed in. His sword was the one constant in an ever-changing world.

Like most samurai boys, Enomoto was given his first sword before he was five years old. This *mamori-gatana*, or charm sword, was worn until Enomoto's *gempuku*, the ceremony that marked his entry into manhood, when he was given his first real sword and his first armor and had his hair dressed in an adult style for the first time.

As a young man, Enomoto dedicated himself to the sword. Early on, Enomoto realized that he had exceptional talent with the katana. Other boys looked clumsy and awkward when practicing their cuts, but to Enomoto using the katana seemed natural and easy. This caused him to redouble his efforts to master its use. He found a Sensei who would train him and then he practiced what the Sensei taught him for endless hours. Soon the sword was an extension of his body and, eventually, it became an extension of his spirit.

Filled with the principles of bushido, the code of the warrior, Enomoto was anxious to put his skills to use in a great war. Hideyoshi, the Taiko, obliged him.

When Hideyoshi had subdued all the daimyo, the Lords of Japan, he immediately embarked on a foreign adventure. He decided to conquer Korea and, after that, he boasted about conquering China itself. The Koreans and Chinese had other ideas.

Hideyoshi mobilized up to one hundred and fifty thousand men for his expedition, and initially his invasion of the Korean peninsula met with great success. At first the Korean army was no match for the fierce Japanese samurai, tempered by hundreds of years of internal clan warfare. From Pusan on the southern tip of Korea the Japanese forces surged northward, capturing Seoul, Pyongyang, and even Wonsan, on Korea's eastern coast.

As a teenager, Enomoto joined the first Korean campaign with enthusiasm. Enomoto's Lord was a great supporter of Hideyoshi, and he committed the bulk of his fighting men to the effort. But even in victory, Enomoto learned that war is not the pageantry of martial display and drumbeats described by storytellers. It was pain, suffering, blood, lopped-off limbs, and exposed viscera.

Still, in the time compression that war causes, Enomoto was able to quickly rise to command a small squad of men, and he happily participated in gathering the severed noses of slain enemies to send back to Hideyoshi to show him how well the campaign was going.

Soon, however, the campaign was not going well. Korean Admiral Yi Sun-sin created a fleet of fierce "turtle boats," warcraft with a covered deck armored with wicker, wood, and even steel plates. The Korean ships played havoc with the Japanese efforts to reinforce and supply their invading army. The Korean army started fighting with the help of Chinese troops, and soon the Japanese were at a stalemate.

When Enomoto was told that Hideyoshi had signed a truce after a year of hard fighting, he could not believe it. When Hideyoshi renewed the war in Korea three years later, it was a disillusioned Enomoto who was sent by his Lord to fight in Korea once more. This time, many of the daimyo tried to avoid sending masses of troops to Korea. Tokugawa Ieyasu was especially successful at keeping his troops in Japan, a fact that gave him a great advantage a few years later at Sekigahara.

The second time in Korea, Enomoto had no childish dreams about the nature of war. What few illusions he had about the nature of honor also dissolved. Enomoto saw officers looting and enriching themselves like common pirates. The noses of Korean women and children were mixed with the noses of warriors to make it look as though battles were bigger and more successful than they really were. The fighting with the Koreans bogged down into an indecisive stalemate almost from the beginning. It was a relief to Enomoto when Hideyoshi died and the Korean expedition was recalled.

Enomoto's last thoughts of honor in war were eliminated at Sekigahara, when highborn daimyo turned traitors to the Toyotomi cause and joined Ieyasu's side for money. Enomoto's Lord was defeated and stripped of his territory, turning Enomoto and the other survivors of Sekigahara into ronin. Lucky to escape with his life, Enomoto decided that the new order of things revolved around money, not antiquated notions of honor, so he happily joined Hishigawa's household when the opportunity presented itself.

Now Enomoto contemplated the problem of this new ronin, Matsuyama Kaze. Enomoto had not seen him handle a sword, but from his bearing and movement, Enomoto was convinced that he was a master swordsman. Matsuyama claimed that his crippling of the ninja in the rooftop battle was just an accident, but Enomoto was convinced that the ronin had done exactly what he wanted to with the ninja, crippling him but not killing him. Only the ninja's suicide had thwarted an attempt to get more information.

Enomoto wondered how good Kaze was with a sword. Was Matsuyama better than Enomoto? Dueling had become increasingly popular, to show the superior skill of one swordsman over another. The question of whose skill was superior to the other could easily be settled by challenging the ronin to a duel. But if he did that, Enomoto was not sure it would enhance his reputation. Killing an unknown ronin was not the same thing as defeating a well-known swordsman or the head of a school of fencing. That kind of killing could translate to a good position with an important daimyo, which would mean money. Still, Enomoto was satisfied with the money he was making with Hishigawa, so there was no need to take a risky course of action with the ronin.

Concentrating his power in his blade, Enomoto pictured the face of the ronin on the straw dummy. Shouting "haup!" for power, Enomoto brought his blade around in a swift arc that caught the straw dummy squarely on the neck, cleanly severing its head with one blow.

"Superb!"

Enomoto turned to see the ronin watching him. Enomoto was perturbed that the man could walk up on him so silently. Even if he couldn't hear him, Enomoto would have expected to feel the presence of a swordsman at his back.

He didn't know if the ronin was able to come upon him unawares because of a lapse in his instincts or if the ronin had the skill to negate those instincts. Either possibility was unnerving. Enomoto said nothing and simply got back into his stance. He expected the ronin to say something more, but instead he remained silent. For some reason, this irritated Enomoto more than if he had said something. Putting a smile on his face, Enomoto relaxed his guard and turned to face the ronin.

"Would you like to try it?" Enomoto said, indicating the straw dummy.

"No, thank you," Kaze said politely.

"Don't you practice?" Enomoto taunted. "Or have you progressed past that point?"

"We both know that no one progresses past the point of practice."

Enomoto laughed. "You're a weird one," he said. "Would you be interested in sparring with me?"

"Your sword looks like a dangerous toy. I think it's best not to play with it. Too much chance for an accident."

"Then why not use bokken, wooden swords?"

"Bokken can kill and maim, too." Kaze smiled. "I still have use for these tired limbs and this poor head."

"But aren't you curious to see how your skill matches mine?"

"I could see you were a superb swordsman the moment I laid eyes on you. Your demonstration of prowess with the practice dummy simply confirmed my initial assessment of you." Kaze bowed. "You are an exceptional swordsman, Enomoto-san."

Surprised, Enomoto reflexively returned the bow. When he straightened up, the ronin turned on his heel and left. Enomoto turned his sword so the cutting edge was facing upward and sheathed it. He was no longer interested in practice.

Ando was supervising the final touches on the food tray. She placed a young maple leaf artfully next to a cube of silken *tofu*. She held the leaf with a pair of chopsticks and skillfully turned the leaf slightly so it was resting against the tofu at an angle, forming a delicate, decorative garnish.

"That looks beautiful," a voice said behind her.

Ando gave a small start. She turned around and saw that pesky ronin standing behind her. His ability to move about silently was unnerving. She turned her attention back to the food tray.

"The Master insists that everything always be of the highest refinement where his wife is concerned," Ando said. She continued fussing with the tray with exaggerated concern. She hoped the ronin would go away. He didn't.

"Hishigawa-san's concern for his wife is admirable," Kaze said. "Is he afraid she might be caught up in the danger he finds himself in?"

Talk of danger to the Young Master caused Ando's ears to prick up. She stopped working on the tray.

"He said he had several attempts on his life," Kaze continued. "At least one was because of his wife. Were the other attempts because of Yuchan, too?"

"We live in a violent age," Ando said vaguely, "so who can tell what is the cause of crazy actions?" She picked up the tray. "Please excuse me, Samurai, because I must deliver this tray to the Master's wife." Ando gave a perfunctory bow and left, holding the tray.

Kaze stood watching her. All Japanese households have secrets. He wondered what were the secrets of this household that caused its inhabitants to remain so closemouthed.

Too proud to cook rice.
Aspire to momentous acts.
Dignity of youth.

Kaze arrived at the temple and found Elder Grandma's grandson, Nagatoki, alone, tending camp. He was watching a kettle of rice boiling on the fire, waiting for the proper moment to put the heavy wooden cover on the pot to let the rice steam. He seemed embarrassed that Kaze had caught him engaging in such a domestic duty, as if it diminished him as a warrior in the older man's eyes. Kaze took the cover out of the young man's hands and placed it on the pot.

"You're letting too much water boil away," Kaze remarked casually. "When you're on a campaign in war, knowing how to feed your men is a critical skill. Hungry men can't fight."

Having rice-making characterized as a martial art seemed to ease Nagatoki's embarrassment.

Kaze had come to tell Elder Grandma that he had made no progress in finding information about Mototane. Finding time on his hands, however, he thought of the Japanese proverb *chiri tsumotte, yama to naru*—dust amassed will make a mountain. He decided to talk to Nagatoki to see if he could learn more details about Mototane.

"I would like to talk to you about Mototane," Kaze said.

"Have you found him?" A touch of excitement entered the young man's voice.

"No, and I'm not likely to unless I learn more about him and his character. What can you tell me about him?"

"Well, he's my cousin."

"Yes."

"Ah, my older cousin." Nagatoki inhaled sharply, making a hissing sound that indicated he was a bit flustered by Kaze's questions.

"Relax. This is not an inquisition. I just want to know more about him as a man, to see if that provides me with any clues about where he is."

"Well, he was a superb swordsman. Not as good as you, Samurai-san, but still excellent. I admired him for his skill."

"Did he have any weaknesses?"

"Weaknesses?"

"Women. Drink. Something that would cause him to abandon his duties."

Nagatoki seemed horrified that Kaze would suggest that his older cousin, whom he obviously idolized, could have a human fault. "Oh, no, Samurai-san! Mototane would never have such vices! Elder Grandma would have never allowed that."

That was something that Kaze could certainly believe. He decided to steer the conversation back to safer ground, to draw out information more gradually.

"You say he was a good fencer?"

"Excellent! Very strong and fearless. Not too many men could hold their own against him in the *dojo*."

"And what do you think happened to him? Why isn't he here?"

Nagatoki bit his lip. Hesitantly, he said, "I can think of no reason he isn't here, unless he's dead. Still, I don't like to think . . ." Nagatoki hung his head, and tears formed on his face. He savagely poked at the rice fire with a small branch. The fire crackled, and a small cloud of red sparks swirled into the air, forming a miniature universe of short-lived suns that flickered into black ash in moments.

Kaze pretended he didn't see Nagatoki's emotion. Instead he said, "If you follow the path of the warrior, death is always a possibility.

But if you think of it, death is the final result of all life. If Mototane is dead, he will come back in another life. From your description of him, his next life will certainly be one of honor and possibility. A man so honorable should have no fear of death. It would be sad if such a promising life ended so soon, but all time is relative, and a short, honorable life is preferable to a long, miserable life."

Nagatoki said nothing, but Kaze's words seemed to comfort him. After a few minutes of sitting in silence, Nagatoki said, "Thank you for letting me have your bed at that teahouse. It was, it was . . . well, it was my first time." It was a reference to their first meeting, when Kaze let Nagatoki swap beds with him because Kaze was trying to avoid an amorous maid.

Kaze laughed.

Nagatoki looked startled, then looked at Kaze's face and blushed. Soon, however, he realized the ronin was not laughing at him, and Nagatoki started laughing too. His melancholy over the possible fate of Mototane was dispersed by the shared secret he had with this strange ronin.

"What is the cause of all this merriment?" Elder Grandma asked as she entered the abandoned temple.

Kaze looked at Nagatoki and said, "Just talk of important military maneuvers and the victories that result." Nagatoki giggled.

Elder Grandma scowled. She didn't like to be excluded. "Have you any news of Mototane?" she said gruffly, trying to regain command of the situation.

"No, Elder Grandma, I'm afraid I don't."

Elder Grandma pursed her lips, clearly displeased. Kaze knew he had tried his best to this point, so her displeasure had no effect on him. It would only be meaningful if he had not done his best.

"Has Hishigawa told you anything?"

"That presents a hard problem," he said. "Getting Hishigawa to trust me will be difficult. I know he wants me to work for him, but that won't release the lock on his tongue. I'll have to wait and see if there's something I can do to gain his confidence. In the meantime, I can try to contact Yuchan for you. The Jade Palace is guarded, but it's hardly a fortress. I think I can sneak in to see her. She seems to be living in absolute splendor and luxury, so perhaps she's happy with the current situation. If she is, you're wasting your time trying to rescue someone who doesn't want to be rescued."

Kaze waited in the boughs of a tree, watching the Jade Palace. The moon was high in the sky; its pale light made observation of the island and the structure on it easy. Kaze had just about decided it was time to enter the water and swim to the island when he saw someone walk out on the veranda that encircled the building. Enomoto.

A building guarded by a sleepy sentry was a simple matter, but a building with Enomoto inside was another proposition. Enomoto was no fool, and it would be infinitely more dangerous to go to the island with him on it.

Kaze didn't understand Enomoto. He was obviously a quality swordsman and made of somewhat the same cloth as Kaze himself. Yet Enomoto could offer his sword and loyalty to a man like Hishigawa. Kaze could not imagine what would make a master fencer work for a man like Hishigawa.

Kaze heard a rustling below him. A figure was making its way through the villa grounds, moving toward the lake and the palace. Kaze gave a small sigh of exasperation because he was sure it was Elder Grandma or one of the other two doing some reconnoitering on their own. The villa was still not tightly guarded, but that would change if it were discovered that intruders were entering.

As Kaze watched the figure, his exasperation turned to interest. In the moonlight he could see it was not one of the trio. Fascinating. He glanced back at the palace and saw Enomoto returning inside.

The figure was a bit late, and he knew the Boss would chastise him for it. They were supposed to meet at the hour of the rat, but now it was almost the hour of the ox. He had been winning big at dice and kept staying to play just one more round. Finally, despite his winning streak, he realized he would never be able to make the appointed time, and he tore himself from the game. Now he was nervous and a bit frightened at what the Boss would say or do about his tardiness.

He knew no guards would be patrolling the back of the villa tonight, so he hoisted himself over the wall and started slipping from tree to tree to reach the appointed spot. He had done this many times before, although he didn't like the cold swim at the end. His movements were almost routine by now.

He found shelter in the darkness of a large pine tree growing next to the lake and placed his sword in a hollow of the tree. He took off his kimono, shivering slightly in the late-night air in his loincloth, and put his rolled-up kimono next to his sword. He was starting to untie his straw sandals when he heard a sound above him. He looked up just as a man landed on him, flattening him on the ground and knocking the wind out of him.

Kaze heard a satisfying "Oommph!" when he landed on the man, and he knew it would be several minutes before the man could muster up the wind to try to get away. He grabbed the man by the arm and dragged him into the moonlight, where he could get a better look at his face. He was surprised.

"Well," Kaze said, "if you're going to be my regular landing cushion when I jump out of trees, then you'd better put some more meat on you." Staring up him was the bandit with the scarred cheek he had jumped on the Tokaido Road.

A half hour later, Kaze was sitting in a room with a sleepy Hishigawa and the frightened bandit.

"I dare not tell!" the bandit said. "The Boss would slit my throat."

Kaze put his hand on the hilt of his sword. He gave the bandit a smile that made the half-naked man shudder. "If you don't tell, I'll start another process," Kaze said menacingly. "I'll start slicing you into thin shavings, like a block of katsuo-bushi. When you were a young boy, you probably watched your mother shaving the bonito block to get flavoring for soup. If you don't tell Hishigawa-san what you told me, then I'm going to cut you into equally thin slices, and each cut will hurt."

The bandit looked at Kaze fearfully, not sure if the samurai was bluffing. He decided not to test this threat. "All right," he said. "Enomoto-san employed us to rob Hishigawa-san of his gold."

"Enomoto-san?" Hishigawa was now fully awake, his eyes round with surprise.

"Yes. I was part of the band that robbed you before. We would have robbed you again, but this samurai stopped us. We were told not to harm you, but we were also told to get the gold."

"But you killed my yojimbo," Hishigawa said.

"Yes. That was part of the plan, so you would never suspect Enomoto-san. When you were moving especially large amounts of gold, Enomoto-san would assign weak men to escort you. He knew they would die, but they were unaware of the planned attack. That way we could rob you many times and you would not suspect it was being arranged from within your own household."

Hishigawa was confused. He looked at Kaze. "What do we do now?" he asked.

"We tie this scum up and then go to sleep. Then we talk to Enomoto-san in the morning. Before we do that, we make sure the household guards understand that they were used as sacrificial *usagi*, rabbits. They were destined by Enomoto-san to eventually have their necks caught in a snare and killed, so that he and his real men could continue robbing you."

Enomoto walked into the reception room of Hishigawa's villa. He was annoyed because his man had missed their appointment, so he could not get the full story of how the ronin had foiled the robbery attempt on the Tokaido. He was even more annoyed that the love-besotted fool of a merchant had decided to have a meeting the first thing in the morning.

He walked into the room and stopped immediately. The atmosphere of the room was charged with tension, and Enomoto's swordsman's eyes took in the scene at one glance.

Hishigawa was sitting on the dais, like some nobleman. Next to him was the ronin, watching Enomoto carefully, with his sword worn at an angle from which he could pull it quickly. The old hag Ando was on the other side, her rat's eyes looking at him with hatred. The household guards were standing in the room, glaring at him. They must know, Enomoto thought. And sitting in front of the ronin was his appointment for the hour of the rat. Tied, half naked, and no doubt singing like a *kusahibari*, a "grass lark," the most popular singing insect that the *mushi-uri*, the insect seller, offered.

"Well, it's over," Enomoto said before any accusations could be made. "I'm glad. I was growing weary of the farce of a man like me working for a worm like you," Enomoto said to Hishigawa.

Hishigawa had a suitable shocked look on his face, and the old harpy Ando actually hissed at him, like a snake expressing its anger.

"You . . . you . . ." Hishigawa started.

"Don't bother," Enomoto interrupted. "I'll be going. Don't complain to the authorities about the money I took or I'll have to talk to them about our little secrets." He turned to go, then stopped. He swiveled his head around to take one more look at the composed face of the ronin, Matsuyama Kaze. His gaze was met steadily by the ronin, who had a face that mirrored neither surprise nor concern. Forgetting his control for an instant, Enomoto's own countenance darkened, like the angry skies during a typhoon. He said nothing to the ronin, but both men knew the depth of Enomoto's hatred for the interloper. Enomoto turned and left, walking out the front door of the villa and past the startled guard at the gate.

W ell, that went well, except for the insolent tongue of that rogue, Enomoto," Hishigawa said.

Kaze made no reply.

"I wonder if you would reconsider my offer to work for me," Hishigawa said.

"I will consider it," Kaze replied. "I also have an idea for you to consider."

"What is that?"

"I wonder why you move gold between Edo, Kamakura, and Kyoto."

"Well," Hishigawa said patiently, as if lecturing a slow child, "the businesses in each city have different needs. Sometimes a business in one city needs gold and a business in another city has too much. So I must transfer the gold from one city to the other."

"That's not what I mean," Kaze said, ignoring Hishigawa's tone. "I was wondering why you physically transfer the gold, running the risk of theft."

"How else would I meet the needs of my businesses in each city?"

"There are other businesses that operate both in Edo and Kyoto or Kyoto and Kamakura?"

"Yes, of course."

"And they have a similar problem, from time to time?"

"Yes, I suppose so. I don't see how any business can always stay in balance among the various branches in each city."

"Then why don't you act as a broker and find these businesses? Then you need never transfer gold again."

"What do you mean?"

"Suppose you have a hundred *ryo* of gold in Edo that you want transferred to Kyoto."

"Yes?"

"Then you find one or more businesses that have a hundred ryo of gold in Kyoto who want that gold in Edo."

Hishigawa looked puzzled. "What good would that do? Then you'd have two shipments of gold you'd have to transport."

Kaze shook his head. "No, then you'd have no shipments of gold to transport. First you collect the hundred ryo of gold in Kyoto that businesses want transported to Edo and you use it in your own business. Then you take the hundred ryo of gold in Edo and give it to the businesses who wanted the gold transported from Kyoto to Edo. All you have to do then is transport paper instructions from Kyoto to Edo, and no actual gold has to be moved."

Hishigawa looked at Kaze and exclaimed, "Brilliant! I can even charge a nice commission for my services, because the businesses in Kyoto don't have to run the risk of transporting their gold." Hishigawa was very excited. "You will make an incredible addition to my business!"

Kaze did not point out he had not agreed to join Hishigawa. He just nodded and let the merchant get swept up in the power and simplicity of the idea. He exchanged several glasses of sakè with the merchant as Hishigawa talked about how he could set up the money exchange service. Finally, when Hishigawa was a little tipsy from the wine, Kaze said, "Enomoto said something about secrets when he left. If I'm to protect you, I have to have an idea about what those secrets are."

Hishigawa looked at Kaze shrewdly and said, "I won't tell you all my secrets yet, but Enomoto was talking about the business I got into after Sekigahara. In addition to my other businesses, I deal in young girls."

Kaze had surmised as much from the girls he saw at the Jade Palace. They were too finely dressed and too bold to be simple maids to Yuchan. Dealing in human flesh was not the highest of social activities, but there was no particular secret involved with it that Kaze could see. "What is the secret in that?" he asked.

Hishigawa smiled and said, "Right after the forces loyal to Hideyoshi were defeated, there were not only a great number of ronin created, but also a great number of families disrupted. Some of the young girls who came on the market at that time were not always properly sold, and many were from good families. Here was all this good merchandise available with no proper outlet, and many merchants in flesh were afraid to get into this trade. I started dabbling in it, supplying brothels in Kyoto, Edo, and here in Kamakura. We have to be discreet about this, because some of the families of the girls might take it into their heads to take revenge for my little business dealings with their daughters.

"I constructed the Jade Palace during that time, to house the girls safely until I was ready to dispose of them. I still use it to store girls I'm transferring between customers, as well as for Yuchan.

"The supply of young girls has dried up over the last year, so now I have agents looking for girls to work as maids. It's much cheaper to buy girls as maids, and families seem to be more willing to sell them if they think they're not going to end up in a brothel. Usually we bring them here to the villa and actually use them as maids for a time. When we've had enough of them, I let the guards break them in." Hishigawa waved his hand. "A few are precocious, but most are still virgins because we buy them so young. I, of course, have Yuchan, so I don't participate in raping the girls and preparing them for their lives as whores, but all the guards enjoy that. You'll enjoy it too."

Kaze's face was impassive, and he had to force himself to refrain from explaining to Hishigawa what he would and would not enjoy.

CHAPTER 23

A strong spirit is
contained in a frail body.
You are beautiful.

I don't like it," Elder Grandma said. "I should be the one to talk to Yuchan."

"That's difficult," Kaze said. "You don't even know if Yuchan is unhappy with the life she's leading. She's treated like a noble, living in her own palace. It's best for you to wait hidden in the villa's grounds until I have a chance to see if Yuchan wants to leave. After I find that out, I'll come to you and we can plan our next action."

Kaze was once again in the tree by the lakeside. The water of the lake was a glistening sheet in the moonlight, and the gentle lapping sound of the water on the shore was restful and soothing. Kaze was relaxed but alert, watching the Jade Palace intently. Elder Grandma, her grandson, and her servant were safely hidden in a grove of trees on the villa grounds, waiting for Kaze to report on his conversation with Yuchan.

The guard at the drum bridge seemed alert but bored, leaning against the bridge and walking about in fits and starts. Without a regular patrol schedule, the problem of getting to the island and the palace was harder. But with only one guard outside it was not impossible. Kaze had no idea how many guards were inside.

The guard sat on the steps on the island part of the drum bridge and took off a sandal, rubbing his foot with obvious satisfaction. Kaze slipped out of the tree and made his way to the far side of the palace. Taking off his kimono, he used the kimono sash to make a neat bundle, tying his sword to his clothes.

Dressed in only his fundoshi, he slipped into the cold water of the lake. The bottom dropped out quickly, and Kaze was soon swimming, holding his kimono and sword above his head to keep them dry. In military training, Kaze had learned to swim while in full armor. He had also learned to swim holding his armor and sword above his head, just as he was doing now. The light weight of the kimono was nothing compared to the weight of a full suit of armor. Kaze made his way across the lake smoothly.

When he reached the opposite shore, he crouched in the deep shadows of the veranda that encircled the palace, making sure that the guard was not on one of his unpredictable patrols of the island. Satisfied that he was unseen, Kaze put on his kimono and replaced his sword in his sash.

He stood on the veranda and walked to a corner. The back of the veranda had shoji screens opening onto it, and these shoji almost certainly opened up into a room. The room might be occupied. On one side of the palace was a door, but he would be seen by the guard if he tried to enter it.

Kaze waited, showing patience until the guard retied his straw sandal and started on one of his patrols of the island. As soon as the guard disappeared around the corner of the palace, Kaze slipped through the door.

He was in a hallway, with shoji opening into rooms on one side and what looked like a closet door on the other. Directly ahead was a wooden grate blocking entrance to the core of the palace, locked shut.

Kaze looked at the closet and decided he would take a lesson from the ninja. He opened the closet door. From the moonlight spilling through the open doorway, Kaze could make out the ceiling slats. Standing on a shelf, he reached upward and pushed one aside. As he did so, the rock that was sitting on the slat to hold it in place slipped off the slat and started falling to the ground. Instantly, Kaze reached out and caught the rock in midair. In the silent palace, the sound of a falling rock could wake the inhabitants. He carefully put the rock on a shelf.

Satisfied that the opening was large enough to allow him to fit into the attic, he closed the closet door and used the shelf as a ladder to enter into the space above the ceiling.

He waited for several minutes, letting his eyes adjust to the gloom of the attic. Like that of the villa, the palace's roof had lattice openings that allowed some of the moonlight to bathe the interior. Moving carefully from rafter to rafter, Kaze made his way to the center of the palace.

There, using his fingers, he felt the ceiling slats, searching out the bamboo pegs that kept them in place. Taking the ko-gatana knife from the sword scabbard, Kaze removed the pegs, using his sense of touch as a guide.

As he removed the pegs, warm yellow light from lanterns started peeking past the edge of the slat. Silently, carefully, Kaze pried up the slat and looked down into the room below.

The room was dark and had a closed, fetid odor that assaulted Kaze's nose. One corner of the room was occupied by a large metal cage. Sitting on a table before the cage was a tray of sumptuous food, expertly prepared and displayed. There was gomoku rice, fresh sea bream, a light soup, and a tiny sweet in the shape of a chrysanthemum.

Next to the table was a beautiful silk robe, elaborately embroidered with peonies, and a mirror with silver mountings and a tortoiseshell comb. Except for the cage, the sparse furnishings in the room, a *tansu* chest and two lanterns with black lacquer frames, were elegant, tasteful, and expensive.

Kaze was puzzled as to what kind of animal would be kept in Yuchan's apartment. He carefully let himself down from the ceiling, dropping lightly to his feet on the tatami below.

Once in the room, he went up to the cage to see its contents. Inside, he was repulsed to see a plate containing the carcasses of two boiled rats. They had been gnawed on, and the pink flesh of the rats lay open like some disgusting flower bursting from a gray skin sheath. In a corner of the cage was a shapeless bundle of hair and rags. It took him a few moments to realize he was looking at a human being curled into the fetal position. His brows creased into a V, and Kaze could not make sense of what he was seeing. Was Yuchan some kind of monster, keeping some miserable human as a kind of bizarre pet?

The creature in the cage looked up at him. Kaze wasn't sure if it was a man or a woman because it had an emaciated face, with the skin stretched parchment-thin across the bones of the skull. Its frightened eyes looked out at him from a tangle of matted and filthy hair.

"Why are you in this cage?" Kaze asked softly.

"To break my spirit," the creature croaked back at him.

"Who wants to break your spirit?"

"Hishigawa. And Ando. They have done this together."

"But why hasn't Yuchan stopped them from committing this cruelty?"

"I am Yuchan."

Kaze was stunned. This pathetic collection of rags and bones was the creature of ethereal beauty that Hishigawa rhapsodized about. For the first time, Kaze understood that Hishigawa's obsession with the woman had slipped over to madness.

"How did you know my name?" the creature continued eagerly.

"Because I'm a friend. Your grandmother has sent me to see if we can get you out of here."

"Elder Grandma?"

"The same."

Tears formed in the dull eyes of Yuchan. "I knew she would help me. I prayed constantly to the Buddha to have pity on me and to send Elder Grandma and the whole Noguchi clan to punish these monsters."

"The whole clan isn't here, but Elder Grandma, Nagatoki, Sadakatsu, and I, Matsuyama Kaze, are here to help you. But I don't understand this. Hishigawa claims he loves you. Why would he do this to you?"

"Because I don't love him. He could abduct me and violate me, but he couldn't get me to love him or even to say I love him. Ando thought of this punishment. She has confined me in this cage for many months. Every day they bring the most sumptuous meals they can devise and leave them just outside my reach. Then they give me disgusting things like those boiled rats to eat. They say if I just tell Hishigawa I love him, they will release me, dress me in the robe you see there, groom me, and feed me this elegant food. But I won't tell him I love him. I'll never tell him I love him. I'll die before I tell him I love him!"

Kaze saw a spark of fire in the dull eyes of Yuchan, and he could tell that she was of the same strong stock as Elder Grandma. He well believed that she would die before bending her will to Hishigawa's desires, because she was near death now and had obviously not been broken.

Kaze came across the room and inspected the lock on the cage. It was one he could not force. "Who has the key to this cage?" he asked.

"Ando. She always carries it with her. Every night she and Hishigawa come to argue with me, trying to get me to say I love the disgusting merchant. Hishigawa seems quite oblivious to my state and acts like I'm still the maiden he first met. He is touched by some evil spirit and crazed. Ando is not touched, but she is a monster, an ogre! I hate her more than Hishigawa. She knows what she's doing, and I think she quite enjoys it."

Kaze digested this declaration and found that he tended to agree that a sane person committing evil was more guilty than someone touched by some evil spirit. Since he could not force the lock, Kaze said, "All right, I'll have to—"

Kaze was interrupted by the door to the room sliding open. There were Hishigawa and Ando. Hishigawa seemed shocked at the sight of

Kaze. If Ando had shown a similar hesitation, Kaze might have been able to cross the room and eliminate them with two sword strokes. But Ando was too quick and started screaming, "Guards! Guards!" as soon as she saw Kaze.

There was a scramble of running feet, and Ando and Hishigawa disappeared from the doorway.

"I'll be back," Kaze told Yuchan.

She reached out and grabbed his arm in a surprisingly fierce grip.

"Don't leave me!" she said.

"I have to for now. The guards will be here in moments, and their companions from the villa will be right behind. I won't abandon you, I promise. I will be back for you soon!" Kaze gently pried loose the fingers of Yuchan's hand, afraid he might break the bony appendages if he yanked his arm away violently.

He ducked out of the doorway and found himself in a dark passageway. He didn't know the direction in which Ando and Hishigawa had disappeared, so he chose one at random and started running. He guessed wrong.

He came to a doorway and opened it. It was some kind of storeroom, with merchandise piled high. He was at a dead end. Kaze turned and looked down the passage, hearing the clatter of running feet and seeing five guards rushing toward him. He stood and prepared to cut his way out of the trap he found himself in.

Seeing the intruder calmly standing in the door of the storeroom, his sword in the point-at-the-eye position and apparently ready for a fight, the guards slowed down. They looked at each other, unsure about how to rush the ronin when only one at a time could enter the door to the storeroom. Finally, the bravest of the guards rushed into the storeroom with a yell.

Kaze caught the attacker's blade and, in one smooth motion, went from the defense to the offense, slashing the man's side and letting the dying man's momentum carry him through the doorway. The man landed on the wooden floor of the storeroom, which did not have tatami mats, and lay there groaning, his lifeblood rapidly leaking out of the large cut in his side. Kaze looked at the remaining four calmly.

"Get out of the way," Ando ordered.

The four guards were eager to obey any order that would delay an attack on the samurai. They parted cleanly, moving to the walls of the passageway.

Ando advanced toward the door. In front of her, she held Yuchan by the hair. She had taken her out of the cage. Yuchan was struggling, but her emaciated state and weakness made it easy for Ando to control her. In Ando's other hand she had a dagger. She stopped and held the dagger to Yuchan's throat. "Surrender," she said, "or I'll cut her throat."

"If you kill Yuchan, Hishigawa will be angry," Kaze pointed out.

"I'll tell him you killed her," Ando said. "He's already mad with jealousy. He thinks you wanted to steal Yuchan from him for yourself. He'll believe you killed Yuchan out of jealousy when you couldn't have her. This insolent girl has been enough of a bother as it is. It will be good to be rid of her so quickly."

Kaze looked in Yuchan's eyes, and he thought he saw in them a look of defiance, encouraging Kaze to fight on, even if it meant her death. But Kaze could not bring himself to cause the death of this pitiful creature. He threw his sword down.

The guards rushed him and roughly dragged him out of the storeroom. They quickly bound him with rope as Ando looked on in triumph, a crying Yuchan still in her grasp. Kaze noted with approval that Yuchan didn't start crying until the crisis was over. He couldn't say if she was crying for him or for herself—perhaps a bit of both.

When Kaze was securely bound, Ando approached him and slapped him across the cheek. Touching a samurai's face was the ultimate insult, but Kaze simply winced at the slap and gave no other indication that he felt Ando's blow.

"Beat him," Ando said. "Do it thoroughly, but don't kill him. I'm sure Hishigawa-san will want to deal personally with the man he thinks tried to steal Yuchan from him."

The men rushed Kaze and started kicking the bound ronin. They wore straw sandals, causing bruising but not broken bones. Kaze simply ducked his head to try to protect his face and gave no other indication that the four men were beating him.

One of the men left and returned with a spear. He brought the butt of the spear down into Kaze's side, bringing a grunt of pain from him. He pointed to the dead body in the storeroom, the first guard that Kaze had killed. "This is for Ichiro!" the guard with the spear said. He brought the spear butt down on Kaze's head, making him see blackness for a brief moment. Kaze fought to keep consciousness, telling himself it was foolish to do so because it wasn't likely that there would be a chance to escape and kill his tormentors in his current circumstances. Eventually, as the fist, feet, and spear butt fell on him, Kaze's effort to remain conscious proved futile.

The pain of good-bye
lingers far longer than the
parting of our souls.

Kaze thought he was being held by a demon of enormous size. The demon was an angry red color and had bulging eyes and two curled, yellowing tusks protruding from its mouth. He held Kaze suspended high in the air with one hand. The hand was so large that the demon could hold Kaze with two fingers. With the other hand, he had Kaze's two arms pinned back behind him and he was pulling on them, trying to rip them out from Kaze's shoulders the way wanton boys will pull the wings off a dragonfly.

The pain was excruciating, and Kaze felt an agony like the pain of fire. He looked in the demon's face and saw an idle curiosity. The pain in his arms and shoulders built and built and built. Kaze closed his eyes tightly and grit his teeth to help him bear it.

Finally, when the pain was unbearable, Kaze popped his eyes open, ready to shout his defiance to the demon, telling the creature to pluck off his arms if he must.

Instead of seeing a demon, however, Kaze discovered he was in an eight-mat room in Hishigawa's villa. His hands were tied behind him. A rope bound his wrists and looped through a hook in a ceiling joist. Kaze had been hauled into the air by the rope. He was dangling above the mats from his arms, and the weight of his body was causing the pain.

He twisted his wrists, but the ropes binding them were too tight. He was trapped.

Kaze closed his eyes and gathered his strength. He felt the tearing pain in his shoulders, but he tried to ignore it. His face and body were bruised, but he dismissed the beating as the work of amateurs. Instead of worrying about the pain, he tried to take his mind to another time and place. He thought briefly of his first view of Kamakura when he arrived a few days before. The green of the foliage, the blues from the sea and sky and some of the tile roofs, the brown of the earth, and the tiny splashes of color from flowers and birds helped settle his mind. He still felt the pain, but now he regarded his position as just an annoyance.

He wondered if the Lady had been able to take her mind to another place when she was captured. She had endured the same thing, and more.

The rain was drumming down with a steady beat on the day that Kaze had tried to save the Lady. He had been crouching under a large bush, smeared in mud as camouflage, watching Okubo's encampment.

The encampment was a large enclosure at the top of a hill. Poles were set in a rectangle, with ropes strung between them. Hanging from the ropes were large pieces of black cloth, to shield the encampment from wind, prying eyes, and an easy shot by a sniper with a musket or bow. On the cloth was the Okubo crest, looking like a large, malevolent spider.

Frightened peasants told Kaze that the Lady had been captured. Okubo had used the ruse that he was making a courtesy call before joining the main battle force arrayed against the Tokugawas. The Lady and her daughter had opened the doors of the castle and come out to greet him. He had seized them and pressed an attack, surprising the garrison and overwhelming them with his superior force. Now the castle was destroyed, and no one quite knew where the Lady and her daughter were.

Kaze had watched Okubo's enclosure all day. Messengers arrived constantly, and the camp seemed to be in a state of intense excitement. If they still lived, Kaze thought the Lady and her daughter would most likely be held prisoner in the encampment. In the late afternoon this suspicion was confirmed in a horrible way.

Activity outside the enclosure seemed at a lull, and Kaze could not see what was happening inside. But he could hear. From inside Okubo's enclosure came a woman's scream. It was a scream of pain, torn from her throat. Kaze wasn't sure if it was the Lady, but even if it was, he told himself to be still and be patient. The second scream almost galvanized him to action, but he knew that attacking the enclosure now would be suicide. Kaze wasn't afraid to die, but he knew he would not save the Lady by making a senseless attack. So he waited. More screams came from the enclosure. He waited some more, his heart tearing with every scream that long, wet afternoon.

Finally, after hours of the sounds of suffering, Okubo and a strong guard left the enclosure. After Okubo left, two guards came from inside the enclosure and made the rounds of the guards posted outside the fabric barrier. They handed them jugs of sakè, and, with Okubo gone, Kaze could see the guards visibly relaxing and celebrating their victory.

Because of the rainy sky, Kaze did not see the sun go down, but by the sudden descent of darkness, he knew it was night. Still he waited.

Finally, in the small hours of the morning, Kaze moved. He carefully made his way to one side of the enclosure, where a single guard was on duty. The guard was wearing a straw rain cape and stood holding his spear with his head bent under his conical metal helmet to shelter his face from the rain. The guard wasn't drunk, but in that pose his field of vision was restricted to just a few feet in front of him. Kaze used that fact.

The guard was bored by the sentry duty and fighting to stay awake.

He had given up trying to stay warm in the rain hours before and had settled into a state of patient acceptance when he heard the sound of running feet. Startled, he looked up just in time to see a samurai descending on him. He opened his mouth to sound the alarm, but before he could shout his throat was cut by the samurai's katana.

Kaze took the guard and leaned him up against one of the poles holding the fabric barrier. If someone spotted him, it would look like he was asleep. It would buy Kaze a few moments before they realized the guard was dead.

Kaze cut one of the cords holding the bottom of a fabric panel to a pole and slipped under the panel. Inside the enclosure Kaze saw a couple of tents and another closed-off area. Unsure of where the woman's screams came from, he decided to try the closed-off area first.

Slipping like a shadow against the background of the black cloth, Kaze went to the small area and entered it. Three long poles had been set up to form a tripod. Hanging from the tripod was the Lady. Her arms were tied behind her and she was hoisted up by those arms. Her kimono was open and hung wet on her body. Her head was bent forward, and she was so still that Kaze thought she might be dead. The cruel rain made her long black hair hang down in front of her face like the hair of a ghost.

Kaze approached her and whispered, "My Lady?"

She moaned and raised her head slightly. Her wet hair still obscured her vision, but she said weakly, "You!"

"Yes. Stay strong. I'll have you down in a minute." Kaze placed one arm around her, and as he drew her close his nose was assaulted by the smell of burnt hair. He reached up with his sword hand and cut the rope suspending her. He stopped her from falling to the earth, but she gave a moan of pain when the rope was cut.

Kaze cut the ties on her wrists and laid her on the ground.

"Can you cover me?" she asked. "I'm afraid my arms are dislocated, so I can't do it myself. I'm sorry."

Kaze wrapped her kimono around her body and as he did so, the cause of the smell of burnt hair became apparent. Her privates had been burned with fire or hot irons.

"My daughter . . ." she said.

"Do you know where she is?" Kaze asked. "I'll get her, too."

"No. They took her yesterday. Okubo told me he was going to sell her. He wouldn't tell me where. He said it was punishment for my husband and me always thinking we were better than him. It's true. We always did think we were better. Now I know we are. But the revenge he took because of that . . ." Her voice trailed off. Then she said, "I think he did this to me because he liked it. He liked it very much."

"My Lady, it's best if you don't talk now. We still have to get out of here, and as soon as they find out you're gone, they'll come looking for us." Kaze picked her up in his arms. He kept his sword in his hand and carefully made his way out of the enclosure. He was halfway to the opening in the outer enclosure when a samurai in armor and a helmet came out of one of the tents.

He saw Kaze and drew his sword. "Alarm! Intruders!" he shouted, and started running toward Kaze.

Kaze took a few seconds to put the Lady down, instead of dropping her, and those few seconds almost cost him his life.

Kaze took the first sword blow while he was still bent. The best he could do was to parry the samurai's blow. A man in armor was hard to kill, because there were only a few vulnerable spots. Even if the armor didn't completely stop a blow, it could lessen its effectiveness, leaving a man with a cut instead of a mortal wound.

Using all his strength, Kaze pushed the man away. He knew he had to end this duel quickly, because he could hear the camp stirring. Reinforcements would be arriving any moment. His katana was made for slashing, not thrusting, but he knew there was one vulnerable spot on the armored man that would end the contest quickly. He stepped back and dropped his guard.

Seeing his chance, the armored samurai attacked, slashing at Kaze with an over-the-head blow. At the ready, Kaze narrowly dodged the blow and lunged forward, the point of his katana aimed at the man's neck, right below the chin. Kaze caught the man in this unarmored spot and shoved his sword home. The man dropped his sword and grabbed at Kaze's blade, now stuck in his neck. Kaze withdrew his sword with a sideways motion, slashing the man's throat. The man collapsed.

Kaze took a second cut at the man's throat, not to deliver another death blow, but to cut the ties that held the man's helmet. He scooped the man's helmet off his head and placed it on his own head just as the troops, roused from a drunken victory stupor, started rushing out of the tents, holding their weapons.

Kaze looked up with the helmet on his head and shouted, "I've killed two of them!" He pointed to the body of the dead samurai and the Lady, who was moaning softly from pain. "Quickly! They've gone into the enclosed area and rescued the Lady! Hurry! There's a dozen of them!" Kaze pointed to the enclosure where he had found the Lady. "They're in there! Hurry! Get them!"

In the dark, with an Okubo helmet on, the troops took Kaze for an officer and immediately rushed to obey. They ran past in a frenzy, bumping into one another in their confusion and bewilderment. As soon as they were past, Kaze scooped up the Lady and made a dash for the place in the compound barrier where he had entered.

Things man does to man.
Human tears would fill Edo
Bay, if gathered there.

The Lady wasn't heavy, but by midday Kaze was weary of carrying her. He had not slept or rested for several days, ever since learning of Okubo's treachery. Kaze had taken to the mountains immediately. He knew that if he stayed on level ground the Okubo troops would soon hunt them down on horseback. In the mountains Kaze had an advantage, because Okubo's troops would have to proceed on foot and Kaze could stretch his meager head start as the troops tried to track him.

The rain had not abated, and the dreary wet weather matched Kaze's mood. His children were dead. His wife was dead. The fate of his Lord was unknown. The Lady's daughter had been kidnapped and presumably sold. The Lady had been tortured and dishonored. In his arms, she made an infrequent moan of pain but never complained as Kaze took her deeper into the mountains to get away from Okubo's men.

Kaze was exhausted, but he would have willed himself to continue, except that the Lady seemed near the end of her strength. He found a sheltered spot under a crooked tree and made a damp nest for the Lady from pine needles and cut branches.

He sat next to her and asked if she wanted him to find something to eat.

"No. Not for me. Find something for yourself."

"I'm not hungry," Kaze lied. "We'll rest here for a while. The rain seems to have made it difficult for Okubo to pursue us. We'll go through the mountains, and I'll find a safe place for you. Then I'll make contact with the Lord. Just recover so we can plan our next move."

"You know, I always admired you for your courage. I don't think I've ever told you that. The Lord and I used to talk about it often. I wish I had some of that courage now. I don't want to die."

"You won't die."

She gave a faint smile. With her drawn face it looked more like a grimace. "You always were a very poor liar," she said. "I can feel my strength and life slipping away. Still, I want to thank you for rescuing me. I wouldn't want to die strung up like that. It's a poor death. An *inujini*. A dog's death."

"Don't die, Lady!"

"I don't think I have a choice. There are still so many wonderful things I want to do. But the biggest reason I want to live is to make sure my daughter is rescued and safe. I can't do that now, so I need your help. I don't know how, but if she's still alive I want you to find her. It's my last wish and my last command to you." She looked at him with feverish eyes black from strain and pain.

Kaze bowed his head in response to the Lady's order. Hot tears flowed down his cheeks and mingled with the icy raindrops striking his face. Despite the pain, the Lady reached up and, using the sleeve of her kimono, brushed the tears from his face. It was a gesture that had no practical purpose, because his face was covered with raindrops as soon as her sleeve moved across it. Yet Kaze found comfort in the gesture. Her touch was so light it felt like a breeze caressing his cheek, the kind of soft breeze he felt when he climbed into treetops and put his face into the wind.

Kaze found it strange that the dying should be comforting the living. With his children gone, his wife gone, his clan defeated and in disarray, and the fate of his Lord unknown, Kaze thought that it might be best to follow the Lady in death when the time came.

As if reading his thoughts, the Lady stopped brushing away his tears and extended a weak hand. It trembled with the effort to keep it in the air. "Give me your wakizashi."

Surprised, Kaze removed his short sword from his sash, putting it in her hand. The weight of the sword caused her hand to drop to the ground, but she clutched the scabbard fiercely. At first Kaze thought the Lady had lost heart and was going to use the short sword to commit suicide, but then she said, "This represents your honor and the ability to take your own life. Your honor is now mine until my daughter is found and safe.

"Promise me!" she said fiercely.

"I promise, Lady. But this is not necessary. I will honor my promise to find your daughter, as I have always honored my pledges. And you will be alive to see her and hold her again."

The Lady looked at him with tired eyes. "I wish that were true." She said no more and closed her eyes to rest. In a few minutes she had fallen into an exhausted sleep. Kaze tried to remove the wakizashi from her hand so she could rest easier, but even in her sleep she gripped the short sword.

Kaze sat next to her. He held his own kimono sleeve above her, holding it out like a tent flap with his other hand, despite his fatigue, to keep the raindrops off her face. In meditation, he had been taught to listen to his own breathing, because breath means life. Now he listened to the Lady's ragged breathing. It became shallower and shallower, until it was barely detectable. Then it ceased altogether.

Kaze sat immobile, watching the pain-racked face relax slightly with the release of death. Then he did something he would never have done while she lived. He placed his hand on her cheek, gently cupping her face. Her position as his Lord's consort made such an action unthinkable to Kaze while she was alive, but now that her spirit had departed her body, touching her face, as she had touched his, seemed the only comfort available to him after days of pain and sorrow.

He stared at her face, seeing her in happier days instead of the visage with black, sunken eyes and tightened jaw muscles before him. The face he tried to see was serene and kind, with the sparkle of good humor in its eyes. It was the same face he carved on the Kannon, the Goddess of Mercy, that he made.

Kaze heard the door of the room slide open. Hishigawa entered, holding a sword. He dropped the sword's scabbard on the floor, unsheathing its blade. Kaze realized it was his own sword, the Fly Cutter. Hishigawa slid the shoji screen closed and turned to look at Kaze. He smiled. "We use this room when we occasionally have a girl that won't cooperate. I told you we buy maids for the villa, and when they are sufficiently seasoned, we convert them for sale to a brothel. Sometimes we have one who is recalcitrant about the new life we have planned for her. An hour or two hanging as you are is usually enough to make her see the error in her ways.

"You tried to steal Yuchan from me. Although it might be mildly amusing to torture you further, I am not a cruel man. I am reasonable. I am a businessman. I deal in judgments about what is profitable or not profitable to pursue. Keeping you alive is not profitable, so I have decided to cut my losses." Hishigawa laughed at his pun.

He hefted the blade, looking at it. It caught the yellow light of the lantern, reflecting a silver arc against the walls and ceiling of the room as Hishigawa moved it around. Even through his pain, Kaze thought the blade beautiful.

"Since I paid for this sword, I thought I would use it," Hishigawa said. "I don't have the skill with the blade that you have, but you'll find that I'll still be able to take your head, even if it might take me two or three blows to sever it. I've ordered many deaths, but I've never killed a man myself, so this will be a novel experience for me."

Hishigawa smiled again. "I know you samurai all like to do your fancy death poems when the end is at hand. But as I said, I am a man who deals in efficiency." He put both hands on the sword hilt. "I believe it would be most efficient to dispatch you without allowing you to declaim the rubbish that you samurai like to yammer as poetry. You see, although I have to deal with you and your stupid wives because they are my customers, I really don't like samurai. You're parasites, feeding off the land and interfering with business every time you start one of your stupid wars."

Hishigawa lifted the blade to the point-at-the-eye position, judging its weight and balance. "I suppose this really is a fine weapon," he said conversationally. "Maybe I'll be able to take your head with only one or two blows, instead of having to hack it off."

Kaze stared at Hishigawa, and, although his body was in pain, he came to an epiphany. He was not afraid. Always in battle there was a chance of him dying, but now he knew that it was a certainty. And yet, despite the knowledge that he would die, Kaze was able to face it with a studied indifference, certain in the fact that life and death were the same and that existence is only an illusion.

Of course, he had been bred as a samurai and trained in the ways of Zen. He had been raised with the thought that the true samurai is always ready to die in the service of his master or his cause. Yet, from personal experience, Kaze knew that such noble sentiments were not always played out in the hearts of men.

At the mere threat of death, some men cowed and broke, their fear overtaking them. In battle Kaze had seen even highborn samurai, new to the violence of war and the clash of arms, shrink from contact with the enemy and shake from fear. It was said that even Tokugawa Ieyasu, when he was a very young man and engaged in his first battle, actually fled the scene of the fighting on his horse. When he reached safety, one of his chief retainers, Honda, looked at the saddle and saw evidence that Ieyasu had lost control of his bowels when fear had overtaken him.

Instead of remonstrating with his young Lord, Honda had simply laughed. Kaze hated Ieyasu for what he and his men had done and yet, even though he was familiar with the story of his first battle, he would not call him a coward—not after the battles he had fought and won subsequently. Any man might lose his nerve the first time he's confronted by war.

Now Kaze was facing something else for the first time. It was the certainty of his immediate demise. He almost marveled that all the things that he had been taught throughout his entire life about how a samurai faces death were now coming to fruition. He was facing his own death with courage and indifference. He did not want to die, but if he was going to die, then it was the fate of all men. It was simply his time. Karma.

He leaned his head to the side to provide a better target for Hishigawa. Instead of stepping forward to take the cut, Hishigawa hesitated, unsure what to make of Kaze's hard eyes staring back at him. The eyes held no fear, no pleading, and no sense of panic, all the things that Hishigawa knew he would display if the situation were reversed.

Instead, the ronin's eyes met his steadily and the ronin's face was impassive, perhaps even tranquil, because of some deep-seated core of courage that Hishigawa could not begin to understand.

Hishigawa raised the sword and started to step forward so he could deliver the blow to the ronin's neck. Suddenly, there was the sound of paper tearing behind him and in the pit of his back there was a burning pain. He was propelled forward and could not bring the sword blade down for the death blow. Instead, he felt his knees grow weak and his grip on the sword become numb. The sword slipped from his hands and tumbled to the tatami mat. Hishigawa fell to his knees.

He reached behind him and felt the shaft of a spear. It had been thrust through the shoji screen because the wielder of the spear had decided there was not enough time to open the door. The silhouette of the man holding the sword was the target, and the spear had been driven home.

Blackness started to descend on Hishigawa as life drained out from the thick hole in his back. He gave a cry of pain mixed with fear at the thought that this blow might be mortal. He tried to give a shout, in a desperate attempt to get help. Instead, all that came from his mouth was a long, slow hiss that ended in death.

The shoji screen was kicked down, and Kaze straightened his head to look into the fierce face of Elder Grandma. She had thick arms, well suited to using a spear, Kaze thought, and the anger and blood lust on her face was as fierce as that found on any warrior.

She looked down at the corpse at her feet. She kicked away a scrap of paper from the shoji that masked the face of her victim, revealing Hishigawa's face. His eyes were still open, but lifeless. His mouth also open, the last scream still on his lips, cut short by death. Seeing Hishigawa, Elder Grandma stopped a moment. Then she placed her foot against Hishigawa's back and, grabbing the spear shaft with both arms, pulled it hard to release it. She looked at Kaze and a grim smile came to her lips.

"It's done," she said. She pointed to the headband that bore the character for "revenge."

"It's done," she said again with a fierce tone to her voice. "It's done. The vendetta is completed and our family is avenged. Our honor is restored."

"If you'll cut me down," Kaze said mildly, "I'll help you see if we can restore your granddaughter, as well as your honor."

Elder Grandma used Kaze's sword to cut him down. When she cut the ropes from his wrists, Kaze's hands burned with pain as the circulation returned to them. He tried to hold his sword, but initially his fingers would not close around the hilt. After the blood returned, he was able to grasp the weapon, and he took a few tentative swings to see how much damage had been done to his shoulders and arms.

"Where's your grandson and the servant?" he asked.

"Like me, they were searching for you to see what happened with Yuchan. We got tired of waiting in that garden. I saw Hishigawa enter this room and decided to take my chance at revenge."

"Go gather Nagatoki and Sadakatsu up before they get into trouble. Yuchan is in the palace on that little island. She is not in good condition and will need help. What I thought was a life of luxury turned out to be a life of horror. There are guards, but I'll take care of them. In fact, it's better if I take care of things here in the villa before going to the island."

"What are you going to do about the guards?"

"I'm going to kill them. Kill them all. Someone told me that only bad ones are here, and I believe it. In the yard I found a shallow grave. The grave seemed too old to be Mototane's, but I was curious about who was buried there. I found the bones of two young people. They were probably girls. Maybe Hishigawa's efforts to persuade girls to co-operate as prostitutes by torturing them resulted in two deaths. Maybe two girls committed suicide when they realized the life they would lead. Regardless of the reason, they buried the two bodies on the villa grounds to hide the deaths, and they probably didn't pay a priest to say the proper prayers for their departed souls. It's a bad business conducted by bad people. It's better if all the rats are cleared out of this den."

"Can you?" Elder Grandma pointed to his arms, which Kaze was still limbering up.

"Yes. Just get the other two and meet me at the drum bridge that leads to the palace."

Elder Grandma didn't question Kaze's claim that he would eliminate the guards. She was like a general who expected her troops to execute their mission. She left to find the two others, and Kaze took a few more moments to assure that he could hold a sword properly. He stuck the katana's scabbard into his kimono sash. Then he stepped into the hall and started making his way toward the main part of the villa.

He turned down a hallway and saw two of the guards approaching. As recognition painted the faces of the two men, Kaze rushed toward them. They shouted and got their swords out just as Kaze reached them. The first was able to parry Kaze's blow. The second guard took a cut at him. Kaze took a step back and caught the blade. He immediately swung from defense to offense and, using the momentum of his attacker's blade, he brought his sword downward and across, cutting open the belly of the surprised guard.

Without a second of hesitation, he then brought his blade upward, catching the first guard in the sternum and delivering a mortal wound. Kaze was already past them and running down the hallway before the two bodies hit the wooden planks of the floor.

Attracted by the shouts, another guard opened a shoji screen and stuck his head into the hallway. His eyes were filled with the image of a samurai rushing toward him, sword upraised. He was able to shout a warning to his companions just as a sword bit into his neck and shoulders.

Kaze jumped over the body blocking the doorway and found himself in a room with four guards scrambling for their swords and a panic-stricken maid who, having dropped a tray of food, was cringing in a corner.

Kaze killed two before they could get their swords out. He sparred briefly with a third before delivering a deathblow and caught the fourth from behind as he tried to flee the room.

The maid watched the carnage with bulging eyes, her mouth open but no sound issuing from it. Kaze looked at her. "I won't hurt you," he said. He pointed at the five dead bodies in the room. "Is this all in the house?"

"Th-th-there are two more," the young maid said, stuttering in her terror.

The two Kaze disposed of in the hall. "And Ando?"

"I don't know, Samurai-sama. I don't know where Ando-san is. Please don't hurt me!"

"I have no intention of hurting you. You go to your room and stay there. Tell all the other maids to stay in their rooms, too. In the morning the authorities will come and things will be all right."

The maid scurried off to do as she was directed, skirting the two bodies at the door. Kaze made his way to the back of the villa and the drum bridge.

CHAPTER 26

The world outside has
winter and unpleasant things.
Freedom brings burdens.

As he approached the drum bridge, he saw a group hiding in the brush, out of the moonlight that bathed the entire garden.

"Psst! We're here!" Elder Grandma said in a harsh whisper.

"Good. Stay there."

He came to the bridge and started climbing up the stairs that led to the central span.

"Who is that?" challenged the guard on the other side of the bridge.

"Death," Kaze answered.

"Huh?"

Disgusted, Kaze said, "Take out your sword and defend yourself. Enomoto-san has not been gone a whole day, and you are already slackening your vigilance."

What the guard lacked in ability to assess the situation, he made up for in ferocity. He drew his sword and rushed at Kaze, yelling and taking the steps of the drum bridge two at a time.

Kaze waited for his opponent to get to the central span of the bridge, where he met his furious attack. The moon silhouetted the two men, standing on the half-round bridge attacking and counterattacking, swords weaving together in a deadly dance amid the music of steel clanging on steel. Kaze knew he was not completely fit, and the torture and exertions with the other guards had taken their toll. Yet he beat the guard back across the span toward the island and delivered a deathblow just as the guard reached the stair portion of the bridge. Staggering backward, the guard stepped off the central span and tumbled down the stairs.

"Come on," Kaze called to the trio hiding in the foliage. "Follow me, in case there are more guards."

Kaze entered the Jade Palace amid a strange silence. After the fighting and shouts and groans of dying men, the palace provided a tranquil respite, despite the fact that Kaze knew it was a place of horror. The wooden grate blocking the hallway was open. He walked down the silent hall, a silence that saved him. As he approached a corner in the hallway, he was able to hear a creak from one of the floorboards.

Kaze didn't change his pace, because that might alert the person waiting in ambush around the curve in the corridor. Suddenly, there was a mad shout, and a spear was thrust at Kaze as he rounded the corner.

Kaze caught the top of the spear shaft with one hand and diverted it slightly, so it missed him. The other hand, holding Fly Cutter, came down, and the shaft of the spear was cut in two.

Kaze threw the spear tip to the ground and looked at his assailant. It was Ando.

She threw away the butt end of the spear and retreated. Kaze stepped forward.

"You wouldn't kill a woman?" she said, holding her hands out in front of her.

"No, but I would kill a monster." Kaze's sword cut a fast arc, and Ando's head and one of her hands went flying down the hallway. A surprised look was still on her face. Kaze stepped past the headless corpse and made his way to Yuchan's room.

The room seemed unchanged. The emaciated creature huddling in the corner of the cell didn't look up.

"Yuchan," Kaze said gently.

She looked up with feverish eyes, half-hopeful at the sound of Kaze's voice.

"Merciful Buddha!" Nagatoki exclaimed. Kaze looked over his shoulder to see the young man, Sadakatsu, and Elder Grandma standing behind him in the doorway. They all had shocked looks on their faces, and Kaze thought he detected tears in Sadakatsu's eyes.

"It's all right, Yuchan," Kaze said. "Your grandmother and cousin are here to bring you home, and you must remember Sadakatsu."

Yuchan looked at the trio, then looked at Kaze. "Is it a dream?" she mused.

"No, it's no dream. You're saved. You will be going home."

Yuchan crawled over to the cage wall closest to the door. She put her fingers around the bars and stared out. The fingers looked like dried twigs, they were so thin.

"Go get the key to the cell," Kaze ordered Nagatoki. "It's probably on that body in the hallway."

"But that body doesn't have a head!" the grandson said.

"Yes, but she probably does have a key. Check her kimono for it."

Nagatoki left, and Sadakatsu went to the cage and fell to his knees, copious tears now streaming down his thin face. Yuchan looked at him and said, "Sadakatsu! Look, Sadakatsu, for once you are not the skinniest one in the room." She held her hands out. Every bone in her hand was visible. "Even you are not as thin as this, Sadakatsu!"

When she made that joke, Kaze immediately knew two things. One, she was indeed from the same strong stock as Elder Grandma. Two, although it would take a long time to recover, Yuchan would eventually prevail over this ordeal. She might never be as pretty again, but she would always be as strong.

Nagatoki came back with the key. He held it away from his body like a repugnant thing. Perhaps it was. Kaze took the key and opened the cage. Yuchan painfully crawled out of the cage, too weak to walk.

"Get up and walk!" Elder Grandma ordered.

Yuchan tried to stand with the help of Sadakatsu but collapsed back to the tatami like a fragile autumn leaf. "I can't," she said.

Kaze picked Yuchan up in his arms. She was as light as a small child. "Thank you," she whispered as he held her.

Elder Grandma handed her spear to Sadakatsu. "Here, let me have her," she said gruffly.

Kaze hesitated a moment, and Elder Grandma turned her back. "Put her on my back. I used to carry her as a baby that way and I can certainly carry her that way again." Kaze took Yuchan over to Elder Grandma and loaded her onto the old woman's back, piggyback style. It seemed to give Yuchan comfort to be next to her grandmother.

"That's fine for getting out of here," Kaze said, "but it won't do for getting you back home. We should all leave Kamakura immediately. I don't know what the authorities will think of all this and don't want to bother finding out. We'll have to roust some porters out of bed and have Yuchan carried in a palanquin. That will take money."

Elder Grandma bit her lip. Her penurious nature did battle with her practical side, and for once practicality won. "All right," she said. "Sadakatsu has the money."

"Good," Kaze said. "You start and I'll join you. I have one last piece of business here." Kaze had no desire to carve a Kannon for the dead in the villa and the palace, but he did want to do one thing.

Kaze left the room with the cell and made his way to the back of the palace. There, in a large common room, he found six girls, all dressed in sumptuous kimonos. They were startled by Kaze's appearance and sat staring at him with wary eyes.

"You're free," Kaze said.

Several of the girls looked at each other, seeming not to understand.

"I said you're free," Kaze repeated. "The men who were guarding you are dead. You can leave any time."

One girl stood with tentative movements. Another girl, with hard eyes, said, "Sit down!" The first girl sat.

Puzzled, Kaze said, "Don't you understand me? You can go at any time."

Hard Eyes said, "Where are we to go? Our parents sold us into prostitution. We have no home now. If we leave, we will have to wander, seeking some housemaid's job, where men will use our bodies just as they do now, except we won't get the fine clothes and luxury our current life can bring us. It's just like a man to announce that we are free to go, but not to tell us where we can go!"

Kaze looked at Hard Eyes until she looked away from his even harder gaze. "Suit yourself," he said. "The door to freedom is open. Freedom is never easy, for a man or a woman. You at least have the chance at it, if you want. If you don't want, then that's your karma." He turned and left, catching up with the others.

Kaze and the four left the Jade Palace and Hishigawa's villa. They went to the outskirts of Kamakura and Kaze found a porters' lodging next to an inn. There he was able to get two palanquin porters out of bed.

At first the two porters were frightened by the sight of Yuchan, but Kaze told them she had been sick and needed to return home immediately to recuperate. After a brief consultation and a few minutes of haggling over price with Elder Grandma, who eventually triumphed by pointing out how light Yuchan was, Yuchan was safely tucked inside the palanquin.

"You should be fine," Kaze said to Elder Grandma. "The authorities will be looking for me, but I doubt they will look for you."

"Will you be fine?"

Kaze rubbed his shoulders. "Like you, I'm tough." Elder Grandma grunted a reply, then went to look after Yuchan.

Nagatoki came up to Kaze and asked, "How many guards did you kill in the villa?"

"Too many. The best blades stay in their scabbard, but I hate to leave a job undone. I did not find out what happened to Mototane, but I decided to clear out that nest of vermin. I think I am still like a Muramasa blade, not a Masamune blade. I am sharp but still have to strengthen my spirit."

"It's too bad Mototane couldn't be here to help us. He would have eliminated that bad lot, too."

"Perhaps."

"It's a shame you couldn't see how Mototane could fight. He was superb. I envied the way he could handle Sakuran."

Sakuran was a word meaning falling cherry blossoms, one of many words used to describe the various states of the cherished *sakura*, the cherry blossom. "Sakuran?" Kaze asked.

"His sword was called Sakuran, Samurai-san."

An awful chill touched Kaze. "What did the tsuba of Sakuran look like?" Kaze asked quietly.

"It was beautiful," Nagatoki said enthusiastically. "It had the branch of a cherry tree around the outside edge and in the middle it had sakuran highlighted in silver."

"Did the branch have gold highlights?"

"Why, yes. How did you know? Have you seen Sakuran?"

"Yes," Kaze said softly. "I've seen it."

Kaze knew Hishigawa was a liar from his first meeting with him. He had called the bandit chief Ishibashi, and that name should have been a clue that Hishigawa was lying. To get to the place where the bandits were attacking Hishigawa, Kaze had crossed a small stone bridge before climbing the hill. "Ishibashi" meant stone bridge. Hishigawa had crossed the same stone bridge and had used "Ishibashi" when he needed another name for Noguchi Mototane.

In Kaze's world, names were important. Men fought and died to protect or enhance a name. In fact, the rulers of the land, the daimyo, had a title that meant "great name." But Kaze, above all in his class, knew that names were ephemeral and not immutable. Kaze now used a name that was plucked from the air on a whim. His past name, which he had once put such store in, was now like the wind. Its effects were still felt, but it had no tangible existence. By the simple expedient of giving Noguchi Mototane the name Ishibashi, Kaze had been fooled and Mototane had died.

As a warrior, Kaze knew death much more intimately than most

men, but even the most sheltered farmer understood that life was fi-
nite. Therefore, death by itself had little meaning to Kaze, but the
manner of death had much meaning. There are good deaths and bad
deaths. The Lady had had a very bad death, and this fact had driven
Kaze to rage more than just the tragedy of her passing.

The death of Noguchi Mototane, Elder Grandma's missing grandson, was a death that now weighed on Kaze's conscience. Kaze had
killed numerous men, but he had never, to his mind, murdered one.

Noguchi Mototane had been on a legal vendetta and had the right
to kill Hishigawa. Kaze had prevented the execution of that right and
in so doing had disturbed something he considered proper and just.
He felt that he had been tricked into committing the murder by the
merchant's assertion that Mototane was a bandit chief. Kaze knew
that if he had understood the circumstances of Mototane's grievance
against Hishigawa, Kaze would have simply stood to one side and let
him kill the merchant.

Kaze's murder of Mototane had disrupted the harmony that was
the linchpin of his existence and philosophy of life. Now he understood why his katana had broken in the fight. It was a sign from
heaven that his actions against Mototane were unjust—a sign Kaze
had chosen to ignore. His *wa* was disturbed, and he had both remorse
for his actions and anger at the merchant who had fooled him into
taking those actions.

Kaze fell to his knees. With both hands in front of him on the
ground, he bowed until his forehead touched the earth. "Please forgive me, Mototane-san. I'm sorry I killed you. I know it was wrong
and that it makes me a murderer. Please forgive me." Kaze aimed his
remarks at the spirit of the dead Mototane, but Nagatoki also heard
the ronin's confession. The young man stared at the repentant ronin.

"You killed Mototane?" Nagatoki said in shock.

"*Nani?* What?" Elder Grandma had returned to the two, with
Sadakatsu at her heels. She had halted at the sight of the ronin hum-
bling himself and her grandson's words now reached incredulous
ears.

Kaze shifted his position to face Elder Grandma. "I just realized that I killed Mototane. It was within minutes of meeting Hishigawa, when he was being attacked by bandits on the Tokaido Road. Mototane must have been shadowing Hishigawa, looking for his chance.

"He had attacked Hishigawa once before, when the merchant was going to Kamakura, but he couldn't kill Hishigawa. On the Tokaido, Mototane attacked right after some bandits had, and Hishigawa told me that Mototane was the head of the bandits. I had killed him in a duel. Hishigawa told me I had killed a man named Ishibashi, but I now know it was Mototane. Talking to Nagatoki, I understand that the sword I threw into the bay was Sakuran and that it was owned by your grandson. That sword is now asleep in Sagami Bay. I threw it there to appease the spirit of the man I killed. I am truly sorry for murdering Mototane."

Elder Grandma strode up to the still-bowed Kaze. In her sash, she had a katana, just like a man. She withdrew her blade and grasped its handle with both hands. Kaze made no move to defend himself or get away.

"You have murdered my grandson. Now I will murder you." Elder Grandma drew her blade back.

Sadakatsu fell to his knees and said, "Elder Grandma, if you are going to kill the samurai, please kill me first."

"What?" Elder Grandma said, startled. "Why?"

"As a protest. I want to die as a protest."

"What are you talking about, you ridiculous old fool?" Elder Grandma chastised.

"I have served the Noguchi my entire life," Sadakatsu explained. "I have always been proud to be a servant in the employ of the Noguchi, just as my father and his father before him served your family. The Noguchi show proper samurai honor and frugality. They also exhibit proper bushido, the way of the warrior. They have never been, to my knowledge, unjust. If you kill this samurai, then you will be unjust, and I want my death to protest this injustice."

"Have you gone senile? What is unfair about dispatching Mototane's murderer into the void?"

"His act was murder, but at the time he thought he was defending an innocent merchant on the highway. How many men would put themselves at risk in similar circumstances? I know that this samurai does things to help the weak that most others will not. He is now being honest with you, and I can tell he has sincere remorse. He took Mototane's sword, which was a valuable one, and flung it into Sagami Bay to try to ease Mototane's spirit.

"He said Mototane died in a duel. That meant that Mototane had an equal chance to kill or be killed. It was Mototane's karma to die, which is something that brings me great sadness. It would also bring me greater sadness if the Noguchi were dishonored by unfairly killing this samurai."

Elder Grandma was nonplussed and stared at her servant as if she had never seen him before. Usually Sadakatsu stayed silent and did what he was told. She couldn't imagine what spirit had gotten into the thin servant that caused him to spout such words.

Her grandson, Nagatoki, came to her and also fell to his knees. He said, "Sadakatsu is right. If you kill this samurai, you will be killing the wrong man. Hishigawa is the man who tricked Matsuyama-san into killing Mototane. It is Hishigawa who is responsible for his death. Hishigawa is now dead, killed by your own hand. If you are going to kill the samurai, then kill me, too, for I could not stand the dishonor of such an act."

Elder Grandma stepped back, looking at the three men kneeling or bowing on the dirt before her. Her sword drooped and, for the first time, she was uncertain about what was right. She suddenly looked and felt as old as she really was.

Finally, she said, "All right, the samurai lives. Our bargain was for him to tell me what happened to Mototane. He has done so, although his news is something totally unexpected." Noticing that the three men had not moved, she said, "Get up." Then, with a touch of her old authority creeping back into her voice, she said, "Get up!"

Kaze did as he was told and looked deeply into the face of the old woman. The challenge to her authority seemed to affect her. Her lined face, once the picture of martial determination, now looked tired. Her hair, once a helmet of steel, was now a bundle of gray strands. Her posture, once as straight-spined as that of any general, was now round-shouldered and sagging. Kaze marveled at how the mind controls the body, but he was not prepared to offer sympathy to Elder Grandma yet. In her life, she must have known many disappointments and challenges. She had now just had both, with the news of her grandson Mototane's death and the rebellion of her little ragtag force. But this woman was resilient, and over the many years she had lived, she had never allowed life or its events to defeat her. She would be back to full vigor soon.

As soon as Kaze thought this, he saw Elder Grandma straighten visibly. "Since you've told me about Mototane, I will tell you about the cloth," she said to Kaze, as if the threat of death and the subsequent rebellion had not just occurred. Kaze marveled at her strength and was reminded that women are truly frightening. No man could recover as quickly.

"That piece of cloth was used to pack gifts that Ando brought when Hishigawa was trying to court Yuchan. I don't know its origin, but I do know its source. It comes from Hishigawa. How he got it, I don't know. It is something you can no longer ask him."

Now it was Kaze's turn to sag. "I know how he came by that cloth," Kaze said. "He told me about his recent business dealings. At the time, I didn't realize that the young girls he talked about brokering included the daughter of my Lady."

Elder Grandma gave a nod, and the palanquin porters hoisted their load. Yuchan was so light, it was if the palanquin were empty. She looked out from the palanquin, a living skeleton. Kaze knew that they'd stop at an inn after they left Kamakura and Yuchan would be able to take a decent bath and put on one of Elder Grandma's kimonos. The dirt of captivity could be washed from her, but she would never regain her beauty or her innocence.

She looked out from the palanquin and said just two words to Kaze. "Thank you." That, and the tears in her eyes, were enough.

As they were about to depart, Elder Grandma gave an almost imperceptible dip of her head in Kaze's direction.

"Elder Grandma," Kaze said.

"What?" she answered gruffly.

"Yuchan needs patience and care. She doesn't need to be bullied into normalcy. She will return to normal on her own. She's more than proven she will not respond to bullying."

"What do you . . . " Elder Grandma's retort died on her lips. She glanced at the palanquin that held her granddaughter. Reluctant to cede to Kaze's authority but cognizant of the soundness of his prescription, she said, "All right."

"Good."

Elder Grandma marched in front of the porters, holding her spear. The servant, Sadakatsu, burdened with his pack, shuffled along behind the palanquin. Only the grandson, Nagatoki, stopped, looking back at Kaze. In the pale gray light that preceded the dawn, he smiled a half smile and waved his hand in farewell. Kaze nodded his understanding and waved back. Then he turned to go.

That peak stands alone.
There is but one highest point
in a mountain range.

He was not anxious to stay in Kamakura. The events at Hishigawa's villa and the Jade Palace would be known to the authorities there. Most likely they were already searching for the perpetrators, although Kaze expected that they would be looking for a group of men, not just one, when they saw the carnage that had been wrought. Elder Grandma had taken her granddaughter out of the north entrance to Kamakura, through the kiridoshi. Kaze decided to go northwest, along the smaller coastal road.

As he walked, he thought about his next move. Perhaps he should return to Kyoto to search for the girl. After all, that's where Hishigawa did much of his business. The light gray of predawn was starting to illuminate the world. Kaze was close enough to the sea to get a waft of salt air that invigorated his spirit and helped him forget about the aches in his shoulders and arms.

Kaze had proceeded along the road for a couple of ri when he became aware that someone was following him. The man was an expert and didn't want to be seen yet, and from that Kaze guessed who it was.

When they came to a remote part of the road, the man showed

himself plainly, and Kaze stopped. He turned to look down the road and saw the man approaching him. It was Enomoto.

A sliver of red sun was over Kaze's left shoulder. Pink streaks of dawn started to marble the clouds.

Enomoto's face was grim—his jaw set, his eyes watching Kaze's every movement. He approached Kaze, then stopped outside the reach of a sword's blade.

"Nani? What?" Kaze asked.

"I'm here to fight you," Enomoto said.

Kaze was a little surprised. "I don't want to do that," Kaze responded.

"But I do," Enomoto said. "In fact, I must."

Kaze sighed. "I wish you could see your way clear not to do this. I really don't want to fight you."

"You ruined a very good thing for me," Enomoto said. "I tried to have you assassinated in Kamakura, but those fools took just three men. I could have told them it would take more than that to kill you. Then I tried a ninja, but that didn't work either. Now I will do the job myself."

"Why do you want me dead?"

"You said you had an idea so Hishigawa wouldn't have to move gold between Edo, Kyoto, and Kamakura. I didn't know what that idea was, but it would have put an end to my profitable game of robbing the merchant. I could have robbed Hishigawa for many years and built up a sizable fortune, not even counting what he paid me."

"It was dirty money," Kaze said.

"But it was still money. And I wanted it."

"Well, I don't want to fight you," Kaze repeated.

"Then you'll die," Enomoto said, "because I intend to attack you. If you don't wish to defend yourself, all the better. But regardless, I will defeat you. I can tell you're tired and worn. I don't know what Hishigawa did to you at his house last night, but I thank him for it."

"Hishigawa's dead," Kaze said.

"Did you kill him?" Enomoto said, surprised.

"No," Kaze answered. "But I did kill the rest."

"I told you once we were all bad there. There were none there that really deserved to live."

"Nonetheless, it made me sad to do it," Kaze said. "I have no feelings about killing evil, but it was sad that there should be so much evil in one place."

"Now you're going to be sad to fight me? To try to kill me?"

"Yes. I'll be sad," Kaze answered. "Because despite everything, I know you are a superb swordsman. I feel no need to confirm my own skills with these silly duels that seem to be so popular now."

"Well, I feel a need," Enomoto said. "The honor of my name demands it."

Kaze sighed. "Well, then. I suppose it's best to get on with it."

Enomoto stood back a few paces. Then, drawing a white sash from a sleeve of his kimono, he tied it under his armpits and across his back in a figure eight, pulling his sleeves up away from his arms and out of the way.

Kaze remained impassive, not bothering to tie his sleeves up.

Enomoto pulled his sword out of his scabbard and stood in the ready position. Kaze did the same.

"I'll give you an extra incentive," Enomoto said.

"What is that?"

"That young girl you're looking for, the one who had the plum family crest?"

"Yes?" Kaze said.

"I know where she is."

"Where is she?" Kaze asked. He studied Enomoto's face to see if he was lying or not. In the eyes looking back at him, impassive but alert, Kaze detected truth.

"Where is she?" Kaze asked again.

"You'll find the answer on a scrap of paper in my sleeve," Enomoto said. "I don't think you'll be reading it. But just in case, you'll find it there."

Kaze saw no further need for conversation and stood at the ready.

The men stood watching each other, looking for the slightest hesitation, the slightest opening, so they could make an attack. With a perfect defense, a swordsman can never be defeated. He might not be able to win, but he will never lose. To go on the offense was to take a risk, but through risk was victory. Kaze was tired but alert, every fiber of his body connected to the sword in his hand. He waited, content to let Enomoto make the first move.

Enomoto suddenly started running six quick steps to the side. Kaze followed, keeping Enomoto in front of him—always watching, waiting for the slightest lapse.

To his left, Kaze could see the sea now marked by a bloody ribbon as the disk of the sun poked its way up the horizon. Enomoto suddenly lunged forward, picking his sword up and bringing it down in one smooth motion. Kaze parried the blow, but his abused body let him down because, instead of smoothly stopping Enomoto's blow, his arms buckled slightly, and he felt Enomoto's blade as it kissed his brow, cutting a small slash. He felt the blood flow down the side of his face, but he made no concession to the wound, maintaining his guard.

"I would have expected you to be much stronger," Enomoto said. "You must be very tired, Matsuyama-san. I guess Hishigawa-san treated you roughly. Now that I've drawn first blood, I know that I will be victorious and kill you."

Kaze made no response. Instead he started moving laterally on his own, with Enomoto following him move for move. As Kaze moved toward the sea, his path made a shallow arc and, instead of having the rising sun to his left, Kaze soon had the sun behind him.

"Very good," Enomoto acknowledged, "but not decisive. Our duel will be over long before the sun can blind me or give you an advantage." He stood at the ready again. The exertions of their maneuvering left a thin sheen of sweat forming on the sides of his neck.

Kaze attacked both to the right and the left. Each blow was parried by Enomoto.

"You're a strong opponent," Enomoto acknowledged. "But there is nothing you can do to defeat me. I'll eventually inflict a mortal blow. We're too evenly matched, but I can see you're weakening. And when you're weak enough, I will prevail."

Kaze said nothing. He concentrated his whole being into his sword. He stood watching his opponent, looking for some small opening so he could once again press his attack. Instead of an opening, he saw that a small fly was buzzing about Enomoto's neck, attracted by the sweat and the heat of his body. Kaze could see the muscles on Enomoto's neck tensing, and he knew that Enomoto would soon be launching an all-out attack. In his weakened state, he also knew he would eventually succumb to that attack and die.

In the sleeve of Enomoto's blue kimono was a scrap of paper that would help him end his quest for the girl. But now his quest and his life would soon be over, and his promise to the Lady would be as dust caught in a whirlwind.

The fly returned and landed on Enomoto's neck. Enomoto twitched slightly to dislodge it, and suddenly Kaze's blade shot out, catching the fly and biting ever so slightly into Enomoto's neck. Kaze's Fly Cutter had lived up to its name.

A red surge of blood pumped from the cut. Enomoto had felt the sting of Kaze's blade, and he was surprised that Kaze had made such a rapid and weak cut. It was a cut that would normally be shrugged off, no more serious than the slash on Kaze's head. The relative weakness of the blow made it seem trivial, but the speed of the blade was a maneuver he had never seen before. At first he didn't realize that, although the cut was relatively shallow, it was nonetheless fatal. It had severed the carotid artery.

As Enomoto stood opposing Kaze, his life's blood was pumping out into a widening stain over his shoulder. With his mind focused, Enomoto did not acknowledge the cut on his neck. Instead, he launched his attack. His blade cut right, then left, then right again. Each time Kaze brought his own blade up to counter the blow and keep Enomoto's sword away from him, but he felt his strength ebbing, and only will kept him from succumbing to Enomoto's attack.

Enomoto had observed Kaze's tired stance, but he was surprised at his own growing light-headedness and weakness as he pressed his attack.

He brought his blade up above his head to launch another onslaught but, instead of bringing it down, Enomoto stopped a moment. His body swaying, a sudden infirmity attacked him. Not thinking of Kaze now, Enomoto brought his sword forward and placed it down on the ground to try to steady himself. He looked down at his kimono and was surprised to see his shoulder and sleeve soaked with blood. It didn't seem possible that all this blood could be his. But his power to comprehend what was happening was rapidly diminishing.

As a dull, gray fog rolled over his consciousness, preventing him from thinking clearly, Enomoto fell to his knees, half expecting Kaze to attack and take his head. Instead, Kaze stood at the ready, closely watching his opponent but not moving to attack.

Enomoto fell forward, the last few measures of his life pumping out of the severed artery and onto the ground. Blackness washed over him. He still had no comprehension of what move Kaze had used to kill him.

Kaze stood a moment and watched Enomoto die. Then he wiped his sword and put the katana in the scabbard, guiding the blade with his left hand while his right held the hilt. He waited to make sure Enomoto was dead, then he walked up to the body and reached into the sleeve.

He found a small piece of folded paper. On the paper, written with a neat brush, were the words "*Edo Yukaku Kobanaya.*" Kaze stared at the seven kanji on the note for several moments, absorbing both their meaning and their implications—"Little Flower Whorehouse Edo."

Kaze went to the side of the road and sat down. The duel had drained his energy, but it was not as great a blow as the note. He looked over at Enomoto. "Thank you for this," he said, bowing and holding the note between his two hands like a prayer offering. "We men can engage in our foolishness, but the child should not suffer for it."

When Kaze had rested a few minutes, he got up and cut a tree branch. Taking the ko-gatana knife from its place in the scabbard, he quickly carved a statue of Kannon, the Goddess of Mercy. The face of the Kannon was the face of the Lady.

Kaze turned Enomoto over and arranged his body into a state of repose. There wasn't much he could do about the blood that stained the kimono, but he wiped the dirt from the dead man's face with his sleeve. He placed the Kannon where she could watch over him until some other traveler discovered the body and reported it to the authorities.

"I'm sorry I don't have the time to prepare you properly," Kaze said. "But now I have to go into the hands of my enemies."

Up the coast road was the junction with the Tokaido Road. At the end of the Tokaido was Edo—the new capital and the stronghold of his bitter enemies, the Tokugawas. His head wound had stopped bleeding, and he felt very tired. Still, he was glad that perhaps his long journey to find the girl might at last be coming to an end. Assuming, that is, that he could somehow survive the blades of his foes in Edo.

Making one last bow of respect to Enomoto, Kaze squared his shoulders and started down the road, which was now bathed in a golden light by the newly risen sun.

The reception given to *Death at the Crossroads,* the first book in this series, by reviewers and readers was gratifying. I found the perceptiveness and knowledge of Japan communicated by some of these readers and reviewers truly astonishing.

Many noticed that my books always have a small scene that emulates something from one of the movies of the late Akira Kurosawa. This is both an homage to Kurosawa, the finest of the Japanese filmmakers, and a reminder that I should strive to capture the same spirit exemplified by a Kurosawa film. A few readers have understood that these books have comic characters in them that echo the buffoonery and delightful silliness of the *kyogen* roles found in Noh plays. Still other readers are practitioners of the martial arts I write about, and they understand the mechanical techniques as well as the spiritual motivation I describe.

This book, *Jade Palace Vendetta,* is the second in a trilogy chronicling the life of the ronin Matsuyama Kaze. It can easily be read as a stand-alone novel, but it also advances the story of Kaze's search for a kidnapped nine-year-old girl.

I was inspired to write this particular book by a walk down a dirt road in rural Japan. The rice growing next to the road was nearing harvest time, and the heavy stalks of grain made the green shoots rustle and bow in the slightest breeze. The windblown ripples in the field looked like a dynamic version of the raked sand of the famous Zen rock garden at the temple Ryoanji in Kyoto. To the side of the road was a Buddhist cemetery, high on a hill. The weathered rock monuments were surrounded by ancient pines, with a few late wildflowers dotting the hillside. In the far distance was a small farm village. Except for the ubiquitous television antennas and lack of thatched roofs in the village, it might have been a scene from a Japanese *ukiyo-e* woodblock carved hundreds of years ago.

The scene made me think of the old Tokaido Road. At one time, the Tokaido was so thick with traffic that people sometimes walked shoulder to shoulder. In 1603, the year I write about in the trilogy, commerce on the Tokaido was not as rich. The famous fifty-three stations of the Tokaido Road were not as established as they would be in later years, and the huge number of ronin in 1603 made travel and commerce difficult and dangerous.

This experience on a country road inspired me to start this book on the Tokaido Road, and my love of Kamakura made me want to conclude it there, even though the road to Kamakura was really an offshoot of the Tokaido Road.

It's my intention to entertain with this series, although I have tried to be as accurate as my research and talents allow. It's my hope that the reader will be transported to a different and unique age. It was an age of turmoil and violence, but so is our age. In 1603 Japan, however, the concepts of honor, loyalty, and duty seemed to have a more tangible existence than they do today.